D0398372

VEN

THE TWILIGHT CIRCUS

BY DI TOFT

Chicken House

SCHOLASTIC INC. | NEW YORK

Text copyright © 2011 by Di Toft

First published in the United Kingdom in 2010 by Chicken House,
2 Palmer Street, Frome, Somerset BA11 1DS.
www.doublecluck.com

Library of Congress Cataloging-in-Publication Data

Toft, Di.
The twilight circus / Di Toft. — 1st American ed.
p. cm. — (Wolven ; #2)
Summary: After a summer spent dodging mutant werewolves and mad scientists,
Nat Carver and shapeshifter Woody join the Twilight Circus of Illusion and are
caught up in a struggle against a black widow vampire and her terrifying hive.

ISBN 978-0-545-29492-8

[1. Supernatural—Fiction. 2. Circus—Fiction. 3. Werewolves—Fiction.
4. Vampires—Fiction. 5. Grandfathers—Fiction. 6. England—Fiction.] I. Title.

PZ7.T5732Wol 2010
[Fic]—dc22

2010054231

10 9 8 7 6 5 4 3 2 1   11 12 13 14 15

Printed in the U.S.A.   23
First American edition, November 2011

The text type was set in Adobe Garamond.
The display type was set in Trajan Pro.
Book design by Phil Falco

PHIL, THIS ONE'S FOR YOU!
—X

CONTENTS

CHAPTER 1

PANIC ON THE PLATFORM

Nat Carver was genius at keeping secrets.

He knew that seeing or feeling stuff before it happened was called *precognition*. And it usually meant that something *bad* was going to happen. Nat and his mum, Jude, were waiting impatiently on the platform for the London-to-Paris Eurostar train when his pulse started to race and he only just managed to control the urge to pant like a wolf. He had felt crazy jumpy ever since leaving Temple Gurney, but had told himself it was just excitement at the thought of seeing his dad and Woody again.

He glanced at his mum and couldn't help wincing at her appearance. Yesterday, Jude Carver had undergone a complete transformation. Her long brown hair had been bleached blond and rolled into dreads. Her dark blue eyes were now emerald green, courtesy of some colored contact lenses, and were framed with unflattering wire-rimmed glasses. Worst of all were the slightly protruding false teeth fixed over her own, which Nat thought made her look a bit like a llama or a slightly insane English teacher. Lady Iona de Gourney, their great friend and ally during the whole Proteus saga, had been responsible for Jude's makeover. She had provided them both with sanctuary until Nat had recovered enough to travel, as well as procured the cleverly forged documents they carried, giving both Nat and Jude brand-new identities.

Nat was thankful he had escaped his own extreme makeover. Over the past few months he had grown taller—his muscles had filled out and he'd grown his hair longer. He was barely recognizable as the puny kid of last summer.

It was freezing, and due to the recent power strikes, the St. Pancras train station was in near darkness. Nat felt the hairs rise up on the back of his neck like hackles. *Why is it,* he thought, *that you only have a premonition when things are going to go wrong?* He scanned the busy platform. It seemed to Nat that *everyone* on it had bad BO. He could see the vapors rising from people and hovering above them like a sort of stanky aura, making him feel as if he was about to lose his breakfast. He tried to concentrate on finding what could be alarming him, but he had brain freeze from overhearing so many snippets of other people's thoughts and conversations. Sifting through all the psychic white noise to zone in on the source took all of Nat's concentration. It was like when you pat yourself on the head with one hand and make circular movements on your stomach with the other. It's impossible to do both things at the same time unless you practice for about three hours every day. Nat couldn't wait to ask Woody how *he* managed to cope with all the extra information.

In the months following the werewolf attack that had almost killed him, Jude had watched Nat carefully. She had heaved a sigh of relief when the first full moon passed and her only child hadn't shown any signs of sprouting fur and turning into a slavering wolf. When the second full moon came and went, she allowed herself to relax, thanking her lucky stars that whatever gifts Nat may have acquired from Woody's Wolven blood, it didn't include shape-shifting.

Nat was also thankful, not least because he had watched Woody's struggle with his own shape-shifting. He had seen up close and personal how uncomfortable, not to mention stomach-churningly weird, stretching out of shape could be. But once Nat had realized how thrilled his mum was when there were no physical changes in the weeks after his emergency blood transfusion, he decided to keep what was *really* going on to himself. His physical recovery following Lucas Scale's attack had been incredibly fast thanks to the new blood . . . but the recurring nightmares had left scars on his soul.

Since the summer, Nat had developed some seriously cool improvements to his human senses, and had so far managed to keep them secret. The cool things were:

- Long-range, high-frequency hearing
- Sixth sense (needed a bit more practice)
- Telepathy, also known as the two-way mind-meld thing (ditto)
- Super-enhanced infrared vision

His eyesight was *awesome*. Nat had needed glasses for school before all the bother at Helleborine Halt; now he could see for miles and, even more amazing, *he could see in the dark!*

But there was a flip side. Nat struggled with self-control, sometimes resenting his new senses as they threatened to take over. Other problems were:

- Occasional dog breath and increased flatulence (the latter more difficult to keep secret)
- Overdeveloped olfactory glands (which made all smells stronger: see above)
- Other people's nasty, dark thoughts (which he really would rather not know)
- The eye thing

Their train was due to leave in a few minutes and Nat was still sensing that something bad was going to happen. More people spilled onto the already crowded platform, some impatiently pushing and shoving. Nat positioned himself between his mum and the platform edge, worried that the crowd was going to push too much and someone would fall onto the tracks. He hoped like crazy that *that* wasn't going to be the bad thing. Then someone shoved past him, causing the crowd to scatter. In the confusion, Nat heard a scream, and he caught the flash of a steel blade as a knife slashed through the leather strap of an elderly woman's bulging handbag. The woman was knocked to the ground, lost in the melee of people struggling to get out of the way of the knife-wielding thief.

Nat's sight locked onto the slightly built figure running away. He was dressed in black, his hood pulled over his head, a scarf covering most of his face. Nat's body was overtaken by an overwhelming urge to make chase. He could feel his heart pumping Wolven blood, preparing his muscles for fight *and* flight. He wanted to *chase*, to run him down—not because the thief had committed a nasty, cowardly crime, but because Nat *needed* to, as though an ON switch had been flicked in his brain. He shoved his way through the crowd and was off on his toes. He could hear his mum screaming for him to stop, but he ignored her and honed in on the hoodie, who by now was near the terminal, glancing over his shoulder to see if he was being followed. When he spotted Nat gaining on him, he sped up, and Nat could smell his fear as he closed in. As Nat ran, he realized there was a strange noise coming from his throat. He was *growling*! It both excited and frightened him.

He launched himself at the hoodie, knocking him to

the ground with a muffled *whump* and wrenching the bag from him. Nat pulled the scarf away from his face. *The thief was a girl!* She stared up at him, panting hard.

"Your eyes!" she said breathlessly.

"What?" snarled Nat.

"Your *eyes* . . . ," she repeated.

Nat sprang to his feet. Other people, including his mum, had joined in the chase and were fast approaching. He examined the backs of his hands as though expecting to see them covered with fur. They weren't. He willed his pulse to slow and his muscles to relax. He glared down at the girl.

"What *about* my eyes?" he demanded.

"They . . . they changed . . . they were *golden*," she gasped.

"And now?" growled Nat.

"N-normal!" she stammered, shocked. "Blue. But when you took me down, they changed."

"You better get out of here," said Nat. The last thing he wanted was to get involved. If the police were called and he was a witness, it could lead to all sorts of unwelcome attention. Luckily, the hoodie didn't need to be told twice. Nat watched her speed off into the afternoon gloom.

CHAPTER 2

THINGS ARE GETTING HAIRY

Nat and Jude Carver were happily unaware that their plans to leave England had already been discovered. A few days before they left the southwest countryside for London, certain information regarding their whereabouts had been passed on to a man named Quentin Crone, the former head of Her Majesty's Military Intelligence, otherwise known as MI5, the British Secret Service.

At a clandestine location in London not far from Fleet Street, Quentin Crone was sitting in his new office, trying hard not to think about the night he had first heard Nat Carver's name. Sighing deeply, he gazed around his new place of work with something like dread. Although it wasn't yet three o'clock in the afternoon, the narrow street outside was dark and eerily deserted. The only light inside was from the embers of the fire and the glow of Crone's computer screen. The rest of the vast room was murky, with shadows in every corner.

Crone glanced nervously around him as he so often did these days, half expecting to see something lurking behind him, hidden in the gloom: a nightmare creature that slavered and snarled, its eyes glowing with violence and hunger.

Stop thinking about it! he told himself sternly. Unfortunately his brain had other ideas. Awake or asleep, Crone was both haunted and taunted by images of creatures that he had believed only existed in the most lurid of horror movies.

The night his world had turned upside down — when he had no choice but to believe that monsters were real — was tattooed on his brain forever. Quentin Crone had seen things he had never thought possible. *Werewolves!* Great big black ones, ten feet tall, loping toward him, *coming for him*, thick ropes of drool swinging rhythmically, almost hypnotically, from their impossible-looking, bloody jaws.

At a remote stately home in deepest, darkest Somerset, experiments to create the ultimate fighting machine for the twenty-first century had gone badly wrong. Barking-mad scientist Dr. Gabriel Gruber had tried to fuse the DNA of crazed werewolves with that of a telepathic Wolven—a noble shape-shifting creature thought (until recently) to exist in legend only. *And the government had known all about it!* Quentin Crone had felt he had no alternative but to resign as soon as he had been decommissioned. Two good things had come out of it, though: The crooked prime minister and his entire corrupt cabinet had all been fired, and, even better—a warm smile lit Crone's tired face whenever he thought of it—the boy, Nat Carver, and the shape-shifting Wolven creature had *escaped*!

His appointment as head of NightShift had followed shortly after, and Crone had hit the ground running. He hadn't even had time to take off his coat on his first day before he had been called out to investigate a nasty poltergeist infestation in Putney.

Not for the first time, Crone wondered what the devil he had been thinking of by accepting the appointment in the first place. He had never even heard of NightShift, for a start, until he had been contacted by an old colleague, a Professor Robert Paxton. According to the professor, the covert agency code-named NightShift had been operating for a number of years, quietly exterminating evil beings or forces without too many humans getting shredded.

The professor had shown Crone disturbing new evidence that supernatural events were on the rise, the threat to humans from malignant forces was now greater than global warming, and vampires and werewolves had overtaken human terrorist activity. In light of recent events (and an unexpected vacancy), Professor Paxton had convinced Quentin Crone he was just the man for the job. An unheated office in Middle Temple Lane was the NightShift headquarters, where Crone was to spend his days and nights making lethal decisions, drinking tea, and counting the dead bodies.

BBBBRRRRRRRRZZZZZZ.

Crone's heart almost leaped up into his throat as the old-fashioned intercom on his desk made him jump.

For heaven's sake, man, get a grip, he told himself sternly. "Yes?" he rasped, sounding more bad-tempered than he felt.

"Cuppa tea, boss?" a bright female voice crackled through to his office.

"I'm awash with the stuff, Fish," he groaned, his voice

sounding echoey and insubstantial in the cavernous room, "but if you're making hot chocolate with sprinkles and marshmallows, I'd be glad of some company."

There was a knack to opening the heavy, studded door to his office, and Crone waited patiently until the sounds of someone grappling with the handle stopped. A slightly built girl tottered across the ancient carpet on the highest, shiniest pair of platform shoes that Crone had ever seen, plonked a tray with two steaming mugs onto his desk, and arranged her skinny body in the chair opposite him.

"*Woohooo*, you're looking a bit rough," blurted Agent Alexandra Fish, studying Crone's features with her beady eyes.

"Not sleeping," said Crone bluntly, distracted by the pile of red files she had also brought with her. Someone had scrawled **Really REALLY Urgent** across the top in thick black marker. "What are those?"

Fish looked down at the folders she'd carried in as though she was surprised they were there. "Oh . . . uh, more cases, boss."

Crone groaned and leaned forward again, pinching the bridge of his nose between his thumb and forefinger.

Fish had only known Quentin Crone for a few days, but she could see how worry and tiredness had drawn lines onto his craggy face. She fervently hoped he wasn't going to quit on them, or worse. Dear old Freddie Alton, the last head of NightShift, had cracked under the incredible pressure of running the agency. The last Fish had heard was that poor Freddie was currently in a high-security facility for the chronically insane, locked in a windowless room with walls made of mattresses, wearing a very tight jacket with lots of buckles and no armholes.

"We have more cases than we have agents," said Crone wearily, gesturing to the pile of red files.

You can say that again, thought Fish, impressed that Crone had already caught on to the freakish trend that was keeping her sleepless: Since she had joined NightShift, there had been a worrying increase in werewolf goings-on, not to mention vampire activity and the number of people affected by demonic possessions and hauntings.

"So, like, things are getting hairy" — she grinned — "if you'll pardon the pun."

At last Crone smiled, his tired eyes crinkling at the corners. "We're learning all the time," he said, "but, as you know from experience, we're only human."

"Obviously!" said Fish in surprise. There was something in Crone's voice that made her look at him more closely from behind her glasses. "What are you getting at?" she queried.

"Well . . . do you not think that perhaps we are at a disadvantage?" asked Crone.

"Huh?" Fish mumbled.

"We're only *human*," he stressed. "Humans investigating supernatural and paranormal activities. Not exactly a fair fight, is it?"

"We do OK." Fish frowned, still not sure what her new boss was going on about. "And NightShift is growing. We've got ten fully trained agents and two trainees."

"Remind me again why NightShift was formed," said Crone, steepling his fingers.

Fish gave him a quizzical look, kicked off her unfeasibly high platform shoes, and curled her stockinged feet underneath her.

"To kill monsters," she said without hesitation.

Crone grinned.

"These are dark days, Fish. The events in Somerset last

summer, proving that werewolves really do exist, meant I had to ask myself a very important question."

"Like, if werewolves really exist, what *else* is real?" Alex Fish said solemnly.

Crone nodded. "And NightShift answered those questions for me. Investigating the paranormal has always been seen as a bit of a joke for those not in the know."

"If the public knew what *really* happened . . . ," began Fish. "Like, if they knew what was *down there* . . ."

Both Crone and Fish allowed their gaze to slide toward the floor. Underneath the faded red-and-gold carpet that covered the mammoth room was a giant trapdoor. If opened, it would reveal seventy-seven steps, each one painstakingly hand-cut into the granite many centuries before. The catacombs beneath were stuffed with more fabulous secrets and priceless artifacts than those allegedly held in the Vatican and Area 51 put together. Crone allowed himself a small shudder whenever he stopped to think about the strange and often terrible things stored *down there . . . in the dark.*

"And since you mentioned Somerset," said Fish, running a hand through her sticky-up hair, "anything new?"

Crone hesitated and chewed on a marshmallow, watching Fish's nimble fingers flick through one of the more urgent files. Although Fish looked as wholesome and shiny as a kindergarten teacher, Crone knew she was shaping up to be one of their toughest and most efficient operatives. She fought dirty, and played dirtier. Just last month, she had successfully trapped and dispatched the Highgate Cemetery Zombies with a simple but brilliant combination of pulleys, string, and trash bags. It had been a scheme of pure genius. On NightShift's last case, she had single-handedly dealt with the Blackwall Tunnel Banshee and sent it screeching back to the underworld where it undoubtedly belonged. Traffic now flowed through the tunnel beautifully, all thanks to Agent Alexandra Fish. Crone considered her sharp little face as she flipped briskly through the file on her lap.

"What do you know about Nat Carver?" asked Crone casually.

Fish dropped the file as if it had suddenly got hot. She stared at Crone, the firelight reflecting in her glasses.

"Not much," she admitted. "Only what I've been *allowed* to know. Why?"

By way of an answer, Crone hunched over his keyboard, his face turning vomit-green as it reflected the screen. He tapped some keys and waited a second for the site to load. Fish watched the big screen on the opposite wall load the site Crone had requested. *BBC News London* flashed up before them. An unremarkable scene unfolded. There appeared to be about forty unremarkable people sitting in the middle of an unremarkable road. There was a lot of chanting about radiation; the crowd seemed to be demonstrating about cell phone towers. Most of the demonstrators were about Fish's parents' age, except for the two people at the front who looked vaguely familiar: a young boy and a woman with the same dark hair and wide, dark blue eyes. Fish narrowed her eyes as the slightly built boy looked directly at the camera with what seemed like acute embarrassment.

"Is that . . . ?" she exclaimed in wonder.

"Nat Carver," confirmed Quentin Crone. "As far as I know, this video, shot a couple of years ago, is the only footage in existence of Jude and Nat Carver."

Crone loaded another site: World's Most Wanted. He scrolled through the usual suspects: the terrorists, the murderers, the pirates, the thieves, and the criminally insane. Then their gaze rested upon a more recent, but hazy, photograph of the same boy, who now looked about thirteen. Nat Carver.

"This photograph was taken on a cell phone," Crone stated. "No other footage of That Night survived."

Fish swallowed hard. She had seen the picture before. According to a witness, Nat Carver had been attacked and his throat almost ripped out by a mutant government agent, Lucas Scale, who mercifully was now deceased.

Uh-oh, thought Fish, *I think I know where he's going with this!*

"Nat Carver's still alive, isn't he?" she gasped. "Where is he?"

Crone smiled thinly. "If I told you that . . . I'd have to kill you."

Fish stared at Crone, wondering if he really would kill to keep the secret. Bright girl that she was, she had already suspected her new boss was privy to more information about Nat Carver than he let on.

"They're on the move," said Crone. "The Wolven — Woody — is currently off our radar. A few weeks ago, though, I received intel that Nat Carver is very much alive and, at present, still here in England."

"Intel from who?" asked Fish suspiciously.

"From *whom*," corrected Crone. "Not government— a safe source. Don't worry."

Fish looked relieved. "So *whom* is going to deal with it . . . I mean, the intelligence?"

"*We* are," said Crone. He got up, stretched his long limbs, and walked stiffly to the far end of his room, where the wall was covered by a faded twelfth-century tapestry of King Richard the Lionheart during the time of the Third Crusade. Fish knew that what interested her boss the most were the animals at the monarch's feet. The first time she had seen it, she had assumed that the pure white canine creatures were wolves. But on closer inspection, she had noticed they were much bigger than ordinary wolves, and that their white fur grew long down their necks, almost like the flaxen mane of a horse. The dozen wolflike creatures were gathered around the king in a protective circle.

"The Wolven dude—Woody?" said Fish. "He's descended from the King's Wolven, right?"

"Right," agreed Crone.

"So he's valuable, but Nat Carver is just a kid, right?"

"Wrong." Crone smiled. "He's very special. I've been told he has enhanced senses, telepathic skills, possibly the ability to change shape. . . ."

"How?" demanded Fish. "The Wolven can shape-shift, but how would Nat Carver get such gifts?"

"Never mind," said Crone mildly. "I shouldn't have said anything."

"You *so* can't leave it there," said Fish menacingly.

Crone took a deep breath. "Nat Carver should have died the night Lucas Scale ripped out his throat," he said. "What wasn't included in my final report of what happened That Night was that he was taken to a safe house and given a blood transfusion that saved his life. Not any old blood, mind you. The blood was a gift. From the Wolven."

"Oh!" squeaked Fish. "Wolven blood? But how d'you know all of this?"

"Intel," Crone said again, tapping his right temple with his finger. "Right now, I know that Nat Carver is experiencing many more changes than a normal thirteen-year-old boy. He's struggling to control his supernatural senses, increased strength, and the potential to communicate telepathically."

"So he *is* as valuable as the Wolven," said Fish. "But why are they on the run? Surely there were other witnesses to testify—"

Crone shook his head. "The web of deceit spun by the government spinners resulted in Nat Carver and the Wolven being blamed for everything," he said. "And as you see, ending up on the World's Most Wanted."

"They were framed like an oil painting, stitched up like a pair of kippers!" cried Fish.

"Woody remains a very valuable commodity," said Crone. "And, since his blood transfusion, so is the boy. They're officially fugitives." He opened his mouth to say something else, hesitated, and closed it again.

"What?" demanded Fish.

Quentin Crone pursed his lips. "You might as well know something else," he said grimly, "but it's for your ears only. Lucas Scale was shot, according to my source, but his body was never found."

Fish, who had seen sights that most humans had only dreamed of in their most horrific nightmares, turned an interesting shade of pale green. When she had seen the images of Lucas Scale contained in the pages of the ultra-secret Proteus files, she had physically recoiled. *That's one sick puppy*, she had thought to herself. The photographs must have been taken sometime before his mutation into a hybrid werewolf, but Alex Fish had been struck by the absence of humanity in Lucas Scale's icy stare. His lights were well and truly off and there was definitely no one home. If he had somehow found a way to cheat death . . . She shivered. She didn't want to dwell on what would happen to Nat Carver or the furry Wolven dude if Scale got hold of them again.

"You mean he may not be dead?" she whispered when she had regained some of her composure.

"Oh, he's dead all right," said Crone grimly. "Part of our job here at NightShift is to find a body to ensure he *stays* dead."

When Fish had gone, Crone got busy. He got a good old blaze going in the fireplace and poured himself a glass of the finest malt whiskey, admiring its topaz glow as the firelight caught the crystal. He sat warming his bones with the pile of red files unopened on his lap, watching thoughtfully as the flames flickered upward, making the grotesque faces of the stone gargoyles gurn and writhe as though they were alive.

We're only human, he had said to Fish earlier. A plan started to form in his mind, and as it grew he felt his courage grow with it. Keeping secrets was just Crone's job; making sure Nat Carver and his Wolven stayed alive was his destiny. If only he could make contact with Nat Carver before he left the country! He glanced at his watch and reached for the telephone.

CHAPTER 3
DEAL OR NO DEAL

There was a welcome warm rush of air as the London-to-Paris Eurostar glided along the freezing platform. Never had Nat been so glad to see a train. After the hoodie had legged it, the other people on the platform had been giving him funny looks, and Jude had given him a right earful. The doors opened and Nat had one ear cocked to his mum moaning on about how lucky he was not to have been killed by the hoodie with the knife—*just because he had been lucky enough to escape death once . . . And what was he flipping well playing at . . . ? Did he think he was indestructible . . . ?*

Nat nodded in all the right places until she had calmed down. He was curious and confused about the girl; his senses had alerted him that something bad was going to happen and he had reacted because of a strange, wild-animal need to give chase. But when he had got close

24

enough to smell her, he knew there was nothing bad about her, even though she was a thief. And there had been something unsettling about the way she had looked at him when she saw his eyes change. He could have sworn she had a look of wonder on her face, not fear.

Forget it, Nat told himself as he followed his mum onto the train. *It'll always be a mystery. Anyway, I'll never see her again.*

Nat and Jude had been touched when they had received their tickets; Iona had booked them the best seats in first class and they were looking forward to traveling to Paris in style.

"This is the life," said Jude, her eyes widening behind the unflattering glasses. "This is a new start, Nat. We're actually doing it. . . . We're running away to join the circus!"

Nat grinned; her excitement was contagious. He settled back in his seat, thinking of how good it would be to see his dad again after so long, and all the questions he had saved up to ask Woody about Wolven stuff. It was weird to think that in a couple of hours, he and his mum would be safe at last. Jude stretched her long legs onto the seats.

"Roll up, roll up, *mesdames et messieurs*, for Carver's Twilight Circus of Illusion . . . the greatest show on the planet."

"Hopefully," said Nat.

They were traveling more than two hundred miles an hour, more than two hundred feet under the English Channel, which made Nat feel queasy. He didn't do travel, especially underground. He tried very hard not to think about the thousands of tons of solid rock above him, and what would happen if it all abruptly collapsed. Suddenly, irrationally, he began to feel panicky and hot. He glanced at Jude. There was a slight curve on her lips and Nat could feel her thoughts inside his own head. She was thinking about his dad, imagining seeing the reassuring bulk of him again after so long. Despite his feeling of panic at being underground, Nat got up from his seat and walked unsteadily through the carriage. It was cooler in the connecting sections between the carriages, and he sat on the floor sipping from a bottle of water until he felt almost human again.

Twenty minutes later, when the train came out of the tunnel, Nat heaved a sigh of relief. He had just got to his feet to find his mum when the connecting door opened and he was joined in the little corridor by a man.

The man nodded affably and Nat nodded back. The man smelled of worry and expensive aftershave. Nat guessed he had come from business premier class because he wore a sharp-looking suit. He had a nice face and floppy hair, which made him look younger than he probably was.

"Amazing feat of engineering, don't you think?" said the man in a posh but pleasant voice. "The tunnel, I mean."

Nat smiled and nodded just to be polite. He made to open the door, but the man put his hand out as if to bar his way.

"Excuse me," said Nat, mildly alarmed.

"Don't be frightened," said the man hastily, withdrawing his hand.

"Why would I be frightened?" asked Nat cautiously. The man was harmless; Nat could feel and smell there was nothing to fear from him.

The man gave a wry laugh. "Good Lord, it's me that should be frightened," he said, almost to himself. "You could probably knock me straight through the side of the train if you wanted to."

Nat decided it was best not to say anything.

"What else can you do?" asked the man, leaning forward conspiratorially. "Telepathy? Can you change your shape?"

Nat tried to keep his face impassive. "I don't know what you mean," he said, "and I don't want to knock you through the side of the train."

"Yes, but you could if you wanted to," insisted the man, smiling slightly. He held out a rectangular card. "Forgive me," he said. "My name is Crone. Quentin Crone."

Nat privately thought what bad luck it was to be saddled with a name like that, but he took the card anyway. "NightShift?"

Crone nodded enthusiastically. "Ex-MI5, now working independently to eradicate the increase in malignant paranormals."

"Good luck with that," said Nat, feigning disinterest.

Crone tried again, feeling slightly unsettled by Nat Carver's presence. He was surprised and a little annoyed at how awed he felt.

"Nat Carver, I need your help," he said. "I'd like to offer you a deal. You and the Wolven, Woody."

Nat was now seriously alarmed, but trying not to show it. He scowled. "See that man through there?" he said, nodding at a random passenger. "If you don't leave me alone, I'll tell him you're bothering me."

Crone looked worried. "Just listen to what I have to say," he said hurriedly. "If you still don't want to know after you've heard me out, then forgive the intrusion, and I'll leave you alone."

Nat said nothing, just glared at Crone with his unnerving dark blue eyes.

"NightShift has no ties with the British government," assured Crone. "We are funded entirely by a private benefactor. But we have a problem. All our operatives are human. If you and Woody would agree to help us, I'll use my influence to guarantee you both amnesty and—"

"No," said Nat firmly. "And my name is *not* Nat Carver."

Quentin Crone smiled sympathetically. "Still a bit of scarring around the old throat area, I see. I imagine that's hard to disguise."

Nat instinctively put his hand up to his neck. Thanks to his Wolven blood the scars had healed fast, but the place where Lucas Scale had nearly ripped his head from his neck still felt raw sometimes, reminding him of how lucky he was to be alive. He stared at Crone, realizing he had blown it. Then he gave up and slumped his shoulders.

"How did you know?" he asked.

"You really don't need to worry," Crone assured him. "Your secret is utterly safe with me."

"I know," said Nat. "You *smell* OK . . . that is . . . I know I can trust you, but you're still wasting your time."

"How are your injuries?" asked Crone.

"I still get some pain," said Nat cautiously. "Apparently it's normal after having your throat torn out."

"NightShift needs people like you and Woody," said Crone. "People with gifts like yours, who have experience in ridding our world of monsters, like Lucas Scale, for example."

Nat's face drained of blood. "That was out of order," he said quietly. "I don't talk about him."

"You know his body was never found," said Crone, hating himself for frightening the boy.

Nat shook his head, squeezing his eyes shut. "Shut up," he said.

"Supernatural events are hotting up faster than you can say global warming," said Crone. "The world is becoming a dark place thanks to creatures like Scale. The malevolent undead who live on the edge of shadows, causing chaos, corrupting and creating others to take part in some hellish crime against humankind. And someone, or *something*, is waking them up."

Nat stared at Crone. "You don't think it's Lucas Scale?" he whispered in dismay.

"I don't know for sure," admitted Crone, "but if you and Woody would agree to work with us, we can find whoever or *whatever* it is and destroy them."

Nat shook his head. "Even if I wanted to, I don't think Woody would agree to it. Not after what happened to his clan at Helleborine Halt. All he wants to do now is forget."

Crone tried another tack. "And what if he has no luck in locating his clan?"

"I don't know." Nat shrugged, wondering how Crone knew all this. "All I do know is that we're moving south when the circus show closes for the winter break. We'll keep looking until we find out what happened to them."

Crone nodded wearily. "Where will you go then?"

Nat shrugged again. He hadn't thought past the winter. He didn't really know where home *was*, now. When his dad had fled the country, they had given up their London flat and moved in temporarily with his nan and granddad to a strange little town in north Somerset called Temple Gurney. Nat had no doubt in his mind that 11 Camellia Lane, his grandparents' house, would be under surveillance for a very long time to come.

"I dunno," said Nat in rather a small voice.

"How does it feel to be a fugitive like your father?" asked Crone.

"We didn't do anything wrong," pointed out Nat.

"The events at Helleborine Halt are going to take years to blow over," said Crone. "A prime minister and his entire cabinet were brought down because of you and Woody. You'll be on the run for the rest of your life. Ask your father what it's like not to be able to go home."

"Home is where my family is. And Woody," said Nat firmly.

"Think of it as a crusade against evil, with NightShift as the special weapons division." Crone grinned.

"You don't give up, do you?" said Nat, smiling slightly. "Anyway, I'm only thirteen."

"You've met one of our team already," said Crone. "She's not much older than you."

Nat narrowed his eyes. *The hoodie!* "The mugger?"

"Not a mugger," said Crone. "Try superhuman hero, black belt in three disciplines, zombie basher, et cetera, et cetera. Her name is Alexandra Fish. She was very keen to meet you, *and* she's one of our best agents."

"Not my idea of a superhero," muttered Nat. "She might have hurt that old lady really badly."

"There *was* no old lady," said Crone. "The person dressed as an old lady was me."

Nat didn't know what to say.

"Fish and I just wanted to see for ourselves the gifts that Professor Paxton said you had," said Crone gently.

"The *prof* told you where to find me?" asked Nat incredulously.

Crone nodded. "Things have changed, Nat. He thought we could help each other. He's also asked me to look out for you."

"More like the other way around from what you've told me," said Nat.

"We do have some successes," said Crone, a little touchily.

"So in return for NightShift's protection we would be sort of like consultants?" asked Nat.

"Exactly," agreed Quentin Crone.

Nat grinned. "We could head up the Shape-shifting Department?"

Crone knew when he was being made fun of. He gave up. "I'll pretend you agreed to the deal and I'll keep my side of the bargain anyway," he said. "I'll do everything in my power to keep your trail cold. I will sabotage any government information about the Wolven and Helleborine Halt and I will permanently remove any images from the World's Most Wanted site. On that, you have my word."

Nat looked at him askance. "Why would you do that?"

"Because we're the good guys." Crone smiled. "You have my card. If you hear anything . . . anything at all about Mr. Scale, it's in your interest to tell me. Do we have a deal?"

"I'll try to keep in touch," said Nat.

The train was slowing down.

"I suppose it's good-bye, then," said Nat awkwardly.

"*Au revoir*, Nat." Crone smiled, shaking Nat's hand. "We've reached the end of the line."

CHAPTER 4

A SINGLE DROP OF BLOOD

Far away from the NightShift HQ in London, and roughly five hundred miles south of Paris, lay the wild and remote region of Salinas. It rested uneasily on a bed of salt plains and squashy, treacherous marshland. Jet-black bulls roamed the white plains, sharing their landscape with all manner of wild creatures from the warty-tusked wild boar and delicate pink flamingo to the rare and beautiful blue-eyed, black palomino, a horse so rarely glimpsed it was rumored to be all but extinct in the wild.

Above the plains of Salinas, not too far from the medieval town of Marais, lay the dried-out husk of an ancient vampire in its filthy coffin. A rough wooden stake was still wedged through its blackened heart, driven there with heroic force more than a century before by a brave man. All this time the vampire had lain moribund and dormant, waiting to be summoned again, to join forces in a reign of promised and unholy evil.

It had long been blind, its eyes having shriveled to calcified balls in its skull, but it could still feel and hear the scurrying and scratching of a hundred tiny creatures as they invaded its coffin. The rats' sharp teeth gnawed through the rotten wood easily, and in minutes they had broken through to where it lay. Dozens of tiny cold feet and long scabrous tails brushed the vampire's desiccated face as the creatures eagerly investigated the rank space.

The rats squealed and fought until, inevitably, a young male was bitten clean through the neck. As its body twisted and turned in agonizing death throes, a single drop of hot, vibrant blood spilled from the doomed rat into the vampire's skeletal chest cavity, where it immediately started to swell. The vampire could feel the life-giving warmth spread through its ancient bones, and it flexed its gnarly old fingers as the rat's blood fizzed like a dark tide around its carcass. Blood filled the eyes and nose of the mummified flesh; muscle and sinew reformed over old bones; and veins and arteries burned with new blood. The crimson tide reached the vampire's mouth, plumping out the lips; its scaly mottled scalp tingled maddeningly as new hair follicles began to sprout. The coffin was so engorged with fresh blood that it spewed rich-red from the cracks.

The ancient vampire drew its lips back in a savage grin of triumph, feeling the sharp incisors as it ran its tongue experimentally around its mouth. As the blood continued to flow, the vampire could feel its old strength and vigor return. It pushed away the coffin lid with a victorious cry, its body dripping and steaming with fresh gore. It rose up and, taking great gusting breaths, filled its lungs with the freezing night air. It reached for the hateful wooden stake still protruding from the hole in its heart and yanked it out with ease, throwing it to the floor with disdain; then it checked and flexed its body parts carefully until it was satisfied all was in order. Rings still shone dully on its fingers, and it was pleased to notice they hadn't been plundered by the human who had imprisoned it in that foul box for a hundred and fifty long years. The vampire stared down in pride and wonder at its female form, now looking as young and perfect as the day it had been slain. Thick black hair streamed from its scalp and snaked down over its milky shoulders in a lustrous curtain. It listened to the low howl of the wind, feeling the old, familiar hunger, and sprang catlike up to the tiny window in the ancient mausoleum, its body now fluid like silver water. It poured itself out into the freezing night, eagerly sniffing the air for more blood.

Time to dig up the servants. There was much work to be done, and it was *starving*.

CHAPTER 5
THE BLACK TENT

Del Underhill was no stranger to the ways of wolves, but he knew very well that the creature snoring outside his trailer door was not strictly a wolf at all. Real wolves were smaller: a *lot* smaller. He opened the door a tiny crack to get another look. Through the gap he saw it was still asleep, a silver thread of drool hanging from the corner of its mouth and twin plumes of condensed air rising dragonlike from its nostrils. Del pushed the door open just enough to insert a cloven hoof, then, as quietly as he could, he squeezed the rest of his body through the tiny space. Holding his breath and trying not to laugh at the same time was difficult, but he managed to step carefully over the threshold, taking care not to tread on the long white fur.

Ha! I'm away free! Del thought triumphantly. He trotted briskly across the stiff grass to the black tent. Then he dared a quick glance backward. Two topaz-colored eyes glowed like jewels through the misty evening gloom.

"*Aaaargh!*" shouted Del. He put his head down and ran as fast as he could, bouncing around like a demented springbok. He could feel the ground tremble and shake behind him, and hot breath steaming at the back of his neck. Before he could leap onto the roof of his neighbor's trailer, an enormous paw batted him on the shoulder and Del was knocked to the frozen ground with a painful, jarring thud.

"Ow, ow, get *off*, you're killin' me!" yelled Del, annoyed.

The Wolven nipped at Del's trousers, threatening to rip the material.

"No, c'mon, Woody," Del said breathlessly. "C'mon, really, that's enough now. I'm due in makeup in five minutes an' I need to change." He brushed the frost from his furry legs and consulted his watch. "Talkin' of which," he added, "you've got a train to meet, so y'have. Hadn't *you* better change an' all?"

The Eurostar slid to a halt at the Gare du Nord, and Nat and Jude jumped gratefully out onto the platform, eager for the next step of their journey. Paris felt cold enough to freeze the marrow in their bones, and the railway station was stuffed with passengers stamping their feet and blowing into their hands in a vain effort to keep warm.

Nat wondered if he would see Quentin Crone again and made a surreptitious scan of the platform; he was disappointed when he didn't appear. Instead, he spied two figures waving at them. One was a tall, broad-shouldered person who appeared to be dressed as an Arctic explorer, the other a slightly wild-looking boy with a choppy mane of pale-blond hair.

Jude gave a shriek of joy and ran toward them, arms outstretched, laughing and crying at the same time. Nat hesitated. He felt funny. He hadn't seen Woody for almost four months; his dad for a lot longer. It was weird to see them together and to think that his dad had known Woody longer than he himself had. Suddenly he felt unbearably shy.

Oh, you gert big soppy weirdo!

Nat grinned in delight, his shyness evaporating. He wondered if he could still do the two-way thing. He sent back his thoughts to Woody: *On your bike, freak!*

Don'tcha mean sur votre bicyclette, *weirdo?* came Woody's reply. It worked!

Nat ran to catch up with Jude. The four of them hugged so enthusiastically they drew smiles from their fellow passengers, despite the miserable conditions. Everyone was talking at once.

"Look at you!" Evan Carver beamed, holding Nat by the shoulders. "I almost didn't recognize you! You've grown so much you're nearly as tall as me!"

Nat was relieved to see his mum had removed the buckteeth she had worn as part of her disguise. She looked almost normal.

"C'mon!" said his dad, still beaming. "We can catch up on all our news in the car. The last show of the season starts in an hour and I don't want you to miss a *second*."

He whisked them off to an enormous black Daimler. Nat and Woody slid comfortably across the old leather seats in the back while Jude and Evan chatted and laughed loudly in the front.

"How's your froat?" asked Woody in a low voice.

"Throat's OK," said Nat, "but I need to talk to you about the other stuff that's going on."

Woody looked alarmed. "You haven't *shifted*?"

"Nearly," said Nat. "But it's all the other stuff that freaks me out sometimes. I just need you to tell me how to turn it all off."

John Carver's Twilight Circus of Illusion had been performing nightly for two weeks in Paris on the last leg of its European tour. The showground lay in the shadow of the Eiffel Tower, and Nat was well impressed before he even got inside.

Which is exactly what Nat's grandfather, John Carver, had intended. He wanted his paying customers to be enthralled and thrilled before they had set foot inside the big top. As they drove into the camp, Nat felt as if he were entering the set of a science-fiction film with a gazillion-dollar budget. The entire area seemed to be filled with silver capsules, which, when they got closer, Nat realized were trailers.

"Are we staying in one of those?" he asked his mum excitedly.

"Mmmm," said his mum, in a slightly less enthusiastic voice than Nat had expected. He was surprised. Who on earth wouldn't feel mega-excited about living in a caravan for the winter!

As Evan Carver parked the Daimler, Woody practically dragged Nat from the car in his eagerness to show him the enormous circus tent. When Nat and Jude set eyes on it for the first time, they gasped in utter amazement.

Nat had been expecting a traditional big white tent with a few Christmas decorations and maybe spotlights, but this tent was *black* and lit up by green and gold spotlights, which made the whole structure—the turrets and the enormous dome—look like an alien spaceship. If you looked up, it was impossible to see where the fabric of the tent ended and the night sky began.

"Well?" asked his dad, shivering slightly as Nat and Jude stared upward, their breath streaming out in the freezing air. "What's the verdict?"

Nat grinned, his face lit up eerily in the green and gold lights.

"It . . . it's . . . ," he spluttered, trying to get the words out, "it's . . . just . . . *brilliant!*"

His dad's smile was wide and relieved. He felt he had

a lot of making up to do to his little family. He had been away from them for too long.

"Jude?" he asked his wife nervously. "What do you think?"

Jude looked at him, her eyes shining with excitement.

"I . . . I never imagined this," she gasped. "I've never seen anything like it in my life. It's the most beautiful thing I've ever seen!"

Hundreds of people were already lining up at the turnstiles, and music filtered out from the massive foyer of the tent. There was such a feeling of intense excitement in the air that Nat thought he could smell it — it reminded him of fireworks, the smoky sulfur smell of gunpowder. An immense noise like a foghorn blasted, making his chest vibrate.

"*Ahwhhhoooo!* There goes the signal," howled Woody. "You don't wanna miss the start!"

Inside the foyer, great fiery torches burned brightly while people dressed in exotic colors and costumes juggled strange and dangerous items, ate fire, or contorted themselves into tiny boxes. There were some wearing animal costumes so strange and realistic that Nat wasn't sure if they *were* costumes at all.

"So, there's, like, no *real* animals in the circus, then?" asked Nat curiously.

Evan smiled mysteriously. "You wait," he said.

"Hey!" said a voice in Nat's left ear. "You must be the famous Nat Carver!"

Nat spun around to see three identical bare-chested young men with pointy beards smiling at him expectantly, their straight white teeth showing. He was fascinated by their ears and tried not to stare too hard in case they thought he was rude, but they were like those of goats, or *sheep*, even! Intricate tattoos covered their entire upper bodies and little horns appeared to sprout from their curly-haired heads. Even more bizarre — and at this point, Nat had to do a double take — below the waist their legs were covered *in thick black fur*.

"H'lo," said the middle one, who looked like the other two but had more of a space between his front teeth.

"Heard a lot about you," said another.

"This is Del, Paddy, and Jerry Underhill," said Woody happily. "And they're the coolest acrobats on the planet."

Nat was well impressed. "Nice to meet you all," he said, and shook hands with the three brothers.

"See y'after," said Del or Paddy or Jerry. Nat watched them as they bounded away, jumping lightly over the barriers, clearing the heads of the stunned queue.

"That's brilliant," he said. "They've got those Poweriser stilts, right?"

"Wrong," laughed Woody. "They're the satyrs. They can do that by themselves."

"Whatyrs?" asked Nat, puzzled.

"Fauns?" said Woody.

Nat still didn't get it. "Fauns?"

"Mr. Tumnus?" Woody grinned.

"Nooooo!" cried Nat, eyes bulging. "You're kidding me. I thought their ears were fake."

Woody shook his head. "Nah, that's what everyone's s'posed to think."

Nat was still trying to get his head around it when he became aware of a very small person by his side. The tiny man — or woman: Nat couldn't tell, as it was dressed in some kind of cowled garment that hid the face — pulled at Nat's sleeve as though he was supposed to follow. The hand was black, skinny, and gnarled. Oddly, its middle finger was about four inches longer than the rest. Nat looked at his dad nervously.

"It's OK," he assured Nat. "That's one of Maccabee's aye-ayes. Not sure which one, but all the performers here double up on floor duties. It's the aye-ayes' turn to show people to their seats. You better watch your loose change, though."

Nat tried to take it all in. He looked at the small figure leading him to his ringside seat. He knew that aye-ayes were some sort of weird primate, but he didn't think he had ever seen one as big as this before. When the hood it wore slipped a bit to reveal its face, Nat flinched visibly. It looked like a very old, very wizened and shriveled alien. The aye-aye possessed a pair of luminous green eyes, a furry black face with disconcertingly vampirelike teeth, and hairless, batlike ears. Scant gray fur stuck up on top of its head and it was about three times the size of the one Nat had seen at Bristol Zoo. And it smelled funny, like musty old attics.

Woody read Nat's mind. "'S part of a troupe of greater aye-ayes," he explained. "They're s'posed to be eggstinked."

Nat swallowed hard. "So this is a circus that has legendary creatures like satyrs and extinct animals like these aye-ayes?"

Woody nodded. "Cryp-tids," he said carefully, concentrating on the word, "that's where—"

"A creature is thought to exist only in fiction or legend, or an *extinct* species claimed by some scientists to still exist," interrupted Nat.

"You got it." Woody grinned. "You are *so* gonna love this."

As soon as they were shown to their seat, the musty aye-aye melted away and the lights dimmed. There wasn't a sound to be heard—not a cough or a fidget—as the audience waited with bated breath.

The foghorn noise sounded again, making everyone jump, and in the middle of the enormous ring there appeared a whirl of gray smoke. Nat gasped. A tall, broad-shouldered figure emerged from the smoke, wearing a black suit. He had wild brown curly hair to his shoulders and piercing gray eyes. It was Nat's paternal grandfather, John Carver. *Or was it?* Nat looked harder through the smoke and realized it *was* his grandfather, but not as he had last seen him. This John Carver flickered slightly and floated upon the smoke a few feet above the ring. *It must be some sort of hologram*, Nat thought to himself as it shimmered and hovered. Then it spoke in the unmistakable voice of his grandfather. It said everything twice, in French and English, and then in a weird mixture of both.

"Bonsoir, mesdames et messieurs! Je suis John Carver. Welcome to the twilight world of dreams and nightmares, of the wondrous and the uncanny. Tonight, we ask you to open your mind and believe the unbelievable, for, ladies and gentlemen, *there is no illusion.* All the incredible things you are about to see are *REAL!"*

CHAPTER 6
SMOKE AND MIRRORS

As the excitement in the tent reached fever pitch, an enormous, transparent sheet descended from high up in the big top, apparently filled with water deep enough for something to swim inside. Flashes of iridescent colors swayed in time to the music, performing a weird sort of hypnotic water ballet. Eventually Nat realized the colors were actually people, and wondered how they could stay underwater for so long with no visible breathing equipment. Were they some kind of marine people who didn't need it? He still wasn't sure if his grandfather had played a joke on the audience by wanting them to think the illusions were real!

The lights got brighter as the transparent pool ascended back into the top of the tent, and the audience clapped wildly as the three bearded satyrs bounced into the ring. *This is more like it*, thought Nat, leaning forward in his seat. He watched in admiration as the satyrs leaped madly around the ring, the audience *oooh*ing and *aaah*ing at their fantastic acrobatics and outrageous sense of humor. At the end of their act they produced sparkly feathers and tickled the kids in the audience until they shrieked. Nat noticed that some of the little ones laughed so much they looked like they were going to puke, which, he had to admit, would have made the satyrs' act even better.

He was doubly thrilled when his *actual* grandfather came striding toward him while his hologram grandfather announced the next act: the Surrealias. It was the first time Nat had seen John Carver for three years.

"Welcome to the family business, Nat." His grandfather smiled, hugging Nat close and planting a firm smacker on the top of his head. "Now, watch this act carefully. There'll be questions later."

Woody was practically frothing at the mouth to tell Nat about all the acts, but he had been forbidden. John Carver wanted to know what Nat made of the whole thing after the show.

The Surrealias turned out to be three young women lowered smoothly from the ceiling on a trapeze. They looked like exotic birds, dressed in blue and turquoise costumes with matching makeup and sequined tail feathers. They swung to and fro on the trapeze out into the audience, once swinging close to Nat. He had thought them beautiful when they first appeared, but close up he could see they were a bit too strange to be beautiful. They all had a bad case of Quasimodo back, and it wasn't just the costumes that were birdlike—their *faces* were birdlike as well. The nose and mouth seemed elongated—pushed out into a sort of beak effect—and the eyes looked as though they had been stretched to the far sides of the head. Nat suspected they wore some sort of clever makeup or masks—it was amazing what could be achieved nowadays. But as the act progressed and the Surrealias defied gravity by leaping from one side of the enormous tent to the other, Nat realized the trapeze was only there for show. His enhanced vision picked up that they weren't touching the ropes at all.

"Might be parachutes," he said to Jude, "'cause *look* . . . there's no safety net."

The bird girls and their uncanny aerobatic skills took any other thoughts away. Then, shockingly, one bird girl appeared to miss her timing, and fell. Nat couldn't bear to look; he covered his eyes until Woody shook him.

"LOOOK," he hissed.

Nat opened one eye and gasped. *What he had thought were parachutes were tiny wings!*

Instead of plummeting to her death, the girl's iridescent wings had unfolded like sycamore seeds, spinning her gently to the floor. And the crowd went wild.

"What *are* they?" Nat asked Woody. "Are they for real?"

"Cryptids," whispered Woody, "but I'm not allowed to tell you what sort. You gotta guess."

Nat didn't recover from his shock until well into the next act, which was the Zombie Dawn Street Dancers. He hoped fervently they weren't *real* zombies. But Nat's favorite acts were the daring and the comical, and although there was a lot of humor in the show, Nat was surprised there were no clowns.

"They're *way* too scary!" Woody shuddered when Nat asked him about it.

One of the audience's favorites, including Jude's, who cried actual hysterical tears of laughter afterward, was the large red-and-gold bird who appeared on the wrist of a man dressed in khaki shorts, a matching shirt, and a hat with corks dangling from it. The bird was too colorful to be a bird of prey, and Nat found himself wondering again if the creature was real, or an elaborate and realistic puppet.

The man walked around with the bird on his wrist, encouraging members of the audience, including Jude, to pet it. In Franglais, he told the audience it was an Oozlum bird, apparently now very rare in Australia.

"Not to be confused with the extinct, short-legged Ooomegoolie bird, which once lived in the Outback," he explained as Jude stroked its impressive plumage.

"The Oozlum is in danger of becoming extinct due to an odd habit it has. Please don't make any sudden moves or it'll—"

There was a *bang* like the report from a gun and the bird shot up into the top of the great tent. The man in the corked hat made a great show of being upset, and spent a long time persuading it to come back. At last, the Oozlum bird circled just above the audience in ever-decreasing circles, smaller and smaller, faster and faster, until it made Nat dizzy. Then it squawked as though in pain. There was a *pop* like a cork coming out of a bottle, and the bird disappeared.

"*Disparu!* Gone!" said the man sadly. "*C'est monté dans son propre derrière!*" The audience, including Woody, was crying with laughter.

"What?" asked Nat.

"What did he say?" asked Jude, stunned.

"It's flown up its own butt," Woody translated once he finally managed to stop laughing. "That's why they're so rare."

When Jude and Nat had recovered from the unfortunate Oozlum bird incident, the acts continued to live up to their introductions. The scary snake-people contortionists reminded Nat too much of the Pyslli clan he had seen at Helleborine Halt to be entertaining, but the next performers were a family of fierce Cossack riders with a troupe of shiny black horses, whose horsemanship and knife-throwing skills kept him on the edge of his seat for their entire act. Nat watched the youngest members of the family, two raven-haired girls of about twelve and fourteen, propel themselves fearlessly under the bellies of their enormous horses, only to end up back in the saddle, their heads still firmly in place on their shoulders, unscathed by the galloping hooves. But for all their stunning stunts and bravery, Nat couldn't spot anything supernatural or cryptid about them. The Cossacks and the horses all *looked* as though they were normal, but tonight Nat had given up trying to guess what was real and what was not.

He didn't have to wait too long to see the strange aye-ayes again. They crept with unnatural grace into the ring behind a man who looked like the human equivalent of an aye-aye, and Nat wasn't the only one in the audience to shiver a bit at his appearance. He was thin and bony with scant aye-aye-type black hair and a ghost-white face. His eyes were made up with black, and his demeanor was rather slow, so that he appeared to creep rather than walk. The John Carver hologram introduced him as Maccabee Hammer, Master Magician, and the aye-ayes as his unlovely assistants. Along with the way the aye-ayes freaked out most people with their bony fingers and uncanny saucer-eyed stares while the magician impressed everyone with his unique type of magic, the part Nat liked best was when Maccabee (who although undeniably weird, was very funny) made the aye-ayes give back all the stuff they had pilfered from people in the audience. *Maybe they have pouches like hamsters or kangaroos*, he thought, but the amount they had pinched seemed to be more than their own body weight, and no one in the audience even realized they'd been robbed.

In any circus the final acts are the best, and Carver's Twilight Circus of Illusion did not disappoint. There followed the nightmare story of "Red Riding Hood," where Granny's big teeth and eyes turned out to be that of a real wolf. Nat knew from experience that the shape-shift had been real; in Granny's bed there was a real, live werewolf. He glanced at his mum, who was clearly thinking the same thing, and he could tell by her expression that she didn't like it at all. *She's still worried about me*, he thought uncomfortably. But the rest of the audience loved it.

Hologram grandpa came into the ring again for the last time to announce the finale.

"Et maintenant, mesdames et messieurs, notre finale — la Femme de Requin! I give you — Shark Woman!"

Inside a large tank swam two women in electric-blue wetsuits, their long blond hair fanning out in the water. The water pulsated with different colors in time to the music while they dived, making it difficult for the audience to see sometimes. Everyone cried out in shock when the water suddenly clouded dark red, and the two girls vanished. The crowd stood in their seats, craning their necks to see what was happening. The water cleared and the audience gasped again. A large gray thing with a dorsal fin and sharp teeth had somehow got into the tank. And there appeared to be only one girl left! *Had the shark eaten the other one?* But Nat, with his supernatural sight, had seen what others could not. Behind the mask of red, one girl had morphed very smoothly into a shark. The water cleared and the audience was treated to the shark playing a game of cat and mouse with the remaining girl. When the audience started screaming, the water clouded again and the girl morphed back. The two performers emerged unscathed and smiling from the tank. The shark, of course, had disappeared.

It had been an adventure and, as Nat stood and clapped with the rest of the thrilled but exhausted audience, someone caught his eye. She was coming toward him, smiling slightly. She had unmistakable fire-engine red hair, shiny black biker boots, and brilliant orange eyes. It was Crescent.

CHAPTER 7
THE *SILVER LADY*

Crescent Domini Moon was the only female werewolf Nat had ever met. Early on in their acquaintance, Nat had decided that if Crescent was typical of the female of the species, he wasn't in a great hurry to meet any more, thank you very much.

So what if Crescent was beautiful? She was also bossy, loud, and extremely vain, and as Nat watched her, she sashayed along, basking in admiring stares from people nearby, acting as though she owned the place. Most onlookers would assume her Halloween-orange eyes owed their color to novelty contact lenses, but the opposite was true. Nat knew that werewolves living in the community usually wore colored contacts or polarized glasses to hide the true color of their eyes.

"Jude!" cried Crescent as she made a big show of air-kissing Jude on both cheeks. *"Mwah, mwah."* Then she turned to Nat, giving him a big hug and a smacking kiss on the lips. Nat blushed to the roots of his hair, deciding maybe he had been wrong about Crescent all along. But when she started bossing them around and taking charge, he changed his mind again.

"Guess *what*," gushed Crescent, "Angelo and Vincent are here! They've taken time off from their restaurant to cook a special welcome dinner in your honor."

Nat was dead chuffed. It was largely due to the heroic acts of the twin werewolves, Angelo and Vincent Spaghetti, that Nat and Woody had escaped from Helleborine Halt with their lives. Far from being the murderous, savage beasts portrayed in the media, many werewolves fit into the community surprisingly well, although of course, there were always exceptions to any rule, as Nat and Woody had found out firsthand.

Then Nat remembered something from the show. "Were you the wolf in the Red Riding Hood act?" he asked her.

Crescent lifted her lip slightly, showing white teeth. "Do me a favor. Do I *look* like a performing animal?"

"It was Otis," said Woody hastily, seeing Nat's

crushed expression, "you know . . . the bass player in the Howlers."

All Nat knew about Otis was that he was a tall, dark-haired, bass-playing werewolf from Cardiff, who seemed to leak vapor trails of cool from every pore in his body.

"Are you and the Howlers staying with the circus, then?" asked Nat.

Crescent flicked her red hair. "We're traveling south with you," she purred. "Isn't that *great*?"

Nat smiled weakly. *Oh yeah, that is* so *great. Not*, he thought to himself. Crescent Domini Moon had just got *way* too big for her biker boots.

Nat and Woody followed Crescent outside. The music still played and great torches blazed fire across the frozen grass, making it sparkle red and gold. The crowd, bundled into thick layers of clothing, followed the torchlit path to the gates, anxious now to be home, safe from the biting cold of the night.

Crescent stopped abruptly, gazing longingly at the moon. *"Look at that sky,"* she murmured in a low, husky growl. Nat and Woody stood either side of her, staring up at the swollen full moon hanging above them. It looked so close that Nat felt he could reach out and touch it. It made him feel restless and weird.

"It's *irresistible*," said Crescent dreamily, and for a moment her face shifted, as though her change was coming and she wasn't going to stop it. Nat caught just a fleeting glimpse of her inner wolf, and then it was gone. She smiled, her teeth glinting dangerously in the light of the moon.

"Want to come?" she asked Woody, and prodded his shoulder.

Nat noticed that for a few seconds her fingernails seemed to lengthen into vicious-looking claws.

Woody shook his head. "It's Nat's first night."

Crescent turned to Nat. "You can come if you want," she said offhandedly.

"Where?" asked Nat, puzzled. "We're going for dinner soon."

"So am I." Crescent grinned, licking her lips. "But I'm talking about *real* food."

"She wants to run with the moon," explained Woody.

"Oh," said Nat, not fully understanding.

"Getting down with my bad self." Crescent grinned

again, her eyes blazing with excitement. "A hunt."

"I can't," said Nat, narrowing his eyes. "You *know* I can't. I won't be able to keep up: I can't change like you."

"Shame." Crescent smirked. "Well, if I can't tempt you, I'm off. I need to, um . . . undress for dinner."

"*You* go if you want," said Nat, turning to Woody.

Woody shook his head.

"D'you go on runs a lot, then?" asked Nat, watching Crescent dash across the grass.

Again, Woody shook his head, and shivered. "I don't think I'd like it."

Nat was surprised. He continued to be thankful his supernatural gifts didn't include a full shape-shift, but all the same he imagined it would be thrilling to run with the pack under a full moon.

"Why not?" he asked curiously.

"They kill stuff," said Woody simply.

Slightly unnerved, Nat watched as Crescent melted into the shadows.

"Come on," said Woody, breaking the mood, "there's your mum and dad. I'll show you where you're gonna live."

Evan had explained that after the final dinner, some

of the circus people would be leaving for their winter homes, while others, including the Carvers and Woody, would prepare for the long drive south to a place called Salinas, their winter quarters. The black tent would be dismantled the next morning and the animals and caravans made ready for the journey.

Small sodium lamps lit the way as Nat followed Woody, their boots crunching across the frosty grass, their breath making whirling patterns in the freezing air. The silver trailers that Nat had spotted on arrival were arranged in neat rows some way behind the black tent, and Nat spotted his grandfather's black Daimler parked regally next to his trailer. In keeping with his status as ringmaster and co-owner, his van was larger than anyone else's, although he lived alone. Nat ran his hand along the freezing mirror-finish of the trailer. He had never seen anything like it. It was like a cross between an enormous tin can and a tiny space capsule.

"All the caravans are made from aluminum alloy," said his dad, who had caught up to them. "They might look brand-new, but they're all pretty much vintage—about fifty years old."

"They look like they're from the future," said Nat. "They're *amazing*."

"This one's ours," said Woody excitedly. "She's called the *Silver Lady*. I'll show you around."

Nat raised his eyebrows. "Show me *around*?" he snorted. "That's not going to take very long!"

He followed Woody into the *Silver Lady*, hoping it—*she*—was going to be a lot bigger than she looked from the outside. She wasn't.

Nat thought he had walked into Santa's Grotto by mistake. The ceiling, walls, and cupboards were strewn with tinsel and baubles, and on the tiny table stood a Christmas tree and one of those glass snow globes you shake to make your own mini snowstorm. Woody took Nat's shocked gasp as one of pleasure, and because Nat didn't want to disappoint him, he laughed weakly.

"Oooh," he said, "Christmas has come early."

"I *knew* you'd like it," said Woody happily. "Want to shake the snow fing?"

Nat picked up the snow globe and shook it once, just to be polite, while Woody waited impatiently for his turn.

"How did you know I always wanted one of these?" Woody smiled, shaking the snow globe so hard that Nat feared for the safety of the tiny reindeer inside.

"I didn't," said Nat in surprise. "Where'd you get it?"

Woody looked confused. "*You* sent it to me."

Nat frowned. "*No*, I think I'd remember if I had."

"It was in a pretty box with a note," insisted Woody.

Nat shook his head. "What did the note say?"

"Can't remember. Something like *see you soon*, I fink."

Nat shrugged. "Well, I'm glad you got a present, but it wasn't from me. Maybe the present was for someone else?"

"No," said Woody firmly. "It's *mine*, 'cause I'm worth it."

Nat grinned, remembering how Woody had learned loads of his English from watching TV commercials. Leaving Woody happily shaking the snow globe, he gazed around the *Silver Lady*.

Obviously designed with hobbits in mind, there were two neatly made-up bunks, a minuscule stove, a table (swallowed by the Christmas tree), and two chairs that looked as though two of the seven dwarfs were coming for tea. There was a washbasin and a closet with a bucket inside, which Nat suspected (hoping he was wrong) was the toilet facility. Almost hidden by eight rows of multi-colored tinsel sat Woody's most prized possession.

"Hey, you got your own TV at last!" cried Nat.

Woody stroked the TV set fondly. "It's *French* TV. They speak French!"

"Oh," said Nat, losing interest, "I don't expect I'll bother with it, then."

"Good commercials, though." Woody beamed. "Nice tunes."

Nat smiled, glad that Woody still liked the commercials best.

He could feel his friend waiting breathlessly for his approval of the rest of the caravan. Due to the explosion of Christmas decorations, Nat had a hard time at first to see the *Star Wars* posters on the walls and closet doors, the brightly colored cushions and blankets on the bunks, and the favorite books arranged on the shelves. The caravan was lit by a small lamp, which flickered cozily in the corner.

"I did it all," said Woody nervously. "I wanted you to like it."

"This," said Nat, beaming, "is *brilliant*. Even

better than brilliant! I thought I'd be sharing with Mum and Dad."

"Thought you and Woody would be OK on your own." Evan appeared in the doorway. "Your mum and I are right next door, so any loud music or loud noises . . ."

"We'll know who to complain to." Nat grinned.

Evan glanced at his watch. "You've got about an hour before we eat," he said. "Why don't you unpack, make yourself at home, and we'll walk across together?"

Nat watched as Woody lit the tiny, wood-burning stove, put the kettle on it, and explained how everything worked. There were solar panels on the roof that supplied most of their electricity, which he said was stored in batteries from decommissioned submarines (another cool fact for Nat to savor). Woody lit some candles to give the gas lamp a bit more oomph, and in no time the trailer was warm and cozy. It felt like home.

After Nat had unpacked the few things he had brought with him, the boys sat down with their drinks to talk properly without being overheard.

Woody had been having the time of his life, by the sound of it. Nat could see that he had grown since he last saw him, and cleaned up his unibrow. He looked almost human in the candlelight, but Nat thought there would always be a wildness about him that would set him apart from true humans. And while Nat had been recovering from his wound in Temple Gurney, Woody had been either loping around the site in Wolven shape or, when he shifted to human shape, busy helping Evan backstage, learning French from TV commercials, and making more friends.

Woody listened intently as Nat told him about the changes he was experiencing.

"These . . . things that've been happening, they're not *all* bad. I don't want my mum and dad to know what's going on, though," he explained. "Just after I got the Wolven blood transfusion, my sense of smell went crazy, and I've got, like, *infrared* vision—I can see things miles and miles away, even in the *dark*. But I get these headaches, 'cause when I'm in a crowd of people, I can't tune stuff out: It's like there's always noise in my head. It's like watching TV while you're eating potato chips—"

"What *you* need is an earworm," interrupted Woody.

Nat stared at his friend askance. He didn't like the

sound of that at all. Was this earworm some sort of parasite that lived in the ear canals of all Wolvens — or his case, half Wolvens? Did it hurt? Was it alive . . . ?

Woody laughed at Nat's slightly worried expression. "An earworm isn't alive, it's a tune."

Nat still looked worried.

"It's, like, you think of the most annoying song you can think of, and after a while it kind of lodges itself inside your head," explained Woody. "Then you can use that to block anyone nosy enough to want to brain-jack your thoughts."

"Like you." Nat grinned.

"Yup," said Woody, nodding, "some fings are private. But what *else* has happened? Have bits of you disappeared, like when my ears don't always go back to normal?"

"No, nothing like *that*." Nat shivered. "It's nothing, really; it's stuff that's easy to hide. I'm physically stronger; I get these premonitions when bad things are going to happen, and—"

"But you definitely haven't shifted?" interrupted Woody again. "'Cause the game will be up when that starts. Trust me, I should know."

"No," admitted Nat, "and I don't think I can, either. But like I hinted in the car, something happened to me at St. Pancras, and then I met this man on the train." He told Woody what had happened and Woody stared, his topaz eyes shimmering in the lamplight.

"He wanted *us* to join this, er . . . NightShift agency?" he asked, astounded.

Nat nodded. "He reckons that there's been an increase in supernatural activity and that the human race is in for a bit of a rough time. He said if we join them, he'd arrange a sort of amnesty—you know, like when people break a law they won't get punished. . . ."

"We didn't *break* any law," pointed out Woody. "We didn't do anything wrong at all. It was Gruber and Scale; they were *killers*."

Nat stared at Woody's sorrowful face. "Crone knows that," he said. "He promised to get rid of any stuff on the Internet about us. I didn't even *know* we were on World's Most Wanted. Iona never told me."

Woody looked stricken with guilt. "I'm sorry," he said. "If it hadn't been for me, you wouldn't be in this mess."

"*What?*" cried Nat. "And miss all this? Anyway, if it hadn't been for you, I'd be dead."

"You'd be normal," pointed out Woody.

"Yeah, normal but dead!" Nat laughed.

"You can do the two-way thing—Crescent can't," said Woody, brightening.

"Sometimes," agreed Nat, "although it looks as though we're limited by distance."

"Can you read my mind?" asked Woody.

"No," admitted Nat, "not as much as you can read mine. And it's like . . . when other voices butt in, I sometimes miss stuff that's more important."

Woody nodded. "That happens to me sometimes. Still got a lot of practicing to do, I s'pose. But I still haven't met anyone else who can do it yet, apart from you."

"Me and—" began Nat.

"Lucas Scale," whispered Woody.

They were silent for a few moments as they remembered the hideous creature that still haunted their nightmares. For a split second Nat wondered if he should tell Woody what Quentin Crone had told him. That Scale's body had never been found. He decided not to tell; after all, it didn't really mean anything. Or did it? He glanced at Woody's face and tried to block his fears by thinking of something else. He didn't want Woody to read his thoughts.

"What about you?" asked Nat, changing the subject well away from Scale. "How's the shifting?"

"Coolio." Woody grinned. "Doesn't hurt at all—seems like I got the knack most of the time. I tried shifting specially today, in case the two-way thing didn't work, but the shifting worked first time!"

"Still prefer to be Wolven shape, then?" asked Nat curiously.

Woody hesitated. "I dunno . . . yeah . . . I guess. It's a lot easier—*simpler*—being Wolven. It's like putting on baggy pajamas when you've been wearing tight an' itchy pants."

Nat nodded. He thought he could understand that feeling.

"It's like . . . a rest," continued Woody. "It's hard work being human."

Nat smiled. "What about your ears?"

"Still got a mind of their own," admitted Woody. "I

want to be able to do it properly for when I meet the rest of my clan."

"*If* you meet them, you mean," pointed out Nat.

"*When* I meet them," said Woody firmly.

"Let's hope," Nat said, and the pair were quiet for a bit, lost in their own thoughts.

The place where the professor and Iona had first found Woody's Wolven clan was close to where the circus would make their winter quarters. But no one knew for sure whether there were any of them left now, or whether Woody was the last of the King's Wolven. While Nat was eager for Woody to find his clan, he had to admit to himself that it was bound to change things between them as friends. Worse still, it was all Woody had thought about since they met. Nat didn't like to think what would happen if they weren't successful.

"Anyway, seems like while I've been holed up with Iona and the prof at Meade Lodge, you've been having a great time," said Nat after a while.

"Yeah," said Woody, smiling. "I tried to tune you in a few times, but Temple Gurney was just too far away to get any reception. It worked at the train place, though."

Nat nodded. That had been *soooo* cool. It was hard to believe that, just a few months ago, Woody had had trouble stringing a few words together. And who'd have thought that choppy haircuts would have become fashionable? With his cool hair and his neatly plucked eyebrows, he was like a different Wolven.

"The Crone man," said Woody seriously, "can we trust him to keep his promise?"

Nat nodded. "He said even if we didn't join NightShift, he'd, like, look out for us."

"*I* don't like the sound of it." Woody shivered. "Anyway, thank goodness we're done with all that dangerous stuff."

CHAPTER 8
THE PEOPLE UNDER THE ICE

In the wild region of Salinas, the ancient vampire was restored; its cheeks glowed with vitality and evil cheer and its body grew stronger. It had been called out in the darkness; something had summoned the creatures of the night with their sharp rodent teeth to sacrifice one of their own and reanimate the empty vampire husk. The vampire wasted no time thinking about why it had been freed from its coffin after a century and a half—it didn't care.

Revenge is a dish best eaten hot and rare, it thought to itself spitefully. Presently it would be time for the sniveling peasants in the town below to pay for its incarceration. And *ooh* . . . how they would pay!

Loud screams interrupted the vampire's thoughts of glorious and bloody revenge, and it grinned delightedly at the sound of human suffering, for a good vampire's assistant needed to be trained like a dog. The human girl in the north tower was proving a difficult vein to tap, but once she calmed down she would see the benefits: She'd get to live forever, never say sorry, travel the world, and earn power and a fortune beyond her wildest dreams. In time, she would be made a half vampire, and then, if she passed the vampire initiation, she would take the blood of a vampire and be complete. For some reason (and the vampire couldn't for the unlife of it understand what it was), this wonderful career opportunity seemed repulsive to the girl in the tower. Still grinning, its teeth giving it a wolfish leer, the vampire inserted ear plugs into its slightly pointed ears and fell into a bloated and dreamless sleep.

The screaming girl in the north tower was called Saffi Besson, and she had been yelling and screaming on and off since the sun rose and the vampire had left her to sleep the sleep of the undead. Until four days ago she had been blissfully unaware that vampires were actually *real*. Her terrifying captor fed and hunted from dusk to dawn and then it would disappear for the day, leaving her alone and waiting in terror for its return when the dark came again. On the fourth day, confident that the pattern would be the same, Saffi had decided to escape the room. Whether she would manage to get outside the chateau would remain to be seen, but leaving the cheerless, freezing prison would be a start. The vampire hadn't shackled her — there was no need. The room in which Saffi had slept fitfully for the last three days had a window, but the jump from it would have killed her — although when the vampire had shared its plans for the future with her, Saffi had vowed to die from the fall rather than become a vampire. The thick oaken door was locked, but on the first day of her imprisonment, Saffi had spotted a possible escape route. A plan had formed in her practical mind, but she had been too scared to try it at first in case she woke the ugly old bloodsucker. To test her theory she had screamed her head off. The vampire had not appeared. Then last night, when it had revealed its dreadful plan, Saffi couldn't afford to wait any longer. She had to get out *now*, before the daylight disappeared.

If she had been equipped with a toolbox and a strong assistant, her plan would have worked within about half an hour. But because she had neither, she estimated it could take all day. On that first day of her imprisonment she had noticed that the door hinges stuck out, slightly proud of the wood, where the old wooden door had expanded and shrunk many times over the centuries. It became a fixation and she had to stop herself from looking at them in case the vampire noticed. If somehow she could remove the hinges before it was too late, she could escape.

Taking a deep breath, she knelt at the old door with its three hinges. One part was pinned to the door, the other to the door frame, the two parts fitting together like puzzle pieces. There was a third part to the hinge, like a long nail that was threaded through, holding it all together. Taking off her boot, Saffi used the heel as a makeshift hammer. At first, the hinge didn't seem to want to budge, but she worked on the theory that if she kept at it, the vibration would shift it slightly. The process was painfully slow. Three hours later, her body oily with sweat, her fingers swollen and bloody, she managed to push one pin up and out of its hinge. *One down, two to go!* The blood was making her hands slippery and she wiped them on her filthy jeans, leaving bloody handprints. Her face set in a grimace of pain and exertion, she set to work again, trying not to notice how the shadows had shortened in her small prison, indicating that the time left was short.

Just before dusk, Saffi released the hinges and jimmied the door open with her ruined boot. A really bad moment followed her initial triumph. She found her legs were so numb from kneeling they wouldn't work. Rubbing them fiercely, she managed to get the blood circulating again. She staggered over to the window — the weak winter sun was just about to dip below the horizon. *It would be waking up!*

Saffi didn't know her way out — she had been unconscious when her captor had brought her here — but she half fell, half ran down the stone staircase, which led to a vast room with austere, ancient furniture. It looked as if no one from this century had ever set foot inside. It was frozen in time. But the good news was that no one was there! Saffi had never seen anyone else apart from her captor, but she had sometimes heard footsteps, maniacal laughter, and the voices of others while the vampire was asleep. But no one ever answered her desperate cries for help. She looked wildly around for a door that would lead her to freedom. Saffi knew she was being held in a large castle, a chateau, for her room had been in a tower, looking across a great roof with turrets, but she had no idea where she was. All around her lay the desolate salt plains covered in snow, with no sign of a house or farm anywhere. Worst of all, she had not seen so much as a glimpse of any other living creature, either human or animal. Never before had Saffi felt so alone. But the act of escaping the awful room and running down the staircase had made the adrenaline kick in.

Come on! she told herself sternly. *You're free, Saffi! Run!* Her senses fueled, she spotted a door and opened it without hesitation. Behind the door was a stone corridor that took Saffi into what looked like a kitchen scullery. At the end of the scullery was another huge door. Unaware she was sobbing, she prayed it would be open. She didn't have much time before . . . *Don't think about it, just do it.*

She rattled the latch and put her shoulder to the door. *Locked!* But then she saw a large ornate key sticking out. In her panic, she had been so sure she wouldn't get out, her eyes had somehow missed the key!

Hope gave Saffi strength as she turned the key in the

lock and burst out onto the treacherous, rock-strewn path outside. She daren't risk a look behind her in case she lost her footing; if she fell now, she wouldn't have the strength left to get up again and . . . She tried not to think about what would happen to her then. Her hot breath plumed out of her body in ragged bursts, turning to crystals as it hit the freezing air. Her blood pounded in her ears as she ran down the steep path, mercifully blocking out the caterwauling wail of the wind shifting and snaking across the deserted plains.

Reaching the bottom, Saffi stopped to catch her breath. Everything around her — the pockets of swirling snow, the trees far ahead in the distance, and the frozen expanse of water at her feet, which she hoped would deliver her to freedom — was drawn lividly against the black canvas of the night. A young moon glared down at her, its fierce light hurting her sore eyes, which had become used to the dark. There was no evidence in the eerie frozen landscape of another living soul.

Saffi allowed herself a backward glance. If she had stayed *up there*, she would have been a life support system for the old bloodsucker and become "one of them" herself.

When her soul finally left her body, it would be fit only for the fires of hell.

"GO!"

Saffi's head snapped back at the sound of the voice. She listened for it again, her head held high and still, her eyes wide, nostrils flaring slightly like those of a frightened deer. Now she was hearing voices!

"RUN, SAFFI!"

It was coming from under the ice.

That's impossible, she reasoned with herself. After all she had been through, was it any wonder her mind was playing tricks on her? *It must be my own subconscious telling me to get a move on.*

Pulling herself together, she put one foot on top of the ice to test its strength, knowing it could be thinner and more liable to crack in the middle of the water. She leaned forward as far as she could without toppling over and lowered her right foot toe first. Then, satisfied it would hold, she placed her heel down gingerly and stood for a second.

"RUN!"

Louder now, but oddly muffled, the voice was underneath her. Saffi froze, peering down at the ice through long, frosted lashes. She gasped as she looked closer. Somehow, impossibly, there *was* a person down there. Someone was calling from below the ice!

Dropping to her knees, Saffi brushed away the thin layer of snow, making a window into the frozen lake. More shapes clamored and pressed upward against the underside of the ice crust, their unformed faces oddly fluid and ghostlike. Saffi sensed that the people trapped under the ice had been human once, but no more.

The faces staring up at her were eerie, but not frightening. Somehow, she knew they held no danger for her. A sense of loss and sadness swept over her as she stumbled awkwardly to her feet again, tears blurring her vision. There was nothing she could do for them. They were revenants — the lost souls of the vampire's dead.

"RUN, SAFFI! RUN!"

She looked down again at the ghostly faces pressed up against the ice, then took off, her feet in their scuffed boots gripping the frozen water surprisingly well. The moon lit her way to the edge and to the sanctuary of the trees. To her astonishment, someone stood on the edge, waving frantically. *A boy!* A boy about her own age, with dark hair and a concerned expression. As she lifted her right foot to take her final step off the ice toward the boy, she stumbled and fell, her frozen cheek pressed to the hard surface.

"Saffi! Come *on*, get *up*!"

In slow, dreamlike motion, Saffi reached for the boy's outstretched hand. She was close enough to look into his dark blue eyes. Tearfully, she gathered her wits and scrabbled to her feet, her hand not quite reaching his. A strange keening sound echoed around the ice from the people below. Way above came a blackness so dark the light from the moon was blotted out. The boy was yelling at her, but Saffi turned around slowly and looked up at the flying shape above, her lips moving silently as the darkness enveloped her. The revenants under the ice were still making their wild keening noises, which echoed around the deserted plain.

By the time the moon shone again, Saffi Besson had vanished. It was as though she had never been there at all.

CHAPTER 9

AN ENGLISH WEREWOLF IN PARIS

Hunger howled deep inside their bellies. No matter how much food they would eat later, it would never be the same as eating meat that was still alive. Just before Crescent lost the power of human speech, she delivered her final instructions to the Howlers.

"Don't do anything to draw attention to yourselves," she growled. "Repeat after me: Don't. Do. Anything. Stupid."

"*GgrrrdondoaneeeyooooohhOOOOOOOOHAAH WOOOOOOOooo!*" howled Otis. It was too late for the others. They were struggling with the early stages of the shift and their human vocal chords had shriveled. Now unable to form words, the werewolves would communicate only by howling until they changed back to human shape.

Their humanity was draining away like sand in an hourglass, and the race was on to find a private spot to shift. Few werewolves were happy to be seen halfway through their change. It could often be a brutal experience to witness, and definitely not recommended.

Crescent chose the trailer farthest from the rest of the camp, near to the large open space of grass and trees known as the *Champ de Mars*. They had run here on other occasions, taking care to keep within sight of each other, and away from humans, not daring to stray into any built-up neighborhoods. The only good thing about the cold snap was that fewer people were about to spot a gang of large furry creatures with big teeth.

Crescent could feel the blood in her veins start to fizz and zing as it always did when her change was imminent. She undressed hurriedly, trembling with the onset of the change and shivering under the cold light of the swollen moon. The first spasm knocked her to her knees, making her howl. It forced her to lie prone on the freezing grass, but she was oblivious to everything apart from the shift. She could see her hands stretch out before her into large paws with long, blackened claws. Then, *CRAAAAACK*... Her neck lengthened and her spine made a bone-crunching, snapping sound that would have set her considerably larger teeth on edge if she hadn't been preoccupied with everything else being rearranged. Her nose and mouth rippled and stretched until they had formed the shape of a snout, and her canine teeth grew into sharp, white points. While luxuriant copper-colored fur grew all over her body, her long, fire-engine red human hair retreated eerily back into her scalp. Seconds later, the long plume of her tail appeared, completing her change. It had taken just minutes, and now she was eager to find the others.

Her sharp ears picked up a guttural half howl. She recognized Otis's gruff voice and loped toward the sound, making a yipping noise in reply. Crescent could see three black wolf shapes silhouetted by the light of the moon. They yipped excitedly, circling each other and snapping at each other's heels, whipping up a frenzy for the night's run. It was not unusual for a she-wolf to be the alpha leader, and there had never been any question from the boys that Crescent would be the boss, although Otis had been a werewolf longer and was older by eighteen months. Ramone, the smallest wolf, acted as lookout; quiet, sensitive Salim was the scout; and Otis was the brains.

Crescent was easily the fastest, and she led them away

from the circus camp to the open spaces of the Champ de Mars. They ran, feeling their energy and power build with each step as they loped out into the parklands. She led the small pack along the border of trees, sniffing the cold air for scents. It was proving disappointing; it seemed it was just too cold for anything to be out. Crescent caught a tantalizing whiff of something promising meat, but it was carrion: the chewed, frozen body of a large rat, its eyes having been taken by whatever had killed it.

Once out of the trees, their mood lifted and excitement returned, although it soon became clear there was no sport to be had. In a moment of madness, Crescent turned tail and made a split decision to head for the frozen streets, her small pack following, inquisitive to find out where she was taking them. Most of the streetlights were unlit these days in a bid to save resources, and they appeared to be headed toward another smell. This time it was gorgeous. It was *alive*. A rich, pungent animal scent filled their nostrils, egging them on, as their great paws flew swiftly across the dark pavements of Paris.

The glorious smell was getting stronger, pulsing with

promise, and Crescent came to a skidding halt by ornate gates flanked by a high wall.

A large sign outside said:

PARC ZOOLOGIQUE

She had taken them to the zoo! Otis hung back, sensing what Crescent had in mind. He bared his teeth at her, warning her not to go any farther. She snarled and trotted away toward the high perimeter wall, then paced up and down, measuring its height. Otis growled again. *Hang on a minute*, he thought, curling his lip and snarling, *this is bad. This isn't my idea of not doing anything stupid. This isn't my idea of not drawing attention to ourselves.*

But Crescent had conveniently forgotten her own words of warning and was eager to break all the rules. Otis stalked her on his belly, licking his lips, tail between his legs, fully aware that Crescent was the alpha wolf. She ran at him, teeth fully bared, daring him to come any closer.

Ramone and Salim fell in behind, showing her their full support, and Otis knew he had lost. They scaled the walls with their strong claws and leaped down easily to the other side, with Otis reluctantly bringing up the rear. By now, the captive animals had been alerted by the angry screeches of the monkeys, who had smelled the werewolves as the pack of four had loped through the gardens. Crescent took no notice as the big cats threw themselves against the bars of their cages, snarling and showing their teeth to ward off these strange intruders who smelled like death. She ignored the warning stamps of the giraffes and rhinos, having no interest in the larger caged animals. Strings of steaming saliva hung from her jaws as she savored the anticipation of the hunt.

A delicious smorgasbord of tastes awaited them in the petting zoo, although their prey was disappointingly easy to catch. Crescent enjoyed three guinea pigs as an appetizer, a slightly gamey-tasting meerkat as her main course, but nothing for dessert — she was saving that for later. The boys had a number of fresh rabbits to start with, and played it safe by having a tasty medley of game birds for their main course. To round off the unexpected but welcome meal, they ripped a vending machine full of chocolate bars from the wall of the café, and ate all of them still wrapped.

At last, feeling satisfied and full, Crescent and the Howlers retreated back to the Twilight Circus as though they had just been for a bracing run in the park.

CHAPTER 10

PEOPLE WHO ARE DIFFERENT

Nat's increased appetite was one Wolven trait he couldn't manage to hide from his mum. But most teenage boys were hungry all the time, so Jude wasn't too surprised to see him stuff his face for the better part of an hour that evening.

The food just kept on coming, from the succulent seafood starters (Woody's favorite) to steaks that were cooked to carnivore perfection—hardly at all—so that the blood ran freely and got soaked up in the fries like red gravy. There were twenty-two different side dishes and profiteroles with six different types of chocolate sauce. The famous Spaghetti brothers and their team worked hard behind the scenes to create a feast Nat would never, ever forget. It was almost midnight by the time they had finished eating, and Nat had passed the point of tiredness hours ago. Sitting at the table surrounded by his family and his best friend, with everyone trying to talk at once, his earlier feeling of unease had passed. In between feeding his face he tried not to stare too much at the more exotic circus people and animals. He spotted Maccabee Hammer minus the aye-ayes, sitting at a table for one. Maccabee was apparently on a diet, for all he had on his table was a glass of red wine—not even so much as a bread roll.

He nudged Woody. "Look," he said. "Maccabee's still got his makeup on."

Woody looked over in surprise. "What makeup?" he asked.

"You mean, he really looks that way?" said Nat in astonishment.

"Well, *duh*," said Woody, his mouth full of custard, "that's the way most vampires look, ain't it?"

Whooooo! Nat didn't really have anything to say to that. He looked over at Maccabee Hammer again and caught his eye. Maccabee raised his glass and winked.

Flippin' heck, thought Nat, smiling hastily before he looked away. He didn't know if Woody was pulling his leg or not. Maccabee did have an otherworldly look about him, but then again so did *most* of the people Nat had seen since he arrived. Over the past months, Nat had learned that humans shared the earth with all sorts of creatures including shape-shifters, so why *not* vampires? Still, Maccabee must be safe—*surely* his granddad wouldn't have given him a job if he wasn't? He was dying for John Carver to hurry up and tell him more about the strange and excellent Twilight Circus of Illusion.

Suddenly, Nat felt himself being lifted high off the floor and onto the broad shoulders of an enormous, hand-some Italian man wearing an apron. Beside him was another enormous Italian, also wearing an apron and a huge toothy smile.

"Angelo! Vincent!" cried Nat in delight.

"No more big adventures for you, eh, Nat Carver?" said Angelo Spaghetti when he had placed Nat safely on his seat again.

Nat nodded happily. "Too right." He beamed.

Vincent Spaghetti gently inspected the scars on Nat's throat. "You heal well, my friend." He smiled. "And no more monsters, eh?"

Monsters. An unwelcome picture of Lucas Scale popped

into Nat's brain, and despite the fact that Vincent's words were supposed to be comforting, Nat shivered. It was like something had stomped over his grave. He hoped for everyone's sakes that NightShift was wrong and Scale was dead and stayed that way. If they were right, maybe his dreams would warn him. He seemed to be getting more tuned into them lately, even more sensitive than Woody, and he was full Wolven, unlike Nat, who was . . . well, he was a sort of mongrel now, neither full human nor full Wolven. And he seemed to have inherited his grandmother's second sight, so maybe that was why he was getting "bad vibes," as his other granddad, Mick, would call them. It seemed longer than just a few months ago that his world had been turned upside down by Wolven and werewolves. The world he had known for thirteen cozy years no longer existed. Stuff was never going to be the same again, that much was a fact, and he had to deal with it.

Suddenly Nat didn't feel so safe. Not safe at all.

When the last plate had been cleared—licked clean, in a few cases—John Carver (or JC, as Nat noticed everyone called him) was ready to talk business. He asked Nat if he had guessed which performances were an illusion and which were not.

"I don't know," admitted Nat. "I think I spotted all the real stuff, but some were so crazy, they *must* have been an illusion."

Nat watched as his grandpa leaned over and pulled out a wad of crisp new euros from Woody's ear. "Was that real?" he asked.

"'Course not." Nat grinned. "You used to do that when I was little."

"Sleight of hand," agreed JC, "but you have to admit, I'm not bad. What about this?" He got up from the table and turned his back to Nat. His feet left the floor and he appeared to levitate a good few inches in the air.

"That's a trick, too," said Nat. "A good one, but it's a technique. Anyone can learn it."

"Good lad." JC beamed, sitting down. "Which act unsettled you most?"

Nat didn't hesitate. "The Surrealias," he said in a low voice, making sure one of them wasn't standing behind him. "They were real cryptids, right? That wasn't makeup or illusion."

"Harpies." His grandpa nodded.

"Harpies," said Nat, his eyes stretching wide. "What on earth are they?"

"Mythic beasts of ancient Greece," explained his grandpa, "half bird, half woman. Also known as 'Snatchers,' who allegedly snatched people off the streets and took 'em to their deaths."

"Nice." Nat shivered.

JC smiled. "You know yourself not to believe stuff like that. Most of those poor myth folk got an appalling press."

Nat grimaced. "Yeah, but their faces are really—" he started to say.

"That's only when they're in the air," interrupted JC. "They look pretty ordinary when they land. Look."

Nat craned his neck to see where his grandfather's gaze rested.

A slim young girl stood talking animatedly to a group of people at the far end of the tent. A pair of iridescent, purply-green wings folded neatly at her shoulders.

"Yeah, dead ordinary apart from the *wings*," said Nat bemusedly.

"Pure victims of prejudice," mused his grandpa. "Their

only crime was to swoop out of the sky and steal food from people."

"Like *really* big seagulls," piped up Woody.

"I *knew* their wings had to be real," said Nat. "I bet other people in the audience thought so, too."

JC shrugged. "People like us who've been exposed to people who are different don't have a problem believing. But the majority of humans know nothing of the supernatural world. As long as they get value for their money and a pleasurable thrill from what they see, or what they *think* they see, they're happy and we're happy," he said. "I tell them they are about to see the most incredible things they will ever experience, that all the illusions are *real*. But their modern, unimaginative brain will dismiss what their eyes see as impossible. Therefore they will remember it as a fantastic, but explainable, illusion."

Double bluff, thought Nat, and grinned delightedly.

"Apart from that small thing, we're like any other circus," said JC. "We treat each other as family and we look out for each other. Any unlikely trouble from anyone outside and we move on. We trust our people not to draw attention to us. And like Woody, they use their gifts for the good of others, never for the Dark Side."

Nat thought that sounded like just about the coolest thing he had ever heard. "So . . . er . . . Maccabee Hammer is safe, then?" he asked, relieved.

JC laughed. "Most vampires are," he said. "It's just the odd few you've got to watch out for. It's very old-fashioned to slurp human blood nowadays, not to mention awfully hard work. Unfortunately there are a few old-style vamps who enjoy spoiling it for all the others."

"So most of the circus is made up of shape-shifters and cryptids?" asked Nat.

His grandpa nodded. "And then we have the waifs and strays, asylum seekers or some people who are simply on the run."

Nat was silent. *Nothing simple about being on the run*, he thought.

Woody was having trouble staying awake, and his huge jaw-unhinging yawns were catching. People were beginning to drift away, calling their good nights.

Nat finally admitted to himself that he could probably sleep for a week, but he felt too full and cozy to move. His mum and dad were wrapping themselves in their layers in readiness for the walk back to their trailer, and Nat pulled himself sleepily to his feet.

He was just pushing back his chair when he saw Crescent and the Howlers appear. He nudged Woody and they both stared. Crescent's normally immaculate hair looked as though it had been pulled through a number of bushes backward *and* forward. Her jeans were ripped and she had mud skid marks on her thick padded jacket. The rest of the Howlers didn't look any better. Ramone was picking what appeared to be fur from his teeth, and Otis had dried blood on his chin. Salim had a glazed, rather guilty look in his orange eyes.

"Hey!" snapped Crescent. "Why didn't you save us any dessert?"

CHAPTER 11

A CHAPTER MAINLY ABOUT VAMPIRES

While Nat Carver and his Wolven buddy were preparing for their journey to Salinas in the south of France, Alexandra Fish had spent the day stalking and staking an ancient vampire nest that had apparently been dormant, but had now woken up after two hundred years. The vampires had been holed up in the basement of an old bank in Threadneedle Street in London, and Fish had been horrified to see so many in one place at a time. She hadn't been alone in this mission—trainee agent Jack Tully had *sort* of helped, although he hadn't really developed the stomach for such gory work. He spent most of the day trembling and being sick every time it was his turn to hammer in a stake. He faffed about with it for so long that Fish had snatched it off him, afraid that dusk would come before they had finished, and the vampires would wake up. Then she and Jack Tully would've been undead meat, depending on how severely they were bitten.

Some time ago, Fish had read an article in a magazine about an extremely sharp physicist who had tried to prove vampires didn't exist by doing a simple calculation. The bright dude had checked the census data on record, and then estimated from the year 1600 AD, when there were approximately five hundred and thirty-six million humans in the world and (hypothetically) one vampire. He assumed that if the single (and rather lonely) vampire fed on human blood once a month and its victim also became a vampire, there would then be two vampires and one less human in the world. The next month it would rise to four vampires and so on and so on. As they say: Do the math. The brainy physicist worked out that it would take only two and a half years of snacking on humans before the humans were wiped out, cutting off the vampire's food source. This meant, he decided, that vampires *could not possibly exist.*

Alex Fish thought his theory sucked big time. It was common knowledge in vampire circles that most vampires were dead cool and not in the least bit malevolent. They limited their blood lust to animals or raided their local hospital blood bank. Modern vampires weren't interested in making *more* vampires or killing humans because, quite frankly, it was just too much trouble. It was the old-type vampires you had to watch: the cranky ancient ones. And now, it seemed, they were being woken up.

Safely back at NightShift HQ, Fish had supper and a long hot shower, glad to be rid of the sticky, congealed gore of the undead. She was due in the boss's office at nine for a meeting that Quentin Crone had stressed was of ultra importance, and she didn't dare be late.

It was nice and toasty in the office. Crone had mastered the art of fire lighting to perfection, though privately Fish thought that he had become obsessive to the point of twitchiness about keeping the flames going. He had abandoned his apartment in favor of his office and had taken to sitting gnome-like, hunched in the corner, stoking the fire with a poker that seemed to be permanently welded to his person. Outside, London sparkled under the dim streetlights with a hard white frost that covered a treacherous layer of thick ice, and no one could get to work in the city even if they wanted to. Elsewhere in the world it was the same story: The weather had gone mad. Apparently even Niagara Falls was frozen solid.

Fish had been summoned to meet someone special, an elderly gentleman with snow-white hair and a neat beard. She was surprised and a little perplexed to see there were no other NightShift agents present in the office. Crone got up from his fireside vigil and introduced Fish as she walked toward them, balancing precariously on her unfeasible platform shoes.

"This," said Crone, "is the young lady I was telling you about."

The old gentleman stood up and shook Alex Fish by the hand.

"Delighted to meet you," he said. "Quentin has told me a great deal about your achievements."

"Alexandra Fish, this is Professor Robert Paxton," Crone told her, "from the original Proteus project."

"Glad to meet you, sir," said Fish, still wondering what this was about.

The three of them sat around the fire, exchanging pleasantries and talking about the weather as every English person is wont to do. Eventually, Crone got to the nub of the matter.

"We are certain that Lucas Scale is back," he blurted. "Back from the dead."

Fish's breath hitched in her narrow chest. *Break it to me gently, why don't you?* she thought to herself.

"We are positive that Scale is behind the increase in malignant occurrences," said Professor Paxton in a more gentle fashion. "We have reliable information that he has been participating in certain . . . ah . . . certain *rituals* to summon up things of the past. Things long dead, like the Threadneedle Street vampire hive."

"But *he's* supposed to be a thing of the past!" said Fish shrilly. "It's not *fair.*"

"Life rarely is," said the professor. "Nor death, in this particular instance. We think Scale made a deal long before he was shot at Helleborine Halt."

"A deal?" said Fish, her voice no more than a whisper.

"With a demon," said Crone.

Deep beneath the blackened, burned-out shell of Helleborine Halt seethed what was left of the black soul of Lucas Scale.

He had been human once, but now all vestiges of humanity had gone. Even before his deal with the demon (whose name sounded like a scream) Lucas Scale had longed for power and glory. And now, it was in his sights again. His recovery from the gunshot wound had been swift and his lair deep beneath the labyrinthine halls safe from discovery. No one but himself and the long-dead architect knew of the neolithic caves deep in the earth below the Halt. It was time to finish the business with the annoying brat Carver and the Wolven. But first there was fun to be had. Lucas Scale pushed his bony behind deeper into the comfy chair that had belonged to Dr. Gabriel Gruber (until, of course, he was ripped to shreds on that fateful night last summer). Scale grinned toothily at the memory. "Insufferable twit. Vain, puffed-up buffoon," he said out loud, his voice echoing eerily around the cave. How he loved this place. It had been his refuge in the days after the fire that had gutted the entire estate. Underneath, in the tortuous maze, he had been resurrected and recuperated by the demon whom he had summoned just days before the tiresome woman with the fat behind had shot him. His rancid orange eye narrowed with malice again as he thought of her. "But no matter," he muttered to himself. In the end hadn't he been cleverer? Oh yes. He had. *He had assured his future. By making a deal with the demon with the unpronounce-able name, Scale had given himself another chance to change the world. The deal hadn't been entirely fair to Scale's way of thinking*—*he had needed to give up most of his soul and agree to spend some time Down Under, and by that, Lucas Scale knew the demon hadn't been referring to Australia. But the gifts it had thrown in outweighed the debt a hundredfold! The demon had shown him how to awaken malignant beings and bring them back from the dead, beings who now roamed the earth again, ready to cause chaos among the living.* "What a lark!" tittered Scale.

He closed his eye. He took a deep phlegmy breath of satisfaction as his other eye—*the eye he had sent out to spy on the tiresome (but, he had to admit, quite resourceful) Nat Carver and his annoying hairy friend*—*did what he had sent it to do.*

CHAPTER 12

EYEBALL, EYEBALL

Back in Paris, far below the twinkling canopy of stars, the strange collection of animals and people from the Twilight Circus slept soundly. A single cloud momentarily blocked the stark light of the full moon, and inside the *Silver Lady* all was still.

There were no sounds in the trailer apart from the soft breathing and occasional snore from Nat and Woody as they slept: Nat in his bunk, the covers pulled up primly to his neck. Woody, now in Wolven form, lay on the floor, all four legs occasionally twitching as he ran in his wild dreams. It was as black as a funeral director's hat in the shadow of the cloud, no chink of light showing through the thick curtains. On the little dining table, the snow globe stood where Woody had left it, the flakes of fake snow lying at the bottom waiting to fly and swirl again when it was shaken.

The darkest hour is just before dawn, which unhappily is when the snow globe began to glow — but not with a warming, bright light. This was a sullen, sick-looking orange; the dull, burnt orange of a dying planet, or the bleary gaze of a corrupt werewolf. Nat moaned feverishly in his sleep, dreaming of dark things that rose from the earth with red, hungry eyes and darker times to come. The dusty orange light in the snow globe increased to reveal an enormous orange eye with a tiny black pupil. It rolled obscenely around the globe, bumping enthusiastically up against the clear plastic, pressing its terrible eyeball as near as it could to see what it needed to see. How it swiveled and rolled until it was satisfied! Now it could see the sleeping boy and his furry friend, innocent little lambs to the slaughter.

Watching you, boys. Watching and waiting. The disembodied eye of Lucas Scale winked twice and blinked out. The snow globe was dark again.

In the murky early-morning light, Nat's nightmares shrank back into the night, and somewhere in the bit between sleeping and waking, he dreamed of a large bacon sandwich dripping with juice and then — *UGH!* — just as he raised the enormous sandwich to his lips, someone started to wash his face with a warm, stinky washcloth. Unfortunately for Nat, the part featuring the awful washcloth wasn't a dream, it was Woody's tongue.

"Ugh!" yelled Nat, frantically wiping his face on his pajama top. "Get off me, dragon breath!"

Woody grinned his wolf grin and waved his tail like a furry banner.

"I s'pose this is your way of getting out of cooking us breakfast," said Nat, hopping on one leg then the other as he pulled on his jeans.

Get fed up with being human? Woody chuffed, wagging his tail again, and Nat saw a brief image in his mind of the swollen moon of the night before.

"Nice one." Nat grinned. "I s'pose it's hard for you to resist a big, fat, full moon."

He shoved three sweaters over his pajama top, deciding it was far too cold to wash, and pushed open the door of the *Silver Lady*. It was snowing, and he was just about to follow Woody out into the frosted landscape when the snow globe caught his eye. Unthinkingly, he picked it up from the table and shook it. The scene was the same as it always was, the snow swirling merrily around a tiny fir tree and a tiny herd of reindeer. Nat stared at it with distaste, but didn't know why. Who *had* sent it to Woody? Maybe it had been an early Christmas present from Iona, or even the Tates? But there was something about the snow globe, something that jangled Nat's warning senses. As if remembering a forgotten dream or lost memory, he opened a cupboard and shoved it roughly to the back. Then he closed the door and followed Woody, who was in search, as always, of food.

Big, fat snowflakes greeted him as he took in the busy scene. Already the black tent had been packed away and the skeletal base structure was being quickly and skillfully dismantled. The adults were already discussing their plans for the journey south over breakfast. Jude supplied Woody and Nat with platefuls of sausages, beans, and bacon, which were immediately wolfed down, followed by steaming mugs of hot chocolate, croissants, and a whole jar of delicious apricot jam.

The first thing Nat noticed was that Woody was a definite favorite with all the circus folk. Everywhere he went with Woody loping along by his side, people would come over and chat, making a huge fuss of the Wolven, patting him, rubbing his belly, and stroking his ears. Nat watched Woody's antics in amusement, hoping they didn't go around doing the same thing when Woody was in human shape. That would be *very* weird. It was strange seeing people in daylight, too, away from the lights and charged atmosphere of the big black tent. Shark Woman turned out to be an Australian girl called Sharon, who wore sensible clothes and a large Russian hat with flaps, and even the Surrealias, their wings hidden under layers of sweaters to keep out the cold, looked quite ordinary, though they giggled a lot. Nat learned that Maccabee Hammer and the aye-ayes were nocturnal, so they hardly ever came out during the day. (*Well,* that *would make sense,* thought Nat to himself, wondering if Mac had a coffin in his caravan.)

The younger Twilighters all had assigned shifts for cleaning animal sheds and stables and making sure they were ready and fit to travel. Nat's dad told him that when it was time to leave, even the stables were to be flat packed and taken with them. After breakfast was cleared away,

Evan sent Nat and Woody to see if they could help with anything, and they drifted across to the stables, which were half dismantled. There didn't appear to be much activity until a girl appeared from one of the loose boxes. Nat recognized her as one of the Cossack bareback riders.

"*Woody!*" The girl ran over and threw her arms round his neck. "I wouldn't dream of hugging Woody when he's boy-shaped," she said shyly when she saw Nat. "He would hate it!"

Or not, thought Nat, smiling. "Uh, I'm—"

"Nat Carver," said the girl, smiling back. "I know." She had long, curly black hair and an accent that Nat assumed was Russian.

"I'm Scarlet," she said, "Scarlet Ribbons."

"Doesn't sound very Russian to me," said Nat doubtfully.

"We have different names in this country," she said in a low voice.

Geez, thought Nat. *Everyone has something to hide here.*

"It seems funny talking to people who know about Woody," he said. "We spent such a long time hiding it from everyone. It's weird."

Scarlet stroked Woody's long white coat. "I thought

now you are here, Woody would want to stay in the shape of a human being."

Nat shrugged. "Sometimes he doesn't have a choice."

"What about you?" asked Scarlet curiously.

"What about me?" said Nat, a bit shortly.

"Pardon me, that was a bit nostrils," said Scarlet, blushing again.

"Nosy," corrected Nat.

"I *said* I was sorry," repeated Scarlet.

"No, I mean . . . ," stammered Nat. "Look, I don't shift, and I don't bite, either."

They watched awkwardly as Woody investigated the stables and went nose to nose with a fine black horse being led by another girl.

"Anyway," said Nat, "what's your story? Don't tell me you can shift into a horse."

"Neeeiggghhhh," whinnied Scarlet seriously, then she smiled and the dodgy moment passed. "This is my sister, Natalie."

Nat grinned. *Natalie.* He suddenly had an image of Teddy Davis, the boy who had bullied him last summer. Teddy had always called him Natalie, because he knew

118

it annoyed him. Now Teddy Davis was a werewolf. Nat wondered what had become of him. He gave the girl a friendly smile. She was slightly older than her sister and she held out a grubby hand.

"Asylum seekers," said Natalie, shaking Nat's hand firmly. "We're headed for Britain after the winter." Then in a whisper, she confided, "We're hiding from the Russian Mafia."

Nat felt his blood run cold. He couldn't think of anything to say.

"We saw something we shouldn't have," said Natalie.

"My grandpa told me there were people here like you," said Nat.

"Like *us*," said Scarlet. "It looks like we are all in this together, Nat Carver."

"Yeah," agreed Nat. "Like *us*." It felt kind of good to admit it. They were all in the same boat.

"Trust you to get out of doing this," muttered Nat to an unbothered Woody as he shoveled another wheelbarrow of steaming horse dung and wet straw. Woody was sitting in the snow, his fur puffed up against the chill wind, perfecting the forgotten art of snowflake-catching-on-tongue. Despite moaning, Nat was quite enjoying the exercise and it turned out that shoveling poo was a good way to keep warm. When they had finished, Scarlet asked Nat if he had met Titus yet.

Nat shook his head. *"Titus?"*

"Another one of us," said Natalie mysteriously. "Come and meet him."

Woody led the way as the girls escorted Nat to a smaller stable block, apparently enclosed by electric fencing.

"Don't worry," said Scarlet, "it's not switched on."

A few dozy-looking horses popped their heads over the stable doors, whickering to them sleepily. Nat wondered if they sensed the Wolven blood—he had worried that they might smell wolf and go mental. In any event, they didn't seem to mind his presence. Nat's own Wolvenish traits were not as advanced as Woody's; he supposed he would seem almost human to them.

At the end of the block there was another loose box.

"In there," said Scarlet, pointing.

"What is it?" asked Nat nervously. He sniffed the air for danger. All he could smell were good smells like fresh meadow hay and bedding straw laced with the sweet whiff of horseflesh and dung.

"You have to get a bit closer than that if you want to meet him," said Natalie. "Go on, don't be a baby."

Nat had been watching Woody's relaxed body language, and his own senses were telling him there was nothing to be afraid of. He repeated Natalie's words to himself: *Go on, don't be a baby*. All the same, he crept reluctantly toward the loose box, not wanting anything to jump out. A different, stronger smell met his nostrils, beefier than the smell of horses. Goodness only knew what was in there: After all the weird creatures he had seen last night, this Titus character could be anything from a dinosaur to a dodo!

He leaned forward gingerly and looked over the top. If it hadn't been for his enhanced eyesight and night vision, he wouldn't have been able to see a thing because it appeared to be pitch-black inside. A dark shape loomed in front of him, but the thing was so big, it was difficult to see where it ended and the stable began.

It had been lying down and now it struggled to its feet, great plumes of steam coming from it with the effort. *No way!* thought Nat. *It's a real live dragon!* He almost toppled over in surprise as a wet nose twice the size of his hand was thrust into his face. Nat noticed that the animal had a big gold ring through its nostrils, which glinted in the weak sun, and ginormous, lethal-looking horns.

"Oh, it's a *bull*!" exclaimed Nat.

"Obviously," Natalie said with a laugh.

"What's so special about . . . Oh no, I don't believe it!" yelped Nat.

"Don't believe what?" Scarlet prompted.

"It's not *that* bull . . . It *is* that bull!" cried Nat. "The one that was supposed to be slaughtered because it had some sort of disease."

"Tuberculosis," agreed Natalie, "but he doesn't have it now."

Nat shook his head in disbelief. "It's been on TV and everything. They've been looking for it for weeks. They want to slaughter it because of the disease."

Both girls nodded solemnly.

"So let me get this straight," said Nat weakly. "We're taking a bull, which is probably wanted over the whole of Europe, to the south of France with us?"

Both girls nodded again. Woody chuffed his agreement.

"A *sacred* bull," said Natalie.

Like that makes all the difference, thought Nat to himself. Then he looked down in dismay. Sacred or not, Titus had deposited a glistening snail trail of bull snot on his sleeve.

"Oh *nice,*" he said, "I've probably got tubercuwhatsits now."

"No," Scarlet assured him, "there is nothing wrong with Titus now. Smell if you don't believe me."

Reluctantly Nat sniffed the slimy piece of material on his jacket.

"Doesn't smell of anything."

"Woody always says that sickness smells *bad,*" explained Natalie. "You have enough Wolven blood in you to be able to smell the difference between bad and good. Titus has been treated by special monks and antibiotics."

"So what will happen to him when we get to Salinas?" asked Nat.

"He will be quarantined for a bit longer, then set free on the plains," said Scarlet, smiling as she scratched the ears of the enormous beast.

• • •

Nat's grandpa, John Carver, had a legendary temper. Whenever he was mad, the big man had a habit of running his hands through his already big, curly hair, making it wilder to match his mood. The daily paper had been delivered, and the newspaper article he had just read had made his blood boil and his hair frizz out to twice its usual size. He was *livid*. Already massively stressed because of the impending journey south and the responsibility of transporting everyone safely and in one piece, the reason for his rage had been on the front page of the leading Paris newspaper, which had described the "Petting Zoo Massacre" at the zoological park in bloody and graphic detail. Having read the distressing story in the paper, he had no doubt who was responsible, which was how Crescent and the rest of the Howlers found themselves hauled in front of an incandescently infuriated JC later in the day. Crescent gulped as she braced herself for the mother of all telling-offs. In fact, JC looked so angry she feared he might spontaneously combust. In no uncertain terms, he spelled out to them that if this sort of thing happened again, they would be asked to leave.

"I cannot have the lives of the rest of us put in danger by

the idiotic actions of a few selfish werewolves!" he raged. "Do you understand?"

"But—" tried Crescent.

"I said, do you understand?"

"Yes, JC," murmured the four culprits, all looking down at their feet.

"All this wildness will stop NOW!" shouted JC. "From now until we reach the south there will be a curfew, and you will stay within the campsite like the rest of the children."

"But . . . I'm *sixteen*," protested Crescent hotly.

"It's your choice," said JC, his gray eyes glittering dangerously. "Stay and behave, or go."

Lucas Scale fought hard not to lose his temper. He had to think, and wigging out was not conducive to the calm approach he needed to solve this annoying setback. Scale had watched helplessly as Nat Carver had rudely shoved his eye—still encased in the plastic snow globe—to the back of the dark, dank cupboard. Darkest demonish magic had enabled Scale to send his eye to spy on them, to listen to their pathetic little plans. In time, as his powers grew, he would send something nasty to finish what he had started last summer. His plans for the world and his place in it would not be hampered by the Carver boy, but his grudge was like an itch that couldn't be scratched. Until Carver and the Wolven were both wiped from this earth, he couldn't concentrate on the bigger picture.

Scale had a few ideas up his snot-encrusted sleeve. A little mischief, perhaps, before their grisly end? He had already used his spectacular new skills, sending some little furry vermin to wake a certain lady vampire of ill repute. He would use her to finish them off. But for now, how about a little fun? Turn them against each other? That would be superbadfun to watch. Or separate them? Take them out of their comfort zone!

Scale admitted he had taken his eye off the game. He should have been able to will the Carver boy to put the snow globe back. Some sense had warned the boy, warned him there was something not quite right about the globe, perhaps? He sneered at the setback. He would put it right, he vowed, get things back on track. He caught sight of his misshapen form reflected in the flickering candlelight. "Good God you're ugly," he told himself fondly.

CHAPTER 13

AGENT FISH

Less than twenty-four hours after her meeting with Professor Paxton and Quentin Crone, Alex Fish found herself traveling in an overcrowded train car on the London-to-Paris Eurostar, feeling about as nervous as a small nun at a penguin shoot. She had left her collection of unfeasible platform shoes behind, filling her suitcase with sensible, fur-lined boots, thermal underwear, and an entire designer ski suit complete with mirrored goggles.

Fish had taken out zombies, vampires, and the odd banshee, but never had she felt so buttock-clenchingly scared as she did now. Going undercover was one thing, but the cold, hard fact that Lucas Scale had cheated a silver bullet and death following a pact with an unknown demon made her quake in her furry new boots. While she froze in the packed train car, her thoughts drifted back to the meeting at the NightShift HQ.

"How do we fight Lucas Scale?" Fish had asked when she had calmed down.

"*We* don't," Crone had replied. "At least *you* won't be. We've got to find him first. He was a slippery enough character when he was human; God knows how he's evolved if he's in league with a demon."

"So why am I here?" asked Fish, suddenly dreading the answer.

Then the boss had dropped a big-time bombshell. "Using my excellent persuasion skills and a considerable amount of bribe money, NightShift has arranged for you to replace Nat Carver's holiday tutor," he said, smiling for the first time. "In fact, you will have a number of pupils, I gather."

"*Whaaaat?*" shrieked Fish. "I'm not much older than they are!"

Crone nodded. "Don't worry," he said soothingly, "just make sure you wear your glasses."

"What difference will that make?" asked Fish.

"You look quite brainy when you wear them." Crone grinned.

"And when I don't?" demanded Fish, a dangerous glint in her eye.

Professor Paxton coughed politely. "I think Quentin means you look more mature, more plausibly academic, when you wear your spectacles."

"But *why* do I have to go?" asked Fish, still bewildered. "Is it because I'm a rubbish agent?"

This time Crone shook his head seriously. "On the contrary. After last night's excellent work with the Threadneedle Street Hive, I truly believe you are our *best* agent."

Fish still managed to look both miserable and confused. "But then . . . ?"

"I think what Quentin is trying to say is that you, and only you, are the best possible person to look out for Nat Carver and Woody," explained the professor gently. "If Lucas Scale is bent on revenge, he will strike. Maybe not immediately, but when we are least expecting it."

"You really think that Carver and the Wolven are at risk?" asked Fish, frowning. "Even if they're out of the country?"

"While I was held at Helleborine Halt, I watched Scale turn into a monster," said the professor, looking slightly sick. "But I truly believe, despite his new powers, that he's frightened of Nat and Woody. They managed to bring down the Proteus project *and* the government, using gifts that Scale wanted for himself. Instead, the summoning of the demon has given him powers of his own, potentially stronger than those he coveted in the first place. He wants revenge—to finish what he started."

"You mean . . . ?" stammered Alex Fish.

"To kill them both," said Crone grimly. "Get them out of the way once and for all, and resume his quest for global power."

"We have to warn them," said Fish. "We'll have to—"

"There is . . . erm, something else you should know, possibly related to . . . ah . . . Scale," interrupted Crone, looking slightly uncomfortable.

"There's *more*?" Fish balked.

"Nat Carver and the Wolven are traveling with the Carver family's circus," said Crone, staring into the fire, "a very *special* circus with people and certain cargo for whom any close investigation by the authorities could be catastrophic. They are headed for a small town in the remote region of Salinas, where John Carver is always assured of total privacy. But . . . in the last few weeks, Salinas has been the focus of unwelcome activity. People have started to disappear."

"Brilliant," said Fish under her breath. "So, what's the story?"

Crone shrugged. "Some of the people missing are transients—hunters, people who come and go with the seasons. There wasn't really any reason to be too worried at first, but then other things started to kick off."

"Malignant activity?" asked Fish.

"Possibly," said Crone. "There've been reports of a disturbing increase in livestock slaughter, too delicately executed to be the work of wolves or werewolves and, chillingly, no tracks or marks in the snow—just dead animals completely drained of blood. Then a young girl disappeared from her family's farm. Just vanished from the face of the earth."

"You think Lucas Scale is behind this?" asked Fish, her pale face looking even paler.

Crone nodded tiredly. "Our cases have increased in

the last few months. We were used to innocent hauntings and manageable encounters between humans and the supernatural. Then Scale comes back from the dead, keen to cause panic and chaos for us humans, and suddenly there are zombies at Highgate, an old vampire hive in Threadneedle Street, et cetera, et cetera. Scale's dealings with the Dark Side may have extended from here in England to continental Europe. The very fact that there may be malignant activity directly where Nat Carver and the Wolven are headed makes me suspicious that Scale knows where they are and *why* they are there."

Fish looked quizzically at her boss. "There's another reason they're going south? Not just the warmer weather?"

Crone nodded. "The Salinas region is wild and remote; that's why it's ideal for John Carver and his cryptid friends. It's also the last place the Wolven clan was seen. John Carver intends to help Woody locate them. If Scale finds them before Woody, he will summon the means to wipe them out. If . . . *when* . . . his powers get stronger, he could use the vampire activity to his advantage; use them as weapons against the Wolven."

Fish's eyeballs were on stalks. She opened her mouth

to say something, then shut it again.

"Lady Iona and I found Woody's clan at a place known for centuries as White Wolf Falls," explained Professor Paxton, "but I have no idea if they are still there. They are a spiritual and shy group of individuals who will migrate if they feel threatened. It'll be a good chance for you to . . . *ahem* . . . to kill two birds with one stone: keep an eye on Nat Carver and the Wolven, and find the missing girl."

"And what shall I do with my spare time?" asked Fish sarcastically.

"Well," said Professor Paxton with the hint of a smile, "if you could help Woody locate his clan, that would be useful."

"I know I'm sending you to the wolves, Alex," said Crone, "quite literally, as it happens. I may be brought up on a misconduct charge from our benefactor if it all goes horribly wrong, but if I send anyone else, I can't rely on the job being done properly, if you get my drift. It's as simple as that."

Alex Fish allowed herself to blush modestly at Crone's words, and then remembered Agent Jack Tully's laughable attempts to stake vampires the previous night.

"So we're talking, what . . . ? One vampire, or a hive?" asked Fish.

"Possible hive," admitted Crone. "You know what ancient vampires are like. They're a bloodthirsty lot. They only need one invitation to get lucky. Spreads like wildfire."

"I just hope Nat and Woody are ready to fight if we need them to," she said.

"Call it their apprenticeship," said Crone, and smiled.

Despite her misgivings, Agent Alexandra Fish felt the familiar stirrings of excitement. She had met Nat Carver, and now she would be meeting the *Wolven*! She tottered across the room and stared up at the ancient tapestry with the proud figure of King Richard the Lionheart and the dozen Wolven at his feet.

Man oh man, she thought excitedly, *I might even get to meet the whole clan!*

CHAPTER 14

THE GIRL FROM ST. PANCRAS

Although Crescent had fumed for hours over being told off, the other Howlers secretly thought JC had been right. Otis had felt ashamed and upset that they had allowed themselves to lose control. It wasn't their way. All prey was fair game except humans (who were forbidden) and captive animals. And JC had been right; it could have been a disaster for everyone if the trail of destruction had led back to the circus. But Crescent remained less than thrilled that JC was treating her like a kid with a curfew.

"And all over a few mangy guinea pigs!" she had ranted to the other Howlers.

Now John Carver had summoned some of the younger members of the circus, and as Crescent stomped reluctantly across the snow to his trailer, she wondered if he was going to tell her off again. But when she arrived, Salim and Ramone were already there, along with several others, including Nat, Woody, Del, Scarlet, and Natalie, all gathered in the living room. Crescent relaxed a little and waited to see what it was all about.

It was cozy in John Carver's trailer. It was bigger than the others, and for most of them it was the first time they had been invited inside. Immaculately furnished, it had room for two leather sofas on which were luxurious cushions and throws. Gleaming cooking utensils hung above the small kitchen area and everything matched beautifully. Dotted around the place were photographs of John Carver posing with various famous people, from Michael Jackson to the Dalai Lama. The large photograph of a smiling woman in a sparkly leotard was Nat's much-lamented grandmother, Nina, who had died in an unfortunate trapeze accident a few years before Nat had been born.

Minutes later there was a sharp rap at the door.

"Come right in," invited JC, smiling at the expectant faces of the others. "It's not locked."

There were sounds of someone outside struggling with the door handle. Nat felt his body tense. In the few seconds it took for the door to be nearly wrenched from its hinges, he *knew*, somehow, who the mysterious visitor was going to be. There was more scrabbling with the handle, and then a short, slightly built person in a bright red ski suit and mirrored goggles came flying through, followed by a smattering of sleety rain and a draft of freezing air.

"Sorry, *sorry*," the person apologized. "I'm not good with door handles."

She pushed her steamed-up goggles on top of her head, flattening her snow-dusted spiky black hair. She smiled brightly at the expectant faces of her future pupils, though she nearly had a fit at the sight of them. There were at least two werewolves, one of them a girl — *That's unusual*, she noted, as she scanned the room, also noticing a tattooed boy with — *Oh my gawd, are they horns?* And, most exciting and amazing of all, standing together were Nat Carver and the Wolven creature. Fish thought she was going to expire with sheer excitement.

JC beamed at them all. "Everyone, this is Alexandra Fish, your tutor for the winter."

The girl from St. Pancras! Nat was so stunned and confused to have his thoughts confirmed by Fish's appearance that he nearly fell over, and Woody, who had obviously sensed something was up, looked at *him* expectantly.

Nat sent his thoughts in a rush, trying not to jumble them: *ThisveryshortpersonwithspikyhairistheNightShiftagent ItoldyouaboutwhopretendedtobeamuggeratSt.Pancras accordingtoQuentinCroneshe'sasuperhumanheroineblack beltinthreedisciplineszombiebasher.*

Woody sent back equally as rushed. *Whattheheckis shedoinghere?*

"What the heck are *you* doing here?" demanded Nat. As soon as their meeting with JC had finished, Nat and Woody had gone to confront their new "tutor."

"It's really great to mee—" began Alex Fish as Nat and Woody barged past her, through the door, and into her trailer.

"—eet you," finished Fish as she pulled out a couple of beanbags for them to sit on. She had expected to see them as soon as they had left JC, and they hadn't disappointed her. She was dead nervous and tried not to stare, especially at Woody. *Woohoo!* she marveled to herself. *A living legend, a mythical Wolven creature, sitting on a beanbag only a few inches away!*

She sat opposite and was aware she was staring after

all. She couldn't help it. How had she imagined Woody in human form? All she had ever seen was a centuries-old tapestry of the Wolven in animal shape, but she would never have been able to imagine him as the strange boy who sat solemnly in her trailer. He was dressed in ordinary clothes, the kind her kid brother would wear, his unusual silvery blond hair cut in a kind of funky, choppy style that was trendy just now. But that was where the resemblance to a human kid stopped. His face was a regular shape — *Nice, really,* thought Fish — but sort of *wild*-looking. *That was it,* she thought, *he looks wrong in his clothes. It's as if he can't wait to run and shift into what he feels happiest as — a wolf creature!*

Nat sat next to him, a tall, slender boy with dark, slightly too long hair and those solemn navy blue eyes, eyes that she had seen turn a bright topaz in the dreary afternoon light of St. Pancras station. In answer to Nat's question, she told them what the boss had told her to tell them.

"So, you're kind of like our *babysitter?*" asked Nat incredulously after Fish had finished talking.

Fish nodded. "Uh-huh, kind of, but keeping an eye on everything else, too."

Nat was dead suspicious. He had tried earlier to brain-jack her thoughts, but all he could get from inside her head was a really annoying Dizzee Rascal earworm. He realized then that Agent Fish had been trained in all manner of disciplines for her job at NightShift. She clearly knew about blocking unwelcome brain-jacking, since she'd activated her own earworm.

"Crone told me that there's more weird stuff happening," said Nat. "*Bad* supernatural stuff, like something waking up evil. He thinks that . . . Lucas Scale might be behind it."

Fish hesitated. "I . . . We don't know for sure. It's just a precaution."

Unconsciously, Nat put his hand to his neck where Scale's teeth had once bitten him. He felt sick, but forced a smile for Woody's benefit. "Since my . . . accident, I get these . . . sort of . . . *premonitions*," he said. "It's a reliable warning that something bad is going to happen."

Alex Fish felt for Nat Carver. The poor kid had been through a werewolf attack that he called his *accident*, although ripping someone's throat apart was rarely an accident. Lucas Scale had meant to finish him off, not leave him alive. *That* was the only accidental bit about the attack.

"And can you feel it now?" asked Fish gently.

Nat shook his head. "I just get nightmares about . . . what happened"—his hand went back to his throat—"and then I think about Lucas Scale again."

"What about you, Woody?" asked Fish.

"Same," agreed Woody. "Nightmares."

Alex Fish looked at the two boys. She swallowed hard. Her discussion with Crone had convinced her there was a malevolent vampire loose in Salinas. But what if they were wrong? What if the missing people *had* just left of their own accord? But that still left the mutilated animals. That definitely sounded like the work of a rogue vampire, but she didn't have *proof.*

She made what her boss called "an executive decision."

As gently as she could under the circumstances, she told the boys what the boss had shared with her on her last day in London.

"So, like, this vampire is going to take us out because of some sort of revenge deal with Lucas Scale?" asked Nat, staring at Fish aghast.

"What about everyone else?" pointed out Woody, his eyes flashing slightly. "The Crone man is putting everyone at risk."

"*If* it is vampire activity, I'll find it and do what I have to do," said Fish grimly. "Alone, if I have to. It's my job."

Woody looked at her, his strange eyes huge and glowing golden in the candlelight.

"You won't have to do anything alone," he said. "Right, Nat?"

Nat closed his eyes. "I thought you didn't want anything to do with this," he said tiredly.

Woody cast him a ghost of a smile. "You didn't leave me alone when I needed help," he said softly.

"Here we go again," said Nat.

CHAPTER 15

JOURNEY SOUTH

John Carver had been puzzled, but not too concerned, when his contact in Salinas had not been in touch as agreed. The severe weather conditions were playing havoc with power and communication systems all over Europe, and the Salinas region was notorious for its lack of a mobile phone signal. If there was anything wrong, he would find out when he arrived — too many people were relying on him to provide a safe haven for the winter months to change things now. Frowning slightly, he pocketed his iPhone and looked up at the sky. The forecast had warned more snow and the leaden sky confirmed it. He pulled his thick sheepskin coat around him and shivered. It was time to hit the road and head south to warmer climes.

Just after dawn on the coldest day of the year, while the people of Paris slept, the Twilighters made the final preparations for their journey south. The horses and Titus the sacred bull were loaded into a luxury horse box, complete with a loft area for Scarlet and Natalie Ribbons to keep their eyes on the precious cargo. Nat and Woody helped Evan and Jude connect their two silver trailers tandem-style on to Evan's Land Rover. At last, when everyone was ready, they waited for John Carver to give the signal. He drove to the front in his gleaming Daimler and sounded the horn long and hard. Nat could feel everyone's excitement deep in the pit of his stomach as the first vehicles moved off, including his dad's truck. As they fell into place behind his grandpa Carver, he caught a glimpse of Scarlet and Natalie, who gave the thumbs-up sign, and saw the dark limo that he knew belonged to Maccabee Hammer. The special blacked-out windows were designed to keep Mac away from bright sunlight, but with their enhanced vision both he and Woody could see the vampire inside. Nat grinned to himself as he caught sight of the aye-ayes snuggled up fast asleep in the backseats like very ugly children. The procession of thirty silver trailers and various cars and trucks made an impressive sight as it snaked alongside the frozen river Seine.

Hours later, Nat was fed up with traveling, and fed

up with the weather and the effect it had on the vehicles. The engines couldn't keep up with the ice and snow, and breakdowns were frequent. Everything was white: fields, rivers, roads. There wasn't anything or anyone to see, and everyone got a bit grumpy and short-tempered, except Woody.

Woody's travel sickness and distrust of cars, boats, trains, and planes — in fact anything with an engine — had always been a big problem. But on this journey, he discovered by accident that shifting from Wolven form to human form had the same sort of effect on him as motion sickness pills. His innards still churned and made funny noises and he had to poke his head out of the window now and then, usually with his tongue flapping out like a Labrador's, but he hardly ever puked now, which was a huge relief for his fellow passengers. He was enjoying the journey so much that he was beginning to get on everyone's nerves.

When they at last reached the final leg of the three-day journey, it was still snowing heavily. Nat had been watching the snowflakes as they hit the windshield, and they were having a sort of hypnotic effect on him;

he kept drifting off into a troubled sleep. Every now and again the vehicle would slide heavily to the other side of the road and he would hear his dad mutter under his breath.

As for Fish, who had the honor of riding in the posh Daimler with JC (much to Crescent's disgust), she thought Quentin Crone would have been proud of her. As she listened to the comforting purr of the engine, she thought about her conversation with Nat and Woody. Her revelations had gone down rather well and she had been pleased to find that Nat Carver and the Wolven dude were *way* more professional and less hysterical than adults. She was used to wasting a lot of valuable time trying to convince adults that things that go bump in the night were *actually real*, but she guessed she should have known that a circus full of freaks would just shrug and take her at her word. For her part, she was excited and proud to be working with Nat and Woody, and despite their fear that Scale might be onto them, she was impressed that in the cold light of day they were acting as though nothing was wrong. Still, in the daylight things looked a whole lot better, as they almost always do.

Nat stretched and yawned and looked out at the desolate landscape. Everyone was cheering up now that the end of the journey was in sight. The sky was a uniform gray instead of the blue they had been hoping for farther south, but at least the wind had dropped. Nat's eyelids went all heavy again, but the road was straight and smooth and for the first time since his Wolven blood transfusion, his brain felt uncluttered by the thoughts of other people. He could unconsciously "tune in," or "tune out" by playing his earworm, and he felt surprisingly good and healthy. Since talking with Alex Fish, both Nat and Woody had a sort of plan.

If Agent Fish and the NightShift people *were* right and they found real and actual evidence of vampire activity, they would share their suspicions about Lucas Scale with Nat's family. It would mean that Nat would have to come clean to his parents about his new Wolven gifts, something he dreaded having to do. The other thing Nat had turned over in his mind concerned Woody. He hadn't spoken it out loud at the time, but he was certain Alex Fish was thinking the same thing. *If they found Woody's clan, would the Wolven help them fight?*

• • •

On and on went the road, flat and bleak and rather like Nat imagined the surface of the moon to be. It started to get a bit more interesting the nearer they got to the town they were destined for, but Nat had a bad moment when he saw what appeared to be rows of shrunken heads on sticks by the side of the road. Then with relief he realized that they were some sort of plant, lining the shallow water outlets like grotesque guards. On top of the long stem of the reedy plant, hard balls of dried-out material naturally formed into tiny, wizened human expressions with frizzy ribbons of grass stuff that looked like hair. *Wimp*, Nat admonished himself and closed his eyes again.

He could hear his dad telling Woody about the traditional Christmas festivals and celebrations he had enjoyed in Salinas in previous years and how he was looking forward to them this time.

"The festival of the bulls is the best," explained Evan. "It's a chance to show off the skill of the *gardians*."

"What are they?" asked Woody curiously.

"The *gardians* are the herders who ride horseback, controlling the cattle," said Evan. "More like cowboys, really. Their name harkens back to their Romanian roots as watchmen. Legend has it they first journeyed to the South of France to battle a vampire outbreak during the Crusades."

"D'they have guns?" asked Woody, impressed.

Evan shook his head. "Nope, but because of the remoteness of the area, they rule the range. They're the ones to go to if you're in trouble!"

"What d'they do with the bulls at the festival?" asked Woody.

"They race 'em." Evan grinned. "Imagine that."

"You could race Titus," said Woody eagerly, "I bet he'd be up for that after being hidden for so long."

"Titus will have a nice long rest, to make sure he's completely better," said Evan. "Then in the spring, he'll be let loose to enjoy the rest of his life."

Woody considered this and felt pleased for poor old Titus. But he had another question, one he had been dying to ask Evan, but kept avoiding because he never felt the time was right. It was such a biggie, he could barely contain himself. It was about the clan. He looked across at Nat and Jude, who both seemed to be asleep.

"When will we start?" he asked in a quiet voice. "I mean, when can we start looking for . . . for my clan?"

Evan Carver turned around to smile at the strange wild boy sitting in the backseat. "As soon as we're settled. How does that sound?"

Woody nodded gratefully. That sounded just right.

LA REGION
NATIONALE
DE PARCS DE SALINAS
LA VILLE DE MARAIS
5 KM

"Welcome to Salinas!" Evan Carver announced from the driver's seat. "Only a few miles to go till our town, Marais. It means 'marsh,' as it sits on ancient marshland."

"But," said Woody, "it's wrong."

"Huh?" said Evan, puzzled. "What d'you mean?"

"It doesn't say what I want it to say," said Woody, looking despondently at the sign.

"Oh," said Evan, realizing what Woody meant. "Marais

is the town we're staying near, but the place of the White Wolf Falls isn't signposted. It never has been, as far as the professor knows."

"Then how're we gonna find it?" asked Woody dolefully.

"I have a cunning plan"—Evan replied with a twinkle in his eye—"and a great big map."

Woody was satisfied, and the talk turned to food. Nat and Jude were waking up.

"You'll love the food here," said Evan, glancing at his wife and son, "the sheep's feet, the garlic and crab soup, the stuffed squid with snail porridge, paella, the cowboy stew. . . ."

"Hang on. Does the cowboy stew have beans in it?" asked Nat weakly.

"Yup," said Evan, "at least four different kinds. Why?"

"Because our trailer has very small windows," said Nat, thinking about Woody's tendency to blow off like a machine gun, especially after eating beans. "I'll be gassed!"

So much for warmer weather. The nearer they got to the small town, the thicker the snow fell, and it was difficult to tell where the salt plains morphed into the wetlands made up of the shallow lagoons and marshes. Most were frozen now, but if the trucks and trailers veered off course, the ice wouldn't support their weight and it would be a catastrophe. But for all that, the icy scenes were Christmas-card gorgeous, and while Evan concentrated on driving through the beautiful but treacherous country, they all gazed out of the windows, watching the different species of birds dot the marshes looking for food. There were thousands of them: buzzards, terns, herons, gulls of all shapes and sizes, wailing dolefully like the souls of drowned sailors. Then Woody exclaimed out loud. Standing on one spindly leg (each, not between them) were hundreds of pink flamingos, dusted with blue-white snow. Away in the distance, a herd of something oil-slick black wound its way across the white plain, and Jude got excited.

"Look! Black palominos," she cried.

"Not unless they've got horns," said Nat, amused. "They're cows, Mum."

"Are you sure?" asked Jude, craning her neck for a better look.

"He's right," said Woody. *"Cows."*

"You two have superb eyesight," marveled Jude,

"especially you, Nat. I haven't seen you wearing your glasses for ages."

"Will we see any palominos?" said Nat, changing the subject quickly.

"I doubt it," said Evan. "They're notorious for being shy and they're quite rare in the wild, although your grandpa tells me the mayor has one on his ranch; remind me to show you when we visit."

From time to time they passed curious-looking thatched buildings with no windows. Each one had a long pole outside and a pair of ferocious pointy bulls' horns nailed to the front door.

"That's so the *gardians* can climb up the poles to check that their animals are safe on the plain," explained Evan.

"What about the horns?" asked Woody. "Why've they got them?"

"To ward off evil spirits," said Evan.

"Why don't they have windows?" wondered Nat.

"To keep out the evil spirits. And the mosquitoes." His dad grinned. "Do you know there's over forty species of the little buggers? The good news is that only ten of those species will bite you, and the really good news is that there's none in the winter months, so we'll be grand."

Nat and Woody looked at each other. They were more worried about the possibility of evil spirits.

"Don't seem to be any people around," remarked Woody. "Maybe 'cause it's so cold."

"It *is* odd," agreed Evan, sounding worried. "It's usually busy at this time of year. At Christmas the streets are decorated with hundreds of lights and there's a big tree in the square. Where on earth is everyone?"

CHAPTER 16
LOOKS LIKE CHRISTMAS IS CANCELED

It was the roadblocks that made Nat wake up again. The roadblocks and the group of unsmiling men with cowboy hats coming toward them: the ones with the guns!

"Now what?" muttered Evan, as one of the men broke from the pack and strode forward, his head lowered to avoid the bitter wind, the brim of his large hat flattened by the gusts.

"Dad, he's got a *gun*," warned Nat in alarm. "I thought you said they didn't have them."

"It's OK," said Evan with a sigh of relief. "Look, seems your grandpa knows him."

Everyone peered out their windows into the snow. John Carver had left his Daimler and was shaking hands with the man with the big hat. Both looked grave.

"Wait here, boys," said Evan, and opened the door of the Land Rover.

The man with the big hat and holstered gun was named Teebo Bon, and he made the law in Salinas. He was the mayor of the whole region and responsible for policing the area, along with four deputies. But he told John Carver his job had been made harder this winter by some mysterious and very worrying occurrences. First it had been the dead animals. Animals that had been mutilated horribly and completely drained of blood. There was a hefty cash reward for anyone who could catch whoever— whatever—was responsible. The mystery darkened when the snow came. *Whatever had done this thing had left no tracks!* And now, people had started to go missing. Fourteen-year-old Saffi Besson had apparently disappeared off the face of the earth. Teebo Bon had had a horrible feeling that she wouldn't be the last, and he had been right. Yesterday, two more kids had gone: brothers. They had been in the hospital, both suffering from a mystery disease that had left them weaker each day, certainly too weak to walk out of the hospital in this weather. Now other people were sick, seemingly affected by the same thing. The doctors were baffled as they watched normally healthy people reduced to pale shadows of their former selves in a matter of days. Things had got severely out of hand after the two young boys disappeared from the hospital, and Teebo felt powerless to stop the rumors flying around Marais.

Rumors that Teebo Bon knew to be true.

A farmer across town reported seeing a ghastly black creature with red eyes scrabbling at his daughter's window, while a *gardian* reported seeing the same creature crawling across the roof of his house, red eyed and fanged.

Teebo Bon knew better than to dismiss their fears as a load of superstitious codswallop. He had seen the puncture wounds on the flesh of the victims for himself. The doctors had tried to blame all sorts of diseases and ailments. But seeing those telltale bite marks had convinced Teebo Bon beyond all reasonable doubt. With a small band of believers, he had watched every night, but still the vampire eluded them. As his great-great-great-grandfather had done over a hundred years ago, he wanted to deal with the thing himself once and forever, and cleanse the town in his own way. *And now this!* He hadn't been able to contact John Carver to warn him off, so the long train of wagons was added to his responsibility.

Nat and Woody watched apprehensively as Evan and

JC appeared to argue with the man, waving their hands around, as though there was a BIG problem.

With their keen hearing, they were able to hear most of what the tall man with the gun said. As he spoke, he fiddled nervously with the large gold cross he wore around his neck.

"I'm sorry, my friend," he said, "there is sickness in the town. You must go back. It's too dangerous to continue."

"I'm sorry, too," said John Carver firmly, "but going back isn't an option. We don't have any more water for the animals and the weather is getting worse. It's too dangerous to travel."

Teebo Bon's expression was resigned. "If you still want to stay, that must be your choice," he told them. "But my advice to you is to keep out of the town and keep your people safe and, *je vous en supplie*—I beg of you—do not venture out after dark."

Sickness! Nat tried a quick brain-jack, but could see only worry in the big man's mind. Still, it was obvious he was hiding something—the *real* reason why he had wanted them to turn back. Nat and Woody exchanged worried glances again, both thinking the same thing. *Vampire!*

Their falling spirits were lifted slightly when Teebo and his men escorted them to their camp. Despite the deep snow, Nat was able to make out the wooden cabins that would be home to them for the Christmas break. They were set inside a heavily wooded area, giving much-needed shelter from the snow. Nat didn't know what sort of trees they were—they were tall and shaped like Christmas trees, but instead of being spiky, the branches were fluffy and formed a sort of canopy high overhead. Woody refused to move from the *Silver Lady*, so he and Nat helped Evan and Jude move into their cabin. As soon as they were in, had lit a fire, and got the kettle on and the oat biscuits out, everyone felt much better.

Over the next few days, despite their odd welcome, the Twilighters relaxed after being on the road for so long. Evan and Jude Carver were busy planning a special holiday hog roast for everyone. Nat slipped easily into life in the camp with his family and Woody, and continued to make new friends. One of the most unlikely friendships Nat and Woody had formed since joining the circus was with the vampire, Maccabee Hammer. Nat had got over the worry of Mac trying to drain his blood dry, a thing that would never happen, Mac assured him, because he was allergic to human blood (Nat didn't like to ask him how he had found out) and only ever drank that of animals. Under the vampire magician's tuition, Nat learned new and wonderful sleight-of-hand techniques, thieving personal items from friends and family as skillfully as the Artful Dodger.

But with the town out of bounds and the weather showing no signs of improvement, people began to make noises about moving farther south. JC didn't blame them, but for now it was out of the question. The snow had worsened and a weird fog shrouded the plain most days, making visibility difficult and traveling dangerous. JC had offered to send search parties out for the missing children, but only Crescent and her Howlers and Woody were qualified to go. With their extraordinary senses of smell and supernatural eyesight, they scoured the plain and woods, but could find no trace of the missing.

Nat felt left out. Unless he came clean to his parents about his Wolven traits, he had no choice but to stay at camp. Woody was in a strange mood, too. He had hoped to start the search for his clan, and was sure when each day dawned it would be THE day he would find them. He spent time with Nat and his family planning the strategy, but continued to be disappointed that he still couldn't feel their presence, despite trying for hours to "tune in."

"They're probably just out of range," Nat kept reassuring him as Woody polished his shifting skills. It didn't matter to Nat which form Woody took—he was so familiar with his friend's body language as a Wolven that it was almost as good as talking, and they practiced the two-way thing whenever they could.

When Fish wasn't tutoring (she was surprisingly good) she was swotting up on the case. All her research pointed to vampire activity. She hunched over her files making notes in her scrawly handwriting, cursing frequently about the lack of Internet access.

1. *Exsanguinated animals—drained completely of blood, chewed, partially eaten throats*
2. *No tracks in snow (possible airborne attack???)*
3. *Missing people—no traces of violent scuffles*
4. *Mystery wasting disease*
5. *History of vampire activity (reanimated ancient hive?)*

6. NC and Woody—premonitions?

7. Conclusion: vampires—definitely

Fish put down her pen thoughtfully. If it wasn't vampires to blame for what had been going on, she would eat her snow goggles. It was time to do something positive, and she was itching to find proper evidence of vampire activity so they could fight.

She wouldn't have long to wait.

CHAPTER 17

THE CARDBOARD BOX CLUB

Only yesterday, the wild boar now roasting on the spit had been running with hardly a care in the world through the forest—that was, before Crescent Moon got her teeth into it. On one of the Howlers' luckless trips to track down the missing children, Crescent had managed to hunt down a big fat wild boar, bringing it back to camp already gutted and only a bit chewed around the edges. After at least ten hours roasting on the spit and driving anyone who wasn't a vegetarian mad with the delicious sweet smell of roasting pork, it was finally ready to eat. The Twilighters enjoyed the tender, hot meat served in fresh, crusty baguettes. Heaps of baked potatoes were consumed along with the special *gardian* cowboy stew with plenty of beans. Despite the worry of the last few days, the atmosphere was lighthearted and there was no shortage of laughter and high-spirited chatter among the gathering at the enormous fire. Curiously, Nat noticed that the younger Twilighters were leaving the warmth of the fire and was puzzled to see Scarlet and Natalie return to the fireside, jabbering away to each other in Russian, each carrying a box under one arm and a cushion under the other. Then he spotted a few others also carrying cardboard boxes, all painted in bright colors and cut to form a crude bucket shape.

"What's all that about?" he asked Woody.

Woody smiled. "Cardboard Box Club."

Nat looked puzzled.

"Now we've all stuffed our faces, it's time for the real fun to begin." Woody grinned wolfishly.

"But what is it?"

"*Ghosts.*" Woody shuddered. "It's a sort of ghost story club. Everyone takes a turn to tell one."

Nat brightened. "Have you told one yet?"

Woody's eyes flashed. "*Noooo.* Ghosts scare me to death."

"So, you don't go to this club, then?" asked Nat.

"'*Course,*" said Woody, "I always go."

"Why d'you go if it scares you?" asked Nat.

Woody grinned sheepishly. "It's *soooo* fun being scared."

"Anyway, even if ghosts *were* real," said Nat, "they can't hurt you; they're, like . . . well, kind of insubstantial. They can't touch you."

Woody ignored him. "Anyway, everyone takes a turn to tell a story."

Nat frowned. "So you make one up, obviously."

Woody shook his head in surprise. "No, all the stories have been true!"

"Oh yeah, *right*," said Nat. "You are *so* naive."

Woody looked hurt. "Well, don't come, then."

"No, no," said Nat, "it'll be a good laugh. But what are the cardboard boxes for?"

"To sit in, of course. Keeps the cold off your back," said Woody, surprised at the question. "You are *so* naive."

The very young children were safely tucked in their bunks, the older ones anticipating staying up as late as possible. The night was dark already, and thanks to the low cloud and canopy of trees, it was just about warm enough to sit in front of the fire. Nat and Woody joined Scarlet and Natalie, who were sitting in their boxes, hugging their knees and drinking hot chocolate from flasks. It wasn't long before Nat could see the point of the boxes. Although the fire was keeping everyone warm on their fronts, being wrapped around your back with cardboard and a cushion did a good job of keeping out the chills. The cardboard kept the heat of your body in, and any cold drafts out. There were maybe ten or twelve other kids around the far end of the fire, including Nat and Woody. Most of them were familiar to Nat: Scarlet and Natalie, Del and his brothers, a couple of kids from Zombie Dawn, and an aye-aye. They were just about to start the story when they heard howls coming from the edge of the camp. It was Crescent and the Howlers.

"Oooh good, we haven't missed anything, have we?" panted Crescent, throwing herself down beside Woody. Nat was surprised the Howlers had shown up at all. He would have thought this sort of thing was too juvenile for them, Crescent especially.

"It's Del's turn tonight," said Salim, rubbing his hands in front of the fire, grinning expectantly. "His stories are always the spookiest!"

Nat looked around at everyone, their faces glowing in the firelight. All of them had eyes like saucers, and the earlier giggling from the girls was replaced with an air of thrills and excitement. Even Crescent was quiet for a change.

Del skedaddled forward in his box. None of the satyrs ever wore shirts, only trousers and woolly hats; they didn't seem to feel the cold at all. Del's tattoos flickered and shifted in the glow of the flames, and Nat had to remind himself again that the three brothers weren't a figment of his imagination.

"Tonight," said Del, in a scary, wavering voice, "for your delight and delectation, I've a story *so* bloodcurdling, *so* chilling, it'll knock yer socks off, so it will."

Despite his initial scoffing, Nat felt excited. Salim had been right. Like most satyrs, Del was a natural storyteller. Everyone was quiet, although you could hear the sounds of the adults talking and the occasional plucking of a guitar and the cozy crackle of the flames.

"It all kicked off two summers ago," said Del, edging nearer the fire. "We'd left Ireland in a hurry, and y'all know what that's like."

Most people listening nodded gravely. They all knew what it was like to run and hide; it was what drew them together.

"We lived in a safe house which might o' been safe, but it was filthy dirty and *phew*! It stank, specially in summertime. There was a great deal o' flies . . ." Del shuddered at the memory. "We hated living there, but we had no choice until we were moved again. Me mam worked long hours during the day and was always tired. In the evening we would open all the windows to try to get rid of the smell, but it was no use, it still stank. I'd lots o' bad dreams when we first left the auld country, but I began dreaming about dead children. I dreamt they were in me bedroom, just kind of milling around, over by the window. Then I realized one night it wasn't a dream. Or p'raps a . . . what do you call a waking dream?"

"Daydream!" chorused several voices.

Del nodded. "Aye, one o' them. I knew I was awake, though, and not asleep. I opened me eyes and saw the first one, like a sorta shadow at first. First of all I thought it was the pattern on the wallpaper. Then it moved—all jerky like, *unnatural*. Then more shadows appeared, came out, as though they were comin' through the wall! I closed me eyes tight shut, trying to blot out the memory, but every time I opened 'em they were still there. I got out of me bed and went knocking on me mam's door. She said it was just a product of my overactive imagination gland. But every night after, as soon as I put the light out, I would see the outlines of small figures, silhouetted like, between the window and the dressing table. They appeared not to notice me, an' I'd try not to move. Then, one night, they edged just a little bit closer, then the next night, closer still. I kind of knew, I just knew in the bottom of me gut, that if . . . *when* . . . they reached the bed, I'd be a goner."

There were horrified gasps from Scarlet and Natalie, who had somehow managed to squeeze into the same box.

"I tried to tell me mam how scared I was, but she had too much on her mind, so I stopped worrying her. I went to the library to see if I could find anything out about our apartment. What I found told me I was in greater danger than I'd realized." Del paused to take a swig of his drink.

"Go *on*," shouted Crescent, orange eyes flashing. "What happened next?"

"I found a newspaper cutting from 1963," continued Del. "There had been complaints from residents that the apartments smelled bad, specially on the ground floor, where we were. Back then it was thought that the drains were the culprits, but the next year when the smell was worse than ever there was an official investigation. What was found was something so *terrible*, so *frightening*, I . . . Well, I can hardly bring me self to say it out loud."

Del paused for dramatic effect and sipped his drink again, thoughtfully and deliberately, as if remembering.

"*Del!*" shouted Scarlet. "What was it?"

"Bones of dead kids," said Del, his eyes huge in the fire-light, "loads of 'em . . . thousands . . . *millions* probably."

"Oooooh no." Nat shivered. "That's horrible."

"The apartments were built on a medieval plague pit," continued Del in hushed, creepy tones. "On thousands o' dead bodies."

"And you think that the children you saw every night were . . . plague victims?" Crescent shuddered.

"I *know* they were," said Del grimly. "Because that night, I asked me mam if I could sleep on the sofa. Even then I was scared. I tried to keep awake, knowing they were getting closer. I could hear them behind me bedroom door, scratchin' . . . tappin' . . . like they were trying to get in . . . to get me. The next night as I lay on the sofa, the door slowly opened and . . ."

Del took another swig.

"It was them!" cried Woody, his eyes flashing slightly.

Del nodded gravely. "Aye, they came through," he said. "They gathered at the bottom of the sofa and I could feel them . . . smell them, as they moved toward me. Then . . . I felt a cold finger touch my forehead."

"Eeeeuw!" yelled Natalie and Scarlet.

"What happened then?" asked Salim, wide-eyed.

Del got out of his box and slowly walked toward him. He whipped off his woolly hat, revealing a livid purple mark in the middle of his forehead.

"THIS!" he cried.

Salim scooted back, trying to get out of his way, and promptly toppled over.

"This is the mark of the plague child," intoned Del, jabbing his finger at the terrified Salim.

"Geddoff!" yelled Salim, his eyes flashing, indicating his change was near. "Go 'way!"

There were peals of mirth from the other Howlers as Salim ran off into the night, moaning. Del, weak with laughter, showed the others the "plague child" mark. It was drawn on with a purple marker.

· · ·

With the storytelling over, the talk turned to what might have happened to the missing kids.

"Well, they've not been in the forest, that's for sure," said Crescent, licking the pork grease from her fingers. "There's no fresh smell of humans anywhere."

"No sign," agreed Ramone.

"They might have run away," suggested Natalie.

"What, in their *pajamas*? Would you look at this weather?" said Del, raising an eyebrow. "Nah, the vampires have had 'em, for sure."

Nat froze at the word *vampires*. "You reckon?"

"Did you not listen to what your man Teebo Bon said?" asked Del in surprise. "He might think he's fooled us by telling us there's a mystery sickness about the place, but I've seen this sort o' thing before. All the evidence points to it."

"He's right," agreed Crescent, wiping her mouth daintily. "All those animals mutilated? People sick in their beds, kids missing . . . ugh, I hate 'em. All except Mac, of course."

"You don't know any vampires apart from me," came a disembodied voice from somewhere out of the darkness.

"Hey, Mac," said Nat. The orange brilliance of the bonfire obscured the night around them, but thanks to Nat's Wolvenish eyes, he could see the thin shape of the vampire as he sauntered elegantly toward the fire.

"What d'you think?" he asked Maccabee Hammer.

"Del's right," said Mac, his expression grim.

The others watched as the willowy vampire slid his long body in one fluid movement into a sitting position and joined them.

"Really?" asked Woody in a small voice.

Mac nodded, the flames from the fire reflecting in his pale face. "'Fraid so," he agreed. "There's an atmosphere about this place, a *bad* atmosphere, you know? A pall of sadness hangs about the air, and sometimes . . . sometimes when the wind is in a certain direction, I can hear the revenants calling."

"What are *they*?" asked Crescent.

Mac's red lips stretched into a sad smile.

"In ancient times, vampires operated in a very different way from how they do now," he explained. "The old vampire way was violent and bloody. They infected humans with their greed for blood and made more vampires from humans, sometimes creating a hive—a small army of vampires with a king or queen giving the orders to workers and soldier vampires—"

"How old are you?" interrupted Crescent.

"A mere baby," said Mac. "I was three hundred and fourteen last dieday."

"Cool," breathed Nat, "but how come you're not an ancient? Because . . . erm . . . you're, well . . . *old.*"

"I've never been slain," said Mac simply. "Looks to me like the old vampire hives slain years ago are being reawakened to avenge their deaths."

"But who would do that?" asked Salim, his eyes flashing with fright.

Maccabee glanced at Nat and Woody. "Someone out to cause chaos . . . and revenge."

He knows! Nat realized with panic. *He knows about Scale!*

"But what about the *revenants*?" asked Crescent impatiently. "What are they?"

"I was telling you, before you interrupted," said Mac mildly, "revenants are tragic creatures—discarded servants of the vampire."

"So they're like *ghosts*?" Woody shivered. *"Eeurgh."*

"They serve the vampire for about a century," explained Mac, "and then they begin to age, to break down and crumble, because the vampire never allows them to drink its blood. When they're no longer useful, the vampire abandons them and finds another companion—usually a healthy young person who will provide them with their life's blood."

"Oh God!" cried Nat. "You mean a *child*?"

"Yes," agreed Mac, "a child would be perfect. But if the head vampire is slain, the revenants find peace—their souls will be released from purgatory." The gathering grew quiet as everyone digested Mac's information.

"Well, soon as the weather gets better, we're outta here," said Crescent, shivering.

"When the going gets tough, the wimps get going," taunted Del.

"Bite me," snarled Crescent, her eyes burning orange.

"Don't you want to stay to see if you can help look for the missing?" asked Woody, chewing on a glistening piece of cracknel. "It might not be too late."

"Not really," said Crescent in disdain.

"We're riding out again tomorrow, depending on the weather," said Scarlet. "Uncle Sergei is organizing another search."

"More like he's searching for the black palominos," said Crescent, with a little sarcastic laugh. "You sure he's looking for the kids?"

Natalie ignored her. "And Uncle Sergei asks: Would Nat and Woody like to come?"

Nat was thrilled. "I'd like that," he said. "Woody?"

Woody nodded. He was thinking it might be an opportunity to hunt for his clan at the same time. "Gonna run, though, not ride."

"What about *me*?" asked Crescent hotly. "*I* want to ride a horse."

"You want to ride?" asked Natalie, looking doubtful. "I don't—"

"You don't what?" asked Crescent.

"You . . . well . . . you're . . . a—" Natalie broke off, embarrassed.

"A werewolf?" asked Crescent, a dangerous glint in her eye.

"I think what Natalie's trying to say," said Nat diplomatically, "is that horses are scared of werewolves."

"Woody doesn't scare them," protested Crescent.

"Woody isn't a werewolf," pointed out Nat. "He's Wolven."

"What*ever*," said Crescent rudely. "I'll tell Sergei I'm coming." She turned and looked directly at Natalie. "I *love* horses," she said sweetly. "I just couldn't manage a whole one."

CHAPTER 18
FRIGHTENING THE HORSES

But Uncle Sergei had agreed with his nieces, and Crescent was still smarting at being left out of the search party the next morning. She had seethed all night at Del's remarks, and was still in a black mood as she sat by the tiny stove in the *Silver Lady*. Nat was bundling himself in layers in preparation for the ride out in the freezing snow, while Woody played outside, making snow angels with his tail.

"It's not fair," said Crescent for the umpteenth time. "Stupid, stupid horses. It's not like I'm gonna eat them."

"They just hate werewolves," Nat reminded her, smiling. He was secretly pleased that Crescent wasn't coming. At best she was hard work, at her worst she was a bloody liability. "It's not their fault," he added, "they don't like the smell."

Nat winced as Crescent's eyes blazed. He felt a bit guilty; it hadn't been a very nice thing to say. And when

Nat had cause to think about it afterward, much later on, after Crescent had done what she did, he felt that maybe it had been his fault.

Crescent had watched resentfully from the doorway of the *Silver Lady* as Nat, with Woody bounding along at his side, made his way across the fresh snow to join the others at the stables. She reached back to pull the door closed when a sound from inside the trailer made her hesitate. A thud—as though something heavy had fallen onto the floor. It was dark inside the little trailer, but Crescent's werewolf eyes had no trouble picking out what had made the noise. She bent down and picked up the snow globe, which had apparently fallen from the cupboard above the sink. She shook it in delight, forgetting her bad mood. The snow inside the dome glittered and swirled, the tiny wintry scene disappearing momentarily, obliterated by the make-believe blizzard. Then her smile froze on her lips as the globe began to glow with a malevolent orange light. She tried to let go of it as it started to feel unpleasantly hot in her hand. To her horror and dismay, something was floating in the scummy liquid. Crescent started to whimper as the swirling shape formed itself into an eyeball;

a living, blinking, *staring* bloodshot orb, which held her horrified orange gaze with its own.

Nat Carver was as nervous as a long-tailed wolf in a room full of rocking chairs. He took a deep breath and tried not to act as worried as he felt in front of Natalie and Scarlet. Like, how was he going to get on the horse, for a start? The one and only time he had ever ridden a horse was eight hundred years ago during the Third Crusade, but he thought it probably wasn't a good idea to mention this to Scarlet or Natalie on the grounds that:

a. they wouldn't believe him, or

b. they would think he was mental.

He wondered if it would all come back to him, like riding a bike, but then remembered he had been in the body of a Knight Templar at the time. So he, Nat Carver, actually had *zero* riding skills. As he waited to be dragged or pulled aboard one of the horses, a glossy black stallion with rippling muscles (but dark, kind-looking eyes), he hoped like mad that he wouldn't make a fool of himself by falling off. Getting onto the horse would be one thing. Staying on it would be another. He envied

Woody, who could manage on his own four legs, wishing he could run alongside, too, and not have to ride.

"Don't worry." Sergei winked as he gave Nat a leg up. "This is Rudi. He's bombproof. He'll look after you."

Nat still felt dead out of place, like a pimple on top of a mountain, but Rudi stood as still as a rock, patiently waiting for Sergei to tighten his girth and adjust Nat's stirrups. Scarlet and Natalie sat astride their own horses, chatting to each other, while Woody, keen to be off, was trotting up and down, yipping and chuffing, trying to hurry everyone up.

Nat sat down in the saddle and tried squeezing his legs. To his amazement it worked, and Rudi walked sedately forward. Nat gently pulled the reins and Rudi stopped immediately. *Ha, I've still got it!* Nat thought to himself, pleased.

Then without warning, Rudi started to tremble beneath him, his ears flattened back to his head, which he was tossing wildly. Confused, Nat tried to rein him in, then he heard familiar laughter. It was Crescent. She looked wild.

"Ride 'im, cowboy!" she shrieked raucously. "C'mon, Nat, you'll have to do better than that!"

Rudi reacted to Crescent's werewolf voice by giving a single, screaming whinny, kicking up his heels, and promptly jumping the nearest fence with Nat clinging terrified around his neck. Old, "dependable" Rudi had gone berserk—he may have been bombproof, but he sure wasn't werewolf-proof. As the horse shot away, Nat was dimly aware of the openmouthed stares of his mum and dad, and Crescent screaming with maniacal laughter. The other three horses belted helter-skelter in three different directions, with Uncle Sergei in vain pursuit on foot. Nat tried tugging on Rudi's reins, but the horse was too strong. Nat crouched low in the saddle and wove his frozen fingers into Rudi's long black mane. He was almost blinded, the cold air making his eyes stream as they whizzed along. Opening one eye, he was relieved to see a streak of white alongside at stirrup height as Woody caught up with Rudi, trying to nudge him back to camp. But it was no good. The horse wasn't having any of it. Rudi's reaction to Crescent was terror, and his instincts were fight or flight. Apparently Rudi had chosen flight.

On and on he galloped, showing no sign of stopping. Nat clung on for dear life for what seemed like hours, frozen in an uncomfortable jockey position, not daring to move in case he fell, but comforted a bit to feel Woody was nearby.

Nat guessed they had traveled for at least three miles before Rudi showed any signs of stopping. At last, his flanks heaving, white lather on his chest, and plumes of condensed air streaming from his flaring nostrils, he came to a shuddering halt. Nat gratefully disentangled his raw fingers from the horse's mane and shakily slid to the ground, his legs hardly holding him up.

Woody had been slightly ahead and was now trotting back through the snow.

"Crescent did that on purpose!" raged Nat when he'd got his breath back.

Woody chuffed and sat down.

"I can't believe she did that," said Nat, calming down a bit. "I could've been killed!"

Woody chuffed again, blinked, and made his supersonic jet noise as he yawned.

"Glad you agree," said Nat, and forced a smile. Not wanting to spoil the day, he pushed all thoughts of Crescent to the back of his mind and wondered why it was taking him longer to get his breath back than Rudi and Woody, who had actually been running while he had just been riding. He supposed it was because he was still the most human. Nat stamped around a bit to warm himself up; it was getting colder. The watery sun had lost any of the warmth that it had at midday, and the plains were deserted. With the aid of his enhanced eyesight, Nat could see as far as the sea, stretching beyond the salt plains and the marshes, the sea lavender softening the edges with a purple barrier. Rudi had come to rest at the top of a slight incline. Nearer, down toward the forest, Nat saw a rough path winding upward to a sort of plateau or steppe. And beyond, surrounded by an enormous frozen expanse of water, was an imposing building rather like a castle. Nat knew that French people called large castle-like houses *chateaux*, and this one looked as though it was made out of shiny black granite. It loomed darkly in sharp contrast to the glistening white of the ice, the outside showing no signs of life.

Then someone coughed behind him and he yelped in surprise.

Spinning around, he was shocked to see Woody

standing there naked and pale blue with cold, disheveled and shivering.

"I don't s'pose you brought any spare cloves, did you?" asked Woody apologetically.

Nat stared at his friend in dismay. "What did you do that for?"

"Dunno," said Woody glumly. "Took me by surprise."

"Aw *nooo*," groaned Nat. "Try changing back again — you'll freeze!"

Woody closed his eyes and tried willing himself back to Wolven shape, but nothing happened. Not so much as a shimmer of a shift was coming through.

"Can I have some of your cloves, please?" asked Woody.

Nat frowned, muttering under his breath. Why was it that in werewolf movies they never showed the impractical side of shape-shifting, especially the nakedness part? He supposed that movie werewolves never had to scurry around looking for clothes, because that would take up the entire movie. But he was annoyed at himself. Since he and Woody had met, Nat had usually taken extra clothes in case of unscheduled shifts like this, but because Woody seemed to be more in control these days, he had forgotten.

True, Nat was dressed in about four layers, but since they had all calmed down he was feeling quite cold and couldn't wait to be back at the *Silver Lady* with a mug of his mum's special hot chocolate laced with whipped cream.

Still muttering, he began stripping off his layers, passing one lot to Woody, who gratefully put them on.

"You'll have to wrap the scarves around your feet," said Nat. "We've only got one pair of boots between us."

With the boys both dressed again, Woody got up behind Nat on Rudi, who seemed to have forgotten his panic. Nat winced as his tender behind hit the saddle again, and imagined it had started to glow red like a baboon's. His legs ached, too, and he didn't fancy galloping all the way back again, but if they were to get back to the circus by nightfall before the temperature plummeted again, they would have to get a move on.

"We could always ask for directions in there," he said to Woody, pointing to the black house.

"*Brrr,*" Woody shivered. "Count me out, it looks creepy."

Nat had to agree. There were no visible signs of life outside. *Maybe it's closed up for the winter*, he thought. He was confident they were headed in the right direction, although he had had his eyes closed against the cold wind for most of the ride. Lately, it was as though a GPS had been fitted in his brain, another Wolven trait he could add to his growing list of cool stuff.

Riding Rudi down from the incline was sheltered and they found themselves nearer to the chateau than they had first thought. The wind had sculpted the plain into a kind of natural basin and the horse's iron-shod hooves clattered and echoed satisfyingly. Instead of one horse, it sounded like a whole cavalry rode the pass.

"OOOh oooooooh. Is there anybody here?" called Woody up to the chateau.

Bodyyyyyyyyy-heeeeeeere, -ere, -ere? bounced back the echo.

"Heeeee-eeeeey," shouted Nat. "Yoo-hoo!"

Heeeee-eeeeeeey-hoooooooooooooooooooooooo, yelled the echo.

"Poop!" yelled Woody.

Pooop, -ooooop, -ooooop, came back the echo.

"Fartz!" yelled Woody.

Fartz, -artz, -artz.

"No no no!" Nat laughed. "It's much better if you shout

a word with two syllables, like this." He stood up in his stirrups, cupped his mouth with his hands, and shouted.

"Butt-face!"

Bbbutt-face, -utt-face, -utt-face, came the cheerful echo back.

The boys cracked up, their laughter echoing eerily around the plain.

"Jockstrap!" yelled Woody.

Jjjjjoooocckkkkssssstttttttrrrraaappp, obliged the echo.

The boys tried several more words—some of which were quite bad swearwords—but when the echoes had died away and it was silent again, it didn't seem quite so funny anymore. They stood in the shadow of the Black Chateau, which seemed to glower its disapproval at their juvenile behavior, and even Rudi had a long face.

"C'mon," said Nat uneasily, suddenly feeling the cold, "let's go home."

Saffi Besson thought she was still dreaming at first when she heard the shouts and laughter from below her tower prison. She had been dreaming about the dark-haired boy she had seen or *thought* she had seen down at the frozen lake, just before her capture. Since then she had thought about him often, praying he hadn't been a figment of her imagination, praying he would get help and rescue her from the Black Chateau. But God hadn't been listening to her prayers. Saffi's time was near. Soon the vampire would force her to drink its blood. Then she, Saffi Besson, would become a full vampire. *Wait! There it was again—she wasn't dreaming.* She struggled painfully to her feet, trying to reach the window. *There were people down there—real people!* Her earlier escape and brief spell of freedom had come at a price, and her captor had shackled her in leg irons and heavy chains that chafed her ankles painfully. If she stretched, she could just reach the tiny turret window, but it was splayed inward and angled wrongly for her to be able to see anything properly. She thought or *imagined* she saw a black horse with two figures astride it, but it quickly went out of her line of vision. She was horrified to find that when she opened her mouth to shout, nothing came out except a thin mewling sound, which no one would ever hear. Her throat was red raw, her voice ruined by days of hopeless screaming for help. Silent tears streamed down her face when she finally realized that she was beaten. There was nothing in the bare room to bang or make a noise with in an attempt to alert whoever was below the chateau. Saffi hung her head in defeat and felt for the gold crucifix her grandmother had given her. She remembered the scorn the vampire had shown when she had defiantly held up the cross to ward it off, like people in horror movies.

"You think you can stop me with that cheap trinket?" the vampire had sneered dismissively. But Saffi knew the little cross had powers; she could *feel* it, and she was sure it had kept the creature away from her. It felt strangely warm as she traced its comforting shape with her cold fingers. She took it off, marveling at the lovely warm glow, which threw a welcome beacon of light in the fading daylight.

"Hold on," said Woody. "Can you hear that? I thought I heard something."

"What?" asked Nat. "Like an echo?"

"Nope," said Woody, cocking his head, "someone calling . . . there!"

Nat concentrated. He thought he could hear something, but it was so insubstantial, so indistinct, he couldn't be sure. "It's the wind," he said. "It makes all different sounds on the plain."

They listened for a few minutes, but the sound Woody had heard, or thought he'd heard, didn't repeat itself again.

"Can we go home now?" asked Woody. "Or your mum and dad'll think we've disappeared, too."

"Yea—hey! Wait up," said Nat urgently, "what was *that*?"

Seconds earlier, Saffi had hauled herself up again to the tiny window and watched in wonder as the glowing crucifix changed from yellow to a searing white light. She held it up and pushed her arm out of the window as far as it would go, willing someone to notice it flashing white in the darkening shadows. If there really *were* people down there, they would see the crucifix arc slowly into the air, as it fell like a dying star to the ground.

"Did you see it?" demanded Nat, blinking furiously to get rid of the spots in front of his eyes. "It was like something was thrown out of the window, like a sparkler!"

Woody screwed up his eyes to where Nat pointed. The Black Chateau still looked as it had when they had first spotted it, lonely and sinister with no outward signs of life.

"You think it came from that direction?" asked Woody.

"From the window," said Nat, "from one of the tower windows—see? The small one on the left-hand side . . . that one."

"It was probably the sun reflected in the window," said Woody reasonably.

"No, don't think so, the sun's too low," pointed out Nat, and scanned all the windows again. "What if . . . what if it's someone trying to signal us? What if it's one of those kids who've gone missing?"

Woody swallowed. "Please tell me we aren't gonna go and check it out?"

CHAPTER 19
THE BLACK CHATEAU

Nat didn't need any special Wolven powers to sense that Woody wasn't exactly jumping with joy at the prospect of meeting whoever lived inside the Black Chateau. In fact, it couldn't have been plainer if the words I DO NOT WANT TO GO NEAR THAT CREEPY HORRIBLE HOUSE had been tattooed across his forehead.

By contrast, Woody could tell from Nat's face it was a foregone conclusion.

He groaned. "We *are* gonna go and check it out, aren't we?"

Nat nodded apologetically.

"Maybe we better go back and get your dad or JC," suggested Woody, "or better still, both of them."

Nat thought for a second, then shook his head. "It'll take ages to ride back to camp and then back here again. I'll just knock on the door."

"Are you *crazy?*" cried Woody. "What you gonna say? Oh, h'lo, we think you're holding someone prisoner in your creepy, horrible old house?"

"Oh," said Nat, "I see what you mean. We'll sneak around the back. See if we can work out where the light was coming from."

"But—" began Woody, but Nat had already slithered from Rudi's saddle and was busy leading him away so that he wouldn't be spotted. Woody helped him secure Rudi's reins to a tree and then they tiptoed across to the only cover they could find, a dead-looking bunch of shrub. There had been no further sounds or mysterious sparkle of white light. Nat was beginning to think he had imagined it, like the voice they both thought they had heard.

"Can *you* feel anything weird?" he asked Woody.

Woody shook his head. "Nope, but there's something funny about how quiet it all seems. *Too* quiet, you know?"

"Yeah," agreed Nat, "like something's blocking us out."

"Like what?" said Woody with a shiver.

"Someone, or something, that doesn't want us here," said Nat grimly.

"I don't wanna walk up to the front," whispered Woody,

as they approached the entrance. "There's a sort of archway over there; I bet that leads around the back."

The back of the chateau was even less welcoming than the front. Nat wondered what sort of person would have such a totally miserable garden. There were some hideous statues of armless ladies with twisted, ugly faces, and all the trees looked as though someone had set fire to them. Their blackened branches raised up in cruel, spiky fingers, just like they were waiting to pinch or grab you as you walked by. Worst of all, there was a funny, burned smell about the place and both boys wrinkled their noses in disgust. Nat caught a strong whiff of old socks and sulfur.

"*Phwoo*, smells like fartz," said Woody, catching Nat's thoughts and smothering a hysterical giggle.

"Shhhh," hissed Nat, "I think we should—uh? What's that noise?"

Out of the silence came a high whining sound, almost like the dentist's drill. The type of annoying noise that burrows inside your ear, making the tiny hairs vibrate and then tunnels clean through your eardrum.

"*Don't like it,*" moaned Woody. "Think we should go now, please, Nat. *Please?*"

Nat felt thoroughly unnerved, and was just about to agree when —

"*OW!*" Woody yelped.

"What . . . what's the matter?" asked Nat in alarm.

Woody started hopping about on one leg and slapping his neck with his hand. "Ow, Nat . . . *Wha . . . ? Geddit off me,* get it off . . . *ugh!*"

"Hold still," said Nat. "Oh. My. *God!*"

"What?" yelped Woody, spooked even further by Nat's disgusted cry.

"It . . . it's some sort of insect," said Nat. "Hang on, don't struggle, I'll grab it."

Nat had to hop to keep time with Woody. They ended up doing a sort of Irish jig of disgust. Nat really didn't want to touch whatever it was on Woody's neck. It looked like an enormous mosquito. He remembered what his dad had said about them when they had arrived. *Forty different species, ten of which bite. OK, great. This monster must be a biter.*

His face working in disgust, Nat tried to dislodge the insect from Woody's neck. It took a while because his fingers were stiff with cold. It felt horrible, *hot,* almost, and he could feel it actually swell in his fingers as it gorged on Woody's blood. Nat let go again.

"Hurry up," moaned Woody. "Get it *offff*!"

Nat went in again—his forefinger and thumb poised for a pincer movement. He grasped the thing, which was firmly latched on to the side of Woody's neck, and pulled with all his might. It came off suddenly with a wet popping noise. Nat threw it away in disgust.

"UUUUUUUrghh!" The two boys danced about in horror as the giant insect lay on its back, its loathsome, spindly legs waving in the air, its heavy body bloated with Woody's blood.

"That's *disgusting*." Nat shuddered.

"What is it?" asked Woody, rubbing his neck. "Is it a fly?"

"I think it's a mosquito," said Nat, walking over to a rock, where the thing was still trying to right itself.

"Look," he said, staring at it in a sort of horrified glee, "it's so full of your blood, it can't get off its back, let alone fly!" Then he stamped on it. The creature exploded as it split, and the snow was stained with bright red poppies of Woody's blood.

Nat glanced at Woody's shocked expression and started to grin. Then they both started to laugh weakly, Woody with the huge relief of not having the giant bug attached to his neck, and Nat because he had been the one to have to touch its horrible, bloated body. When they were done, Woody let Nat examine his neck. The mosquito had bitten him twice, but the tiny puncture wounds were almost gone as Woody's Wolven skin started to repair itself.

Then Woody put his hand on Nat's arm, his head cocked to one side as though he was listening to something.

"It's not over," said Woody, his eyes flashing topaz, "I think that was just a scout. *Listen.*"

But Nat could hear it already. This was a thousand times stronger than the dentist-drill whine of the single giant mosquito. It was the kind of noise a swarm of giant mosquitoes might make.

"C'mon," shouted Woody, pushing Nat in front of him, *"quick!"*

As Nat ran, Woody *puuushed* with all his might, combining his will to shift with the sudden overload of powerful adrenaline shooting like liquid fire through his veins. Within seconds, he was shaking off his ruined clothes as they ripped and split from his powerful Wolven body and he shot past Nat, overtaking him on four legs. The boy and the Wolven raced over to Rudi, who was spooked by the noise and trying to pull his bridle off in an effort to get away from the cloud of angry insects. Nat pulled desperately with frozen fingers at the knot, trying to calm the horse, who in his terror was rearing away from him and pulling the knot tighter, while all the time the sound was getting louder. Then, through the angry droning he heard a distinct voice growl in his brain:

GET ON!

Woody! Nat didn't need to be told twice. He vaulted onto Rudi's back like he had been doing it all his life and saw Woody's sharp white teeth flash as they sheared through the leather reins. Nat nearly fell off backward with the momentum as the horse suddenly became free from its tether, then Rudi followed Woody at a breakneck gallop back down the incline. Roughly thirty seconds later the air behind them appeared thick and black with the six-legged, winged bloodsuckers. Pushing Rudi faster, Nat was galloping neck and neck with Woody as they fled from the cloud, which had formed itself into the uncanny shape of a huge shadowy bat.

From the tiny window in her tower cell, Saffi had heard the peculiar whining drone and guessed her last chance of being saved had been cruelly snatched away. The voices she had heard—or *thought* she had heard—had faded away and the loss was almost too great for Ṣaffi to bear. She watched the shadows as the sun disappeared and dusk settled in the tower room. A strange calm settled on her as she waited for the vampire to appear, realizing that without her cross she was doomed.

With every day and every hour that passed, Scale's eye, now released from its hateful cupboard, could see out into the wide blue yonder—farther than the plastic snow globe, through the flimsy walls of the Silver Lady and out onto the wonderful things he had conjured. He felt like the conductor of an enormous orchestra, where the instruments were finely tuned and played pitch perfect. In fact, Scale was so beside himself with delight that he could almost see himself sitting next to himself. Oh, things were turning out just dandy. He capered around his cave like a demented dervish, singing in a tuneless growl. He had freed the eye from its prison by using telekinesis—another splendid party trick he had learned from the demon (whose name sounded like a scream), and now, to add to the vampire and her hive, he had the female wolf in his thrall. And, best of all, Carver and the Wolven were clueless about his clever manipulations. He had been right to play with them. How had he ever been worried about two ickle bitty babies?

CHAPTER 20
BITTEN

If Nat hadn't been concentrating on not falling off and breaking every bone in his body by clinging on to Rudi's mane, he would have been awed by Woody's speed and cunning. He had streaked through the snow ahead of Rudi like white lightning and if he sensed at any time that the horse was tiring, he would circle back and snap at his heels. With the freezing wind searing the insides of his nose and lungs like cold fire as they careered along the plain, Nat's brain was invaded by a string of jumbled thoughts from Woody, mixing with his own to form a string of scrambled words inside his head.

Rrrruuuuuuuuuuun! Rrrruuuuuuuuun! Rrrruuuuuuun! Ouuuttaheeeere!

It helped to keep thinking it, Woody running in front, Nat riding behind, each urging the other on with the shared rhythm of the words. There was no way they could lead a deadly cloud of mosquitoes with a serious case of the munchies back to camp and endanger everyone else. With the bitten reins trailing out of his reach, Nat relied on his legs to steer the horse after Woody into the forest, his eyes screwed shut, as Rudi weaved and zigzagged, dodging the spiky branches of the trees. As they galloped away from the angry swarm, Nat prayed Rudi wouldn't run out of steam and, though he wore three scarves around his neck, his flesh prickled and crawled at the thought that any second one of the bloodsuckers would latch on to his bare skin and spike him with that horrible proboscis thing. . . .

But suddenly, the noise stopped. It didn't trail off, it just ended. Nat risked a look behind. There was nothing there, just trees and shadows. And blessed silence.

It was dusk when an exhausted, sore, and dispirited Nat led Rudi through the forbidden town of Marais, with Woody loping easily along beside him. They had found their way back from the forest, but if they were to be back at camp before dark, it was quicker to go through the town. Nat felt invisible as people hurried passed him, wrapped up against the cold, rushing to be home before full dark.

The darkening streets were depressing, and as people bustled by, Nat felt the charged atmosphere clinging to him like a heavy coat. It was catching, this somber mood. A smartly dressed woman carrying a few Christmas packages on the other side of the road paused to stare at him.

"Boy," she called out in English, perhaps recognizing him as one of the Twilighters, "go home quickly." Then she hurried off into the gloomy alley.

They passed rows of shops and houses that would normally be buzzing with Christmas activity and decked out with Christmas lights. Instead, the townspeople had nervously locked their doors and shuttered their windows against the onslaught of night. Nat noticed that some of the locals had made a bit of an effort to decorate their doors and windows. Pale wreaths of cream flowers were hung on the doors and garlands of the same creamy color were draped at each window and fastened across the shutters like washed-out imitations of the Christmas decorations Nat's parents had back home in England. Nat felt glad when they had left the town and now headed for the *gardian* settlement and the camp. It was only when they got close to the strange-shaped *gardian* houses with the bulls' horns on the doors that he realized that the same pale garlands and wreaths hanging on the doors, and even from the bulls horns, were made of hundreds of garlic bulbs.

"Couldn't have been mosquitoes," said Fish later, after Nat had told her about their adventure that afternoon. "They're out of season."

"Try telling that to the one that sucked half a bucket of blood out of Woody's neck," said Nat, shuddering. "It was weird, though, Fish. The way they suddenly disappeared when we were safely out of the way. It's as though something conjured them up just to scare us."

"I've heard of stranger things," said Fish softly. "More likely they were conjured up to stop you investigating the voice you thought you heard."

"Who could do that?" asked Nat, puzzled.

"Think about it," said Fish, running her fingers through her hair, "who would have the powers to block Wolven telepathy?"

"Well . . . ," said Nat hesitantly, "a vampire might?"

"Or," said Fish, "a certain wolf with demonic energy?"

"Scale," said Nat in a flat voice. "But that's impossible.

Even if he is still alive somehow, how could he know where we are, or what we're doing?"

Woody was growling, his fur bristling. He appeared enormous in the small confines of Fish's trailer, and for the first time Fish saw the true power of a Wolven. Woody's eyes glowed orange with anger, his lip lifting in a snarl.

"There was something else," remembered Nat. "There was a light, or something shiny and bright, that flashed from one of the towers."

"What was it?" asked Fish. "It could be important."

"We don't know," admitted Nat, "we didn't get to find out. The mosquitoes came, and we got out quick."

"Still, you thought you'd investigate." Fish grinned. "We'll make NightShift operatives of you yet."

Woody growled and chuffed as he lay down by Fish's feet.

"Though I don't think Woody's too into that suggestion," Fish remarked fondly. Having experienced Woody in both his forms, Fish, like everyone else (especially girls, Nat noticed), couldn't stop herself from wanting to pet him. As they talked, Nat watched Alex Fish unconsciously fiddling with the long fur on Woody's neck;

it was as though he was giving her strength by the reassuring solidness of him, like a big furry touchstone. All Fish knew was that Woody had an aura about him, something that made her feel *safe* and kind of *glad* . . . glad in her heart, even when they were facing unspeakable danger.

"According to Teebo Bon's investigation, all the properties within a ten-mile radius have been thoroughly searched more than once," said Fish, consulting her notes. "This, er . . . Black Chateau is actually derelict—no one has lived there for years. I've done a bit of rooting around in the town's archives and Marais seems to have had more than its fair share of people going missing. Although people had different ideas about what had happened to them, most suspected vampire activity. It was hushed up as much as possible because the main suspect was a very important person."

"And you think it's the same one come back from the undead?" Nat shuddered.

Fish nodded eagerly. "I reckon Maccabee's right. If the vampire has been reanimated somehow, it's taking young people because it needs their blood to stay young."

"And it keeps them alive," said Nat excitedly. "It

wouldn't be much point making them into vampires or draining them dry because it would need them alive."

"Whatever drove you away from the Black Castle—or whatever it's called—is responsible," said Fish urgently. "We need to get the sheriff dude to search again. If the vampire hasn't forced the kids to drink its blood, they'll still be pure."

"You think there's still hope?" asked Nat.

"I think it's time to let the sheriff know," replied Fish.

"Teebo Bon is the mayor, not the sheriff," pointed out Nat.

"Makes no odds." She grinned. "He's got a gun and a great big hat—seems all the same to me."

Agent Fish's plan would have worked a treat, but for two major developments. First, the weather worsened. The air temperature overnight had dropped to freezing again, and the wind chill was too dangerous to leave camp. The second devastating occurrence was to affect the mayor: the affable but dedicated Teebo Bon. He had received a visitor: a scaly batlike apparition that had sucked his blood for the third night in a row, and whom he, Teebo, had been bewitched to invite inside without any idea of what was happening.

He sat on the end of his bed and rubbed the stubble on his chin absentmindedly. He hadn't slept properly for weeks, and when he did manage to get a few hours, he was plagued by nightmares so terrible he would wake up shouting and waving his arms around as though to fight off an attack from something with hungry red eyes and bad breath. He had gone off his food, and even his wife, a formidable nag and the bane of his life, was worried about him. She told him he was fading before her very eyes. Teebo hauled himself from the bed and wobbled into the bathroom. He surveyed his face in the mirror and inspected his appearance. His face, normally weathered and cheerful, looked haggard, pale, and unkempt. He stared for a while and imagined his wife had been right. He really did look as though he was fading away. For a few seconds, his reflection wavered in the mirror and he could have sworn he could see straight through it, as though his face had faded almost to the point of disappearing. Teebo groaned and reached automatically for his shaving kit. He halfheartedly lathered his chin and dragged the razor across his face, making that lopsided shaving face that all men (and some ladies) do.

Ouch! He leaned closer into the mirror and inspected the site where it had hurt. He turned his head slightly to the left to get a better look and what he saw there made his heart pump twice as fast. He could hear the blood pounding its way through his body, his ears, his temples. There were two puncture wounds on his neck. He touched them in horrified wonder, wincing at the tender red area around the marks. The holes looked nasty, as though they were infected with something toxic. He had been so careful. Teebo Bon suddenly felt very old, and very tired. The light was hurting his eyes, and as he climbed into his bed he made sure he covered his face.

Later that night, Madame Besson, mother of the missing Saffi, put out the stockings for Papa Noël to leave presents. She knew the best present would be for Saffi to come home safe and well. With a heavy heart, she went up the stairs to bed again. She dreaded the day, preferring to sleep through it, feeling strangely alert at night. She lay on her bed, wondering if she would have the same dream she had had for three nights running, that her daughter

Saffi was outside, waiting for her to open the door and invite her in out of the cold. But Madame Besson had been frightened of her dream daughter, for she had a new smile that didn't reach her eyes, and when she opened her mouth Madame Besson could see her teeth were long and pointed.

Still more children were visited by pretty shiny lights as they lay in their warm beds. It wasn't until they unlocked their windows and invited the pretty lights inside their bedrooms that they realized they had invited a black nightmare into their room, a nightmare that carried them away from their safe beds, away on the freezing night air to meet with a hungry monster.

Del Underhill got a visitor, too, as he lay fast asleep in the trailer he shared with his brothers, who snored gently in their bunks. Del was having another dream about the cat he used to have when he was a small boy. In his dream, the cat was scratching at the door as she always did when she wanted to be let inside.

"Go 'way, pussycat," he muttered in his sleep, but still the old cat scratched at the door: *Scratch, scratch, scratch*, went her claws, faster and faster, more insistent, until Del couldn't stand it. *I'll have to let her in*, he thought, raising himself up onto one elbow and opening his eyes groggily. He was dimly aware that it must have been a dream, that the old cat had been dead for years and he wasn't at home, he was miles away, in France, in a caravan. But still he could hear the maddening scratching.

He looked up and froze.

There was something on the roof of the trailer. Something with red eyes, which gleamed malevolently, waiting with greedy impatience for Del to open the skylight and let it in.

CHAPTER 21
THE SLAYER'S APPRENTICES

Nat's dreams often had the habit of turning into nightmares, and this one was a thoroughbred, more like a night*stallion*.

In his dream, Nat stood alone in the snow. It was like when you know you're dreaming and you just *know* it's going to turn nasty, but you can no more scream than you can wake up or run, and everything is in slow motion, even noise.

He knew it was a dream because he still had his pajamas on and his bare feet weren't cold. The short hairs on the back of his neck rose slightly as he got a sense of danger. The danger was behind and it was close.

Nat spun around, his fists already raised, his lips drawn back in a kind of snarl. He was dimly aware of two things. One, that his senses were on overdrive—his body was zinging with strength and energy—and two, that Lucas Scale was standing directly in front of him.

Noooo! Nat blinked hard, as if by doing so the apparition of Lucas Scale would vanish. But no, Scale still stood in front of him, a murderous gleam in his orange eyes and hot drool dripping from his mouth onto the snow, making a slight hiss as the snow melted. Nat stared. Scale didn't move—he just stood there, drooling. Then he smiled.

Why aren't you dead, you monster? Nat asked of Scale with his mind.

Lucas Scale grinned wider, showing his trademark skanky teeth. He raised his right paw and pointed with a deadly claw to his raddled orange eyeball. Then, still drooling hungrily, he pointed at Nat. *Watching you, boy*, he mimed.

Before Nat could react, Scale's body appeared to ripple and warp in the light of the rancid orange moon. As Nat watched, it faded and flickered until, with a slight popping noise, the image of Scale disappeared. Nat's body was pumped—he felt cheated—if only he could have grabbed Scale and . . . then to his dismay he heard a sound riding on the freezing night, a slapping *THWACK*

THWACK of a sound, as if something huge flew over-head. When the stars turned black above the protective canopy of trees, Nat heard himself make a groaning noise of dread. *Something was flying above—only this time it wasn't mosquitoes.*

Nat forced himself to look up to see what was making the air rush around him and the snow swirl around in mad patterns at his feet, as though a helicopter was preparing to land. He felt the cold sting of the snow on his upturned face and he glimpsed the black shadow of something flapping jerkily through the gaps in the trees. There were other black shapes roosting up there, looking down on him with their greedy red eyes and black, shiny wings. *Vampires!*

But they were nothing like the vampires Nat had seen in movies or comics. These were true monsters, with leathery batlike bodies and sharp pointed teeth, not aristocrats in dinner jackets with their hair brushed back neatly from their foreheads. He willed himself to run, but his legs were useless—somehow the snow had become thick and heavy like syrup, and while he tried in vain to wade through it, he realized the vampires were closing in.

They were slithering and sliding through the branches, and as they hit the snowy ground they were changing shape. They were still black and leathery, but now they had morphed into long human shapes, their faces masks of greed and viciousness, their elongated teeth glinting murderously in the orange glare of the moon. Only their eyes remained the same, fiery red orbs, striking Nat as strangely beautiful.

"*Oh God,*" he moaned. "This isn't just a dream. *It's a premonition!*"

They were surrounding him, *he must move . . .* warn everyone . . . he had to . . .

"*AAAARroooooooooooooohhhhhh!*"

At first, Nat didn't know if he were still in the dream and Woody had come into it, too, or whether it was *real* and Woody really *was* howling in terror. With a tremendous effort of concentration, he willed himself out of the nightmare and woke up. He sat up in his bunk, rubbing his eyes, and as they adjusted the first thing he saw was Woody, in human form now, with his eyes bugging out and flashing with terror. Nat gasped when he saw what had terrified the Wolven. A dirty orange light emanated from the top of their dining table. At first Nat had taken it for the weak glow of the lamp, but it was coming from the snow globe that Woody was so fond of. Nat's eyes bulged in terror. There had been something weird about that snow globe, Nat remembered wildly—hadn't he felt it, and buried it inside the cupboard? And now Nat realized what horror it contained! The globe shone with a sullen, rabid light, and in the scummy, greasy liquid floated a monstrous eye, an eye that gleamed malevolently, pressing up hard against the plastic, pushing it outward as if the eye was trying to break out. Nat stared at it, transfixed.

"Look away!" cried Woody.

But Nat couldn't. He could feel the dark, malicious mirth coming from the snow globe and a connection with something he thought he would never have to deal with again. The orange rheumy eye was sickeningly familiar. *It belonged to Lucas Scale.* Nat's senses told him that by some force of tainted magic, Scale had sent it there to spy on them.

Woody sprang from his bunk and grabbed the snow globe. It felt hot and slimy in his hand, as though it leaked oily tears. He pulled open the trailer door and flung it as hard as he could out into the snow, yelping with fear and disgust, wiping his hand frantically on his pajama bottoms.

"He's been watching," cried Nat. "*Scale!* He was in my dream!"

"He knows where we are," Woody whispered, horrified. "You OK?"

"Think so," said Nat in a barely audible voice. "It was horrible. Scale was in my dream and then the vampires came. It wasn't just a dream, it was a premonition!"

"I had it, too," said Woody in a flat, resigned voice. "Scale's set 'em on us. They're coming, ain't they?"

Nat nodded slowly. "I think we need to tell Fish there's more than one."

"The first rule of vampire slaying is that there *are* no rules," explained Maccabee Hammer to the gathering of cold and terrified Twilighters. "Like humans, some vampires are stronger than others. I'd just like to remind you folks that us new-age vampires don't hold with feeding from humans," he added hastily. "Let's make that crystal clear—we don't go around making humans into vampires or sucking their blood." He shuddered at the thought. "That would be considered bad manners nowadays. But if Fish is right, and we're dealing with an ancient, then we're in a heap of trouble. If an ancient has been reawakened, it means that although it was staked, it was asleep in its coffin: That's usually why its body was able to survive the trauma. It will mean its disciples — the original hive of undead — has woken, too, and just one of these ol' bloodsuckers can feed off three, maybe even four humans on a good night. Ancient vamps are blood-crazed monsters: They don't know any better. In the olden days they were hunted down and staked in their coffins. The vampire who attacked Del is a full-on ancient: a vampire who has feasted on the blood of a vampire — usually the head of the hive. If you come face-to-face with one, *DO NOT* look into its eyes if you can help it. If you let yourself become hypnotized by them and invite it in, you've basically had it. The usual remedies for repelling them once you have let them in will be useless. It doesn't matter how much garlic you eat or how many crosses you wear, you will be defenseless. The vamp can, and will, attack. Questions, anyone?"

"How do we kill them?" asked Scarlet, her teeth chattering slightly.

Maccabee Hammer grinned, showing sharp incisors. "A stake through the heart may kill me — might even make me explode, if I'm not in my coffin. It's quite spectacular. Sunlight will melt me, and I can even drown. Water has a strange effect; it would make my body swell up and burst. But I'll never really be dead in the true sense of the word. I can be brought back again by a powerful magus or demon. The only way to ensure I will *never* come back is to burn my body or cut it up into small pieces."

There was silence as everyone digested this grisly information.

"Do you think the missing children are vampires?" asked Jude Carver in a small voice.

"If they are, then they are lost," said Mac. "More likely, they're being held somewhere. The blood of a child is more potent than adult blood, too precious to waste by making them into vampires, too."

"You mean we might be able to *save* them?" asked Woody, his eyes shining with excitement.

Maccabee Hammer smiled. "It's a possibility. All we

need to do is to find the hive and kill the head vamp."

"And that's all there is to it," said Nat under his breath. *It's going to be a flippin' long night*, he thought to himself.

It was three o'clock in the morning. Those who hadn't been woken by Paddy Underhill yelling about the vampire his brother had invited into their caravan had been woken up by Woody's heart-stopping howl. Everyone was bundling themselves into coats over their nightclothes, wondering why all hell had apparently broken loose. After an extended search with the torches and hastily carved stakes, JC and Evan had persuaded everyone that the thing had gone, apparently having got what it had come for: *hot, fresh blood.*

When Nat and Woody shared their premonition with Fish, she immediately ordered fires to be lit in a protective circle around the camp, and Evan organized the bravest men to be posted as lookouts. No one was able to get hold of the mayor, Teebo Bon. His wife said she hadn't seen him, saying he had gone to pick up a pizza, which she suspected was a lie, as there were no pizza parlors in the whole of Marais town.

In the meantime, Agent Fish and JC were preparing

the Twilighters to help fight if their bloodsucking visitor returned with its friends, as Nat and Woody's premonition had warned. A predawn meeting was held in the second-largest tent for those who wanted to help.

Del, who was still pale and shaken from his ordeal, shuddered visibly. "I let it in," he croaked, "it was lookin' at me with those terrible . . . but kind of *beautiful* red eyes, and I *wanted* to open the skylight and let it in. It . . . oh *God* . . . it *bit* me!"

On Fish's instructions, Jude poured disinfectant into the jagged, ugly wound on Del's neck. When she had finished dressing it, she turned to the NightShift agent, her eyes enormous in the lamplight.

"Do you think we have a chance?" she asked.

"Look at us all," said Fish, her beady eyes shining. "We've all got the skills to fight the vampires and win. Between us, we have werewolves, cryptids, Wolven, and human power. Best of all, we've got Mac! C'mon! Let's kick some vampire butt!"

CHAPTER 22

THE FEARLESS VAMPIRE KILLERS

Dusk. Agent Alexandra Fish was taking inventory.

"String?"

"Check," chorused the Twilighters.

"Holy water?"

"Check."

"Stakes?"

"Check."

"Fishing nets?"

"Check."

"Trash bags?"

"Check."

"Electric fences?"

"Check."

"Garlic puree?"

"Uhh . . . no, sorry," answered an apologetic voice from the back of the tent.

"Why not?" asked Alex Fish testily.

"Sold out," replied Scarlet, pushing her way to the front. "Everyone in Marais bought every available bulb of garlic to hang up outside their houses."

"We got an alternative, though," piped up Woody.

"And this would be?" asked Fish, eyebrow raised challengingly.

"This would be onion soup." Woody beamed. "*French* onion soup."

Fish looked less than impressed. "You're joking, right?"

"Nope," said Nat, shaking his head. "It's even better than garlic: We tried a drop on Mac. Covers more of an area. It works even when we mixed it with normal water, not the holy stuff."

"Hmmmm . . ." Fish considered it for a couple of seconds. "Good improvisation. I'm impressed. Every one know their positions?"

"*Check,*" yelled the Twilighters.

The morning had been spent planning and organizing their defense. Wood was gathered around the trailers and cabins and stacked into neat bonfires. The generator was set up and the electric fences unrolled. Water from the nearby church was blessed hurriedly by a very scared, very fat little priest and dragged into camp in a tank by the Russian horses. Evan and John Carver were in charge of the stake-sharpening outfit, while Jude ran an onion-chopping production line. Nat's olfactory glands went into overdrive. His enhanced senses couldn't cope with the smell of the onions; the fumes clung to his clothes and invaded his nostrils. He had to resort to tying a scarf around his nose and mouth, much to the amusement of his mum, who luckily thought he was just trying to get out of chopping the onions. It was at times like this that Nat felt he was being deceitful by not sharing his secret with his mum and dad. He wondered how long it would be before they really noticed he wasn't quite the boy they thought he was.

Fish directed all activities with aplomb, much to Crescent's disgust and annoyance. To anyone who would listen, she'd been voicing her opinion about Fish's certain inability to conduct a successful campaign against vampires as she was, after all, a mere human.

Unfortunately, Fish herself had heard.

"Well, you know, Crescent," she said in a syrupy, condescending voice, "you can always take over if you think you're qualified, but I think you'd better leave this to NightShift, sweetheart. Vampires are slightly harder to kill than ickle furry guinea pigs and meerkats."

A few Twilighters stifled giggles while Crescent flushed, her eyes flashing. She flounced off in a huff, and for once Nat felt a bit sorry for her. It looked like Crescent had met her match in Alex Fish.

"Who died and made *her* queen?" he heard her mutter to Otis, who wisely kept his mouth shut.

Later, Crescent loped sulkily between the rows of caravans, listening to the sounds of activity as the rest of the Twilighters worked in teams to prepare their attack. Not only had John Carver given her a final, final warning after nearly scaring the horseshoes off poor Rudi (*Nat hadn't even fallen off!*), Alex Fish had shown her up in front of everyone, *and* Crescent had glimpsed Nat Carver's expression of sympathy. *Well*, she thought to herself, kicking up the snow in temper, *he can stick his stupid pity, thanks very much.*

Her mood was dark. Her stomach churned and her werewolf senses were reeling. Her head ached and, worst of all . . . she felt like hurting someone. Hurting and *biting . . . ripping . . .* She shook her head, making it ache more, but at least the murderous thoughts receded into the dark part of her werewolf brain. *The part you trained yourself to hide if you were a lycan.*

Something gripped her brain like a vise. Crescent fell to her knees in the snow from the sheer force of it. There was something stuck half in, half out of the snow in front of her, something pushing its way out, like a hand scrabbling from a grave. *The snow globe!* Seeing it again made her feel weird — sort of thrilled, but at the same time ashamed and guilty and frightened. The snow globe had made her forget the things it had told her to do, but she knew they were BAD and if she did them she would be CURSED. She had made herself put the globe back on the table and leave the *Silver Lady*. But she *had* done something bad — not a really big thing — but she could remember how wonderful it felt when she had made Nat Carver's horse bolt, how *good* it had felt to see the look of terror on his face!

Still kneeling in the snow, Crescent looked around

furtively. Although her senses were screaming at her, warning her off, she wanted it. She wanted to pick it up and shake it again, watch the snow swirl around. And then . . . she wanted to see the eye again, although it both revolted and frightened her. She wanted to feel its power and strength creep inside her. It called to her silently, insistently, *cajolingly*. She made her fingers pick it up—part of her still wanted nothing to do with it—and she held it, causing the snow to fly around the scene inside: a tiny family of reindeer and fir trees. As the confetti snow cleared beneath the plastic shell of the globe, the eye of Lucas Scale opened again.

"Nat Carver has set everyone against you," wheedled a syrupy voice in her brain. *"John Carver hates you for what you did to those animals; he wants you gone. Everyone hates you, Crescent, and you smell* very *bad: That's why you had to keep away from the horses."*

After a while, Crescent got to her feet, her face set in an ugly leer. Her body was trying to morph as part of her tried to repel Scale's presence from her body. Her hair stood up on her head and fell in matted clumps around her face. Her hands had changed into twisted paws, her claws unsheathed. When she opened her eyes, they were *changed*.

The Twilighters were as ready as they would ever be. They were prepared for any eventuality, an aerial attack or ground invasion by their bloodsucking visitors, with three lines of defense facing out in a semicircle around the camp. Nat Carver, who was crouched in position with Woody, felt vulnerable and exposed as they waited for the inevitable attack. Nat had learned to trust his premonitions, and with Woody having the same awful dream, their senses were on Wolven overdrive. In the brief and unsettling silence in the still and frozen night, Nat felt Woody clutch the soft flesh at the top of his arm.

"Ow," whispered Nat. "Put your claws away!"

Woody was in the middle of a shift. His hands had already morphed and his sharp claws were sticking into Nat's arm.

"Sorry," Woody growled, and the hairs went up on the back of Nat's neck. No matter how many times his friend shifted, he couldn't help feeling chilled. Woody was always weird when his change was neither here nor there. Half boy, half Wolven, his amber eyes shone out like beams of light and his voice sounded inhuman and scary.

"Listen," growled Woody.

When the vampires came, they came fast. The *THWACK THWACK* sound of their leathery wings reverberated in the still, frozen night. Nat's keen hearing picked up what Woody had already heard: great wings forcing air away as they flapped nearer and nearer.

"Ready?" whispered Fish.

Nat and Woody both flashed her ghostly grins.

"Can you see anything?"

Nat struggled to answer. His mouth was too dry to talk.

Woody answered for him. "Yeah," he said softly. "Look."

Fish peered up to where Woody was staring.

"Oh . . . oh *no*," she breathed.

Fish was used to fighting the unknown. She had been responsible for staking a whole hive of bloodsuckers, hadn't she? But these were different. These would be awake! *How could she ever have thought she would be able to take this on and win?* There were at least fifty of them. Winged horrors with red eyes and black scabrous wings, roosting silently at the tops of the trees, waiting to attack.

Had the Twilighters done enough to ensure a victory? It was time to find out. She gave the signal.

The team members on lights duty turned the headlights on the trucks and cars to high beam. Woody had fully shifted by now, and he leaped forward in the front line with the werewolves, teeth bared, hackles standing up on his shoulders like a demented porcupine.

The vampires' first mistake was that they approached the camp through the trees, planning to take the Twilighters by surprise. They had no idea, until they tried to climb down through their cover, that Fish had designed a cunning cat's cradle of string throughout the entire network of branches. Maccabee Hammer and his aye-ayes had spent the day up in the treetops, until the semicircle of conifers was crisscrossed with hundreds of yards of hairy green string. And it had worked! Designed to slow their inevitable climb down into camp, the Twilighters had a good idea of what they were up against as the harsh halogen lights from the trucks illuminated the creatures trying to disentangle themselves, and watched in fascinated horror at the struggling vampires, who shrieked abominably as their wings and feet became caught in the string. They were just as Nat had described them from his premonition, black leathery devils with burning coals as eyes.

The first line of defense waited while the vampires descended. Dark shapes crashed to the floor as the string lost its strength and snapped.

"Prime the hoses!" yelled Fish as the first vampire crashed through. It rose to its feet as if lifted by an invisible force, its black wings morphing back into its body as it stood up and reached out for Nat with a ragged red grin of triumph.

"*Nat!* Look out!"

Nat was dimly aware of his mum screaming. He ducked just in time as the vampire shot out an impossibly long, thin arm, and turned to run. But the vampire was too quick. This time it managed to grab him roughly, making Nat lose his balance and fall over. It was strong, stronger than Nat, even with his Wolven blood. It tightened its hold around Nat's neck, and he was dimly aware of a reddish-colored wolf shape moving forward close by. *Crescent! Thank goodness! Why wasn't she helping him? WHAT THE FLIPPIN' HECK WAS SHE WAITING*

FOR? A WRITTEN INVITATION? To Nat's horror, she cringed away from him, her lush red tail tucked firmly between her back legs. Nat couldn't believe it. *Crescent had punked out! She was running away!* And the vampire was inches away from Nat's face, its vicious features frozen in a ferocious snarl. He was helpless. *Why hadn't they turned on the hoses?* If he could only move his arms, he could smack the vampire a good one, but his arms were pinned by his sides. Sensing he didn't have long, he pulled his head back as far as he could from the horrific teeth that were trying to latch on to him, and *SMACK!* He head butted the vampire hard enough for it to loosen its grip. Although the vampire looked like it had a headache, it was still hanging on to Nat, moving in again with its fangs.

Then, there was a sudden jolt, like an electric shock, a muffled BANG—and Nat found himself covered in black, sticky goo. The vampire had disappeared, and Fish, also covered in black gore, pulled Nat from the ground.

"Where'd it go?" cried Nat. "What the—"

Fish grinned, her teeth white against her grubby face.

"Exploded," she replied, handing Nat a sharp wooden

stake. "Here," she said. "There's plenty more where this one came from."

More vampires were breaking through the trees. As they advanced on their prey they quickly smelled out the fruity scent of humans, but there was an underlying odor—a meaty, savage whiff of . . . werewolves! The vampires were caught on the back foot again, because they hadn't expected any resistance from the humans, let alone werewolves. They hadn't bargained for the Twilighters to be forewarned by Nat's nightmare, much less on being met by this hostile crowd with their stakes and their rather infantile string traps. *And what was this?* Again, something they hadn't bargained for.

"*Soooooooouuup! FIRE!*"

They didn't have a chance to retreat. The vampires in the front row met the full force of the onion soup. Gallons of foul-smelling, flesh-burning gunk shot out of a dozen hoses, making the vampire lieutenants shriek and sizzle as the French onion soup ravaged their vampire skin. Encouraged by their success, Natalie and her team reloaded with more soup and holy water, ready for the next lot. *"FIRE!"* When it hit the vampires full in the face it hissed horribly, burning off their flesh, and giving them the appearance of melted candles as they writhed on the snowy ground and evaporated. The vampires who escaped this undignified method of vampire-slaying were caught by the three Surrealias as they rose gracefully up into the night sky with a fishing net held in their clawlike hands. Flying high above the camp, they pulled the net taut and dropped it onto the fleeing creatures, for Fish, Evan, and JC to finish off with wooden stakes.

"Is this going to work?" shouted Evan Carver. "I've only ever seen this part in movies!"

"Trust me!" shouted back Fish, "it works. Watch and learn!"

But it was horrible to watch. Alex Fish raised her arm in an arc. She swung it down and staked the nearest vampire trying to bite through the net with razor-sharp incisors. It was as though the stake were a lightning rod. A blue flame sprang out of the vampire's chest, and then it exploded with a muffled *BANG*, covering Fish again with a mixture of vampire innards and French onion soup. After the smoke cleared, all that was left of the deadly beast was an acrid black stain on the pure white snow. The smell was appalling.

"We need to get them all!" Fish commanded. "Don't let any get away!"

"There's too many!" Nat yelled back.

The scene on the ground was horrific. If Nat had been able to watch instead of fighting for his life, he would have seen Woody and the three Howlers dragging the vampires from the trees, leaping up as they broke through the string and mauling them until Fish could stake them. Her tried-and-tested method of shoving trash bags over their heads proved useful for disorienting the vampires, and staking them wasn't so messy, as most of the gore was contained inside the plastic, but it took too long. The vampires who got the full force of the onion soup were taken out quickly, but staking the others as they landed was a bit hit-or-miss. *There had to be a quicker way!*

NAT! STABLES!

"Uh . . . Woody?" Nat caught Woody's message and flung the hose down. "Back in a minute!" he shouted to Scarlet. "Keep it coming!"

He caught a glimpse of white fur as Woody flashed

ahead toward the stables. As he ran, Nat was forming a picture in his mind. Woody was showing him the electric fence and . . . *Wait a minute, he was showing him Titus the bull!*

Woody was in the stable with Titus when Nat arrived, out of breath and running scared.

In his mind, he saw Woody and the bull lower their heads toward each other, as if they were having some sort of silent conversation. Nat wasn't able to pick up any stray thoughts, so he had to be patient. At last, Woody jumped out of Titus's stable and turned to Nat.

NAT! OPEN IT!

"I hope you know what you're doing!" muttered Nat grimly as he opened the stable door. The great black bull walked hesitantly to the open doorway, and Nat stood behind the door as Titus blew steam through his impressive nostrils. He looked mad and bad. His eyes gleamed blackly and his great body trembled as he waited.

What's he waiting for? thought Nat, as he peered into the distance. Then suddenly Titus started to paw the ground. Woody raced off into the darkness. Titus bellowed loud enough to make Nat leap into the air, and then shot off after Woody. Nat followed just in time to see Titus run amok, scattering and confusing the remaining vampires—he was taking no prisoners. With the vampires outsmarted again, they weren't quick enough to morph into their wings. As Titus chased them down and gored them with his devastating sacred horns, they exploded until they were nothing more than splatters of black, undead gore. The ones that managed to get off the ground flew off-course, straight into the electric fence, perishing in a flash of blue fire and black guts.

"D'you want some *more*?" screamed Fish at the retreating vampires. They were off the ground, flying up again into the trees, apparently beaten for tonight.

"They'll be back," she said grimly to the exhausted Twilighters. "We need to find the hive, and quick."

CHAPTER 23
MACCABEE HAMMER

Agent Alex Fish wasted no time in organizing a special vampire-slaying workshop in the candlelit black tent.

"So, what have we found out about our vampire friends?" asked Fish, thoroughly enjoying the tutorial she was giving with Maccabee Hammer. *This is more like it!* she thought to herself as she addressed the sea of weary faces before her. *What a blast!* She was only sorry that the boss would be oblivious to her triumph, as she had no way of contacting him.

It wasn't over, though. There was only so much string and onion soup that would keep the vampires away, and eventually everyone would be defenseless against them. *And that*—Fish shuddered—*would be the end.*

"What we know about real, undead vampires is that they aren't like the ones in the movies," said Fish to her pupils. "The undead in movies are usually middle-aged guys in dinner jackets and shiny shoes, or hip, drop-dead gorgeous ones — no offense, Mac," she added hastily to the vampire magician. He raised a skeletal hand as if to say, *None taken.*

"We outsmarted them." Fish grinned. "They suffered all the casualties. The only injuries our side suffered were minor. Apart from Del, of course, who is showing some unfortunate signs of vampirism. If I'm right and we destroy the entire hive, he'll soon go back to being a normal faun again."

"Come on, people," said Maccabee Hammer impatiently. "What did we learn from the vampire hive?"

"They were butt ugly?" Scarlet shivered.

"Apart from that?" asked Fish. "What else did you notice about them? Did they give any clue as to where they might be holed up?"

Everyone looked at each other, hoping that someone would come up with the answer.

"They had *really* bad hair?" piped up Natalie.

Crescent was strangely quiet. She appeared to have nothing to suggest. She hadn't spoken to Nat to apologize for her wimpy behavior, and was keeping a low profile, probably for the first time in her entire life. She listened to their plans intently, her hand unconsciously stroking the plastic snow globe in her pocket.

"Nat? Woody?" barked Fish. "Anything unusual about them?"

Woody, now back in human form, pondered this for a second, then grinned wolfishly.

"They stank," he said. "They stank really, *really* bad."

"OK," said Fish wearily. "So we've got a bunch of smelly bloodsuckers with bad hair, anything else?"

"I've got a question for Mac," said Nat suddenly.

The vampire magician got to his feet. His face was whiter than usual, his sad expression sadder. "Nat, what can I tell you?"

"C . . . can you do that thing . . . ," stammered Nat, "the changing into a monster thing?"

"What do you think?" asked Mac softly.

"I mean . . . are all vampires the same?"

Mac's face was expressionless. "It's a part of me I am ashamed of," he said. "Like Scarlet said, it's ugly."

Scarlet looked at the floor, slightly embarrassed. No one had ever seen Maccabee Hammer look any different from how he did tonight.

"I guess we could turn this into a show-and-tell session," joked Mac halfheartedly, "but I warn you, it won't be pretty."

Oh my God, thought Nat, *he's going to show us!* His friend Mac was going to turn himself into a monster for the sake of their education! They had all seen the vampires roosting in the trees above camp. The red eyes, strange skeletal faces, how they could morph into their wings when they needed to.

The night seemed to grow colder, if that was possible. It was freezing already. A thin mist had appeared from nowhere. Mac stood in the middle of the clearing, half hidden in shadow from the trees. It was dead quiet. No one spoke; everyone watched as the mist grew denser, rising up, twisting and weaving around Mac's skinny legs. Nat could see Mac's eyes were closed as he concentrated on his monster metamorphosis. The mist was clinging to the vampire's body, and Nat's eyes watered as a sulfurous smell hung in the air. When the mist reached the vampire's head it turned a dirty yellow, and then black. Mac's body seemed to grow and expand. Then, shocking in its speed, the mist disappeared, leaving behind something else.

The thing that stood before the scared Twilighters bore no physical resemblance to Maccabee Hammer, vampire magician, who, although not the most handsome individual in the world, possessed a certain lived-in charm and raffishness. The figure that stood beside the fire had made everyone back away from it in undisguised horror, and Nat was sad about that; Mac didn't deserve to be treated with revulsion. The blackened countenance of the vampire was strange, like a primitive bird. It—*he*, Nat tried to tell himself—reminded him of some sort of flying reptile. Its body was bound with thick, ropelike muscles, no doubt formed to be able to bear the weight of its wings when it flew. As if the vampire had read Nat's mind, a pair of wings spread from its shoulders and shone blackly in the light of the fire. Nat heard everyone take a deep breath. Although undeniably scary, the vampire's wings were beautiful, like those of a dark angel. And when Nat made himself look at his friend's face, he saw that Mac was not like the others. His face—*if you could call it a face,* thought Nat—was turned slightly away, as if ashamed. Nat could see his eyes were red, but not with the greedy malice of the hive. Everyone else had noticed, too, that although he was different, he was still Mac.

Nat was the first to move closer again. He put his hand up and touched the space below the vampire's eyes. Mac flinched away, but Nat had felt how cold and unyielding it felt beneath his fingers, like stone. Then Mac faced them properly, gazing at them with his ruby eyes, and tried to smile.

Mac's show-and-tell was over. The mist enveloped him again and the vampire magician was back to his old self.

Nat broke the silence. "*Wow*. That was *awesome*!"

Woody was curious. "How d'you get to hang on to your cloves?" he asked. "I spend most of my time trying to find mine when I change. How come you're not naked?"

"Vampires transform by dark illusion and magic," Mac explained. "The change from man to wolf, or vice versa in your case, Woody, is supernatural, but physical. That's why it looks so uncomfortable. I guess I'm just a big old freak."

Woody grinned. "I guess you're in good company."

CHAPTER 24
HIVE

Snug and smug in his cave den beneath the snow-covered ruins of Helleborine Halt, Lucas Scale rubbed his misshapen paws together with hectic glee.

What a turn up for the books! The she-werewolf had been an unexpected triumph. She was perfect as a host for his sight: resentful, angry, and frightened; her senses had been ripe for the taking. Lucas Scale leaned back in his chair, congratulating himself on his clever-ness. The female werewolf was the perfect spy. His powers were growing. He no longer needed the plastic snow globe. He could see through her eyes now!

Back in the Carvers' cabin, Nat was trying to rest. If there was to be another vampire attack tonight, as Alex Fish had predicted, he would need all his strength again.

"Nat," came his mum's voice from the tiny kitchen,

"how about a sandwich? I think we need to have a chat."

Oh great, groaned Nat to himself, *here we go.* His body ached with the exertion of the previous night's slayings, and he was so far down in the doldrums that he didn't want any lunch, but he couldn't sleep, either. In Wolven form, Woody could sleep anywhere at any time, as he was now, dozing at Nat's feet.

This wasn't supposed to happen, thought Nat gloomily. He had accepted the fact that since he had met Woody his life would never be quite the same again, but this vampire thing was taking over their entire holiday! Not only that, but it had been hard work fighting them off, and he wasn't looking forward to another session tonight. And now his mum would want to ask him loads of questions about what he had dreaded: his Wolvenness.

He pulled himself from his bunk and forced a wan smile.

"Come on, Nat," Jude prompted. "You must eat, especially after all the slaying you've been doing lately."

Nat met her blue gaze with his own and suddenly felt an overwhelming urge to confess everything. "Sorry I didn't tell you," he said awkwardly. "I didn't know how to start. I mean, about the changes and peculiar stuff I can do now."

"Can you stop it?" asked his mum softly.

Nat shook his head.

"Do you want to?" asked Jude, her face white and strained.

Nat shook his head again, almost ashamed. "No," he said simply. "I guess not. I . . . I'm sorry."

Jude took his hands. "You've got nothing to be sorry about," she said. "I suppose it must have been difficult."

"You *think*?" said Nat with a tiny smile. "I wish I'd told you and Dad, but I thought it would worry you a bit."

It was his mum's turn to smile. "Just a *bit*," she agreed. "I . . . I can't imagine how it must have been for you. But no more secrets, Nat. Not after all we've been through."

"OK," said Nat, his face solemn now. "But I don't know how far this is going to go."

Jude's face went even paler. "You mean . . . ?"

Nat nodded slowly. "What if it goes all the way?"

Jude swallowed. "You . . . you mean if you change into a wolf?"

There, it's out in the open, thought Nat, strangely relieved. "Yeah," he said.

"Then," said Jude bravely, "I'll deal with it."

"Bit freaky." Nat grinned.

"No," said his mum softly, "there was nothing freaky about you last night. I wanted to tell you how proud we are . . . how you fought alongside Woody—it was kind of incredible."

"The worst part was . . ." Nat shuddered, remembering. "The worst part was when they came out of the dark . . . the vampires, I mean. I saw how dead they really are. I never noticed with Mac."

"What do you mean?" asked Jude gently.

"In the dark, with my new vision—it's like infrared, you know?" said Nat. "Living creatures like me and you and Woody and Del, our hearts glow red in the dark. Those things . . . those dead things . . . there was nothing there . . . just *black*."

Jude pulled him close. "We showed 'em, didn't we?" she said. "And we'll do it again. Now eat."

Suddenly ravenous, Nat accepted the enormous mound of sandwiches gratefully. He felt a whole lot better now that he didn't have to pretend anymore.

As he munched, he thought about the previous night's

work. His thoughts turned once again to the vampire hive. Although the Twilighters had suffered a couple of casualties during the fighting, no one had actually been bitten. But the news from Marais was grave. Two more children had been taken, whisked off into the night, which meant the vampires were increasing, the hive becoming stronger. Nat was trying to tune in and spot something—*anything*—that would give them a clue to where the hive roosted.

His nose wrinkled. *Ugh! There it was again! That stink!* Just by focusing on them, he could smell the vampires. He turned around slowly, worried that there were a couple of bloodsuckers waiting to jump on him, so ripe was the smell. He looked down at his plate of sandwiches with a quizzical expression on his face. *Blimey! It was the cheese!*

Cheese. The cheese in this sandwich. *Ugh, did it stink!* His appetite vanished again. Nat loved cheese normally. When he stayed with Mick and Apple in Somerset, he'd eat Apple's homemade cheese, "Gurney Stinker," by the ton. It was strong enough to make your eyes water and your tongue itch, but this stuff was *waaay* stronger than

Gurney Stinker. It smelled of rotting vegetables, dirty rabbit cages, sweaty gym socks . . . and, well, *vampires!*

"*Mum!*" he cried urgently. "Where did you get this cheese from?"

"I *know.*" Jude smiled apologetically. "It *is* a bit strong, isn't it?"

"No . . . yes . . . never mind that," said Nat, his eyes glowing topaz.

"I'm sure that thing you do with your eyes isn't good for them," said Jude worriedly. "I really think—"

"It doesn't *hurt!*" cried Nat. *"Where did the cheese come from?"*

1500 hours—three o'clock in the afternoon. According to the local almanac, sunset was estimated at 1700 hours—five p.m. The snow had stopped falling at last and the sun was shyly peeping from behind pinky-gray clouds when the chosen group of vampire slayers marched grimly toward the town. Behind Nat and Woody came Maccabee Hammer, shrouded in his coat, and Fish. Bringing up the rear were Nat's dad and his grandpa, JC. Jude had protested at being left behind, but Fish had persuaded her to stay and nurse Del, whose condition had worsened. It was later than Fish would have liked—the journey had taken them much longer than anticipated because the snow was so deep in some parts of town that it was impossible to walk through it at any great pace. According to her guide-book, there were a few shops that sold the stinky cheese, but only one place where it was actually made. She was directing them to a little factory on the outskirts of the town where the most stench-ridden of cheeses was produced. *Vieux fromage à la croûte croustillante* roughly translated as "old crusty rind cheese," which even to Woody at his hungriest sounded gut-churningly unappetizing. Nat prayed that his hunch would pay off and they would do what they needed to by dusk. Up above them, the weak winter sun still rode between clouds, teasing them with light.

"I dunno if I'll be able to . . . you know . . . stake 'em," said Woody nervously, his breath pluming out in front of him.

"We've got to find them first," said Fish, her voice muffled slightly through her scarves.

"We're nearly there," said Nat, wrinkling his nose. "Can't you smell it?"

In fact, both Woody and Nat were suffering an olfactory overload. The stink emanating from the factory was a cocktail of the worst smells in the world. Rotting vegetables, dirty rabbit cages, and sweaty socks. Nat didn't know if it was the cold weather or the searing stench that made his eyes water.

"They're here," he said through gritted teeth, "I'm sure of it."

Woody stopped suddenly. "I got a joke," he said.

"Why is it you always feel the need to tell a joke at times like this?" inquired Nat, smiling slightly.

"I dunno," said Woody shyly. "It's like our tradition, isn't it? It just makes me feel good to laugh."

"Go on, then," said Evan shakily. "We could do with a laugh."

Woody grinned. "There's these two nuns goin' through Transylvania in their car. It's the dead of night and they stop at a red traffic light. They're just about to drive off when a vampire jumps onto the hood of their car and hisses at 'em through the windshield.

"'Quick!' shouts the passenger nun. 'Turn the

windshield wipeys on. That'll get rid of the terrible ab . . . abomination.'

"The driving nun turns on the switch, making the horrible old vampire go to and fro, but still he hangs on, baring his teef.

"'Quick!' says the passenger nun. 'Switch on the windshield washer. I filled it up with holy water, just in case this sort of fing happened.'

"The first nun turns on the windshield washer. The vampire screams as the water burns holes in his skin, but he clings on and keeps hissin' at the nuns.

"'Now what?' shouts the second nun.

"'Show him your cross!' cries the first nun.

"'Right I will, Sister,' says the second nun, windin' down the passenger window, and she shouts crossly, *'Get lost, you ugly git!'*"

There was silence for a split second while they all digested the punch line, and then they all laughed long and hard—probably much louder than if they had been told the joke in normal circumstances. Best of all, the laughter echoed in the still air and had an almost magical effect on them all, warming them and lifting their spirits as they all laughed together. Fish felt heartily glad to be one of them. She cast her mind back to the cheerless destruction of the Threadneedle Street Hive with Agent Tully. She was struck by Nat and Woody's bravery and teamwork and knew that whatever happened, it was going to be difficult to work with anyone else again. Woody was right—laughter was the best medicine. It made them feel *stronger* somehow.

When they finally reached the deserted factory, they all solemnly hugged each other and wished each other luck. Bravely, Woody walked over to the reception entrance and gingerly tried the door. As he expected, it was locked. Taking a deep breath, he kicked it once with such force that the lock broke and the door flew across the floor in an instant. Warily, the others followed him across the threshold, expecting a vampire to knock into them at any minute.

"We need to split up," whispered Fish.

"No *way*," said Nat, horrified. "Splitting up is asking for trouble! Don't you ever watch any horror movies?"

"I vote we stick together, too," said Evan. "Likely the vampires'll be together if they're here at all."

"Oh, they're here all right," said Maccabee grimly.

Fish shrugged and they all moved nervously down the corridor. There were doors on either side and Fish and JC opened each one, everyone else standing well back in case anything sprang out. The first-floor corridor was clean. Deeper into the building they went, until they could hear the low hum of the refrigeration units.

"They're here," agreed Woody, "I can feel 'em *and* smell 'em."

The underlying stink of cheese and vampire was much stronger in this corridor. Fish shrugged off her rucksack and took out a red velvet pouch, which she opened almost reverently. Inside the soft velvet there lay fifteen or so beautifully carved stakes. Their pointed ends looked lethal, but everyone was thinking the same thing. It wasn't much of an artillery to face who knew how many bloodsucking vampires. And the thought of all that black gunk sploshing everywhere when the vampires were staked wasn't doing much to enhance their mood, either. The doors on this corridor looked as though they were reinforced with steel. There were no visible handles or locks on the front, just cold, flat metal.

"*Great,*" said Fish, "reinforced fire doors. There's not even a bloomin' lock we can pick. How're we going to get in?"

Nat listened. All he could hear was the insidious buzz of refrigerators. Carefully, he put his hand on the nearest door, laying it flat.

"What're you *doing*?" hissed Fish impatiently. "Let's go."

"Shhhh," hissed back Nat, "sometimes I can feel vibrations, feel stuff through my fingers."

"*And?*" said Fish. "Can you feel anything?"

Nat's fingers tingled. He closed his eyes. It was as though his fingers had turned into radio antennae and were converting the energy of whatever was behind the door into information. *Whispering. Sleep talking. Dreaming.* Nat smiled grimly to himself. The vampires *were* behind this steel door. And he could tell by their thought patterns that they were fast asleep. *They think they're safe*, thought Nat.

Come on. Woody's voice was in his head. He, too, had picked up the vibes from the undead behind the door. *Let's do it!*

Nat nodded at Woody, smiling. Without a word the others watched in wonder as both boys backed up and loped back the way they had come. Fish watched them in confusion.

Now what? she thought irritably. Something had passed between them; they'd done the two-way thing and now they seemed to be legging it.

"Chaaaaaaaaaaaarge!!"

Fish and the others watched as Nat and Woody turned around at the end of the corridor and shot back toward the door, their faces and bodies a blur as the door caved in beneath their combined strength. Fish rushed in afterward as both boys skidded across the floor and landed in a heap. The room was windowless and the darkness that greeted them inside felt thick and oily. Leaping to their feet, Nat and Woody could see they were surrounded. At first, Nat thought he was seeing meat hanging from hooks, like in a butcher's shop. He was right in one sense — but it was *un*dead meat. The things hanging from the ceiling like great sides of beef were vampires. And there were definitely more than fifteen. *More like fifty.*

"We're going to need more stakes," breathed Nat.

He stared at the sleeping vampires. The vampire legends

and folklore seemed to be right about this, at least. They still slept peacefully; not even the door being broken down had so much as made them stir. Nat looked at his watch. Sunset was coming and they had to act now—cleanse the entire hive before dark came and the vampires awoke. *Were they going to have enough time?* Nat shuddered as he watched the nearest vampire sleep. It slept in the form it had been when it had first been made into a vampire—not quite human, but not the monster it could morph into when it was awake. It was hanging by its bare, elongated toes, rather like those of one of Mac's aye-ayes. Its face was a dead, bluish color and its evil teeth protruded from its cruel lips, which were curved into a humorless smile. It didn't appear to need to breathe, and not for the first time Nat asked himself, *How do you kill something that's already dead?*

"After you," said Mac, holding out a wicked-looking stake.

Nat stared at it. It was one thing being able to stake the vampires when they were attacking, but this was another. This creature was defenseless.

Nat looked at it miserably. "I don't think I can do it," he said, shaking his head.

"I'll go first," said Fish, grabbing the stake. "Watch and learn."

The others watched as she raised the stake high above her head. With a sharp cry of effort, she brought the stake down and punctured the vampire's heart, making it shatter inside its chest. In the split second before it exploded in a rain of gore, the vampire opened its eyes and stared straight at Nat, its red gaze burning as it cried out in pain and hate.

"There," said Fish triumphantly. "That's how you do it."

But Fish had made it look too easy. The others tried their best to stake the vampires quickly and efficiently. But it was grim and filthy work, hampered by the way the vampires were roosting; it was difficult to aim the stake properly while they were hanging. *It was taking too long!*

"What time is it?" asked Fish through gritted teeth.

"Time to worry," said Mac. "I can feel them getting ready to wake up."

"Keep going," yelled Fish. "We've got no choice."

"There's always a choice," said Mac mysteriously, putting down his stake.

The others watched as he leaped like a scraggy cat onto a large refrigerator. Lifting his spindly arms, he pushed upward. To Nat's surprise, he started smashing through the ceiling with his fists. The noise was atrocious, but Mac worked like a machine, his vampire strength making short work of the demolition.

"What're you doing?" shouted Woody. "They'll wake up!"

"Plan B," yelled back Mac. "Help me to smash the ceiling out!"

Still not knowing why, Nat and Woody used their enhanced strength to help Mac smash through the ceiling, shielding him from the sun as he broke through the roof tiles. When they had pulled off the tiles and the sky above was exposed, beams of watery sunlight shone through the massive hole. Sunlight: Plan B!

As the weak beams fell on the vampires, they started to wail: a thin but desperate caterwauling that set everyone's teeth on edge.

Nat put both hands over his ears to protect them from the noise. Everyone watched as the vampires fell from their roosts, squirming on the floor like weird snakes to get away from the rays of weak but deadly sunlight. Nat saw Fish's triumphant grin as the sun did its job. Writhing in agony, the vampires burned in the rich blue flame, leaving nothing but a scorch mark on the floor. As JC and Evan made the hole bigger, more vampires got torched. Confusion reigned as the monsters tried to get away from the burning light, many of them pushing others into the sun-filled space as they tried to escape.

"Up here, Nat!" shouted Fish. "We can get out through the roof!"

Nat looked toward her just in time to see Fish's triumphant smile turn to horror as the sun disappeared behind a cloud, plunging the windowless room into darkness again.

The vampires came again from the shadows with a horrid stealth. They were making a nasty guttural sound in their throats, their hands outstretched and their lip-less mouths gaping to show their vicious incisors. Nat found himself cornered. As the snarling vampires approached him, Nat had a sudden crazy thought. He wished he had something more substantial than a handful of flimsy wooden stakes—maybe a .44 Magnum with silver bullets! Then *KAAAAABOOM!* They'd be history. His granddad Mick's fourth-favorite Clint Eastwood movie was *Dirty Harry*. Dirty Harry Callahan was a tough American cop who had little time for rules, but always got results—which was mainly, Nat always suspected, because of the sheer size of his gun. He stood up straight and looked the vampires sternly in the eye.

"I know what you're thinking," he drawled in his best Dirty Harry voice. "Does he have six stakes or only five? Well, to tell you the truth, in all this excitement I kinda lost track myself. But being as this is a very sharp stake, the most powerful stake in the world and would blow your filthy hearts clean open, you've got to ask yourself one question: Do I feel lucky? Well, do ya, punks?"

The vampires stopped making the weird *guuuring* noise in their throats and looked confused. They had stopped undead in their tracks as though they had forgotten why they were there. Nat was dimly aware that a white blur had arrived at his side. *Woody! Thank God!* Woody had shifted into an enormous Wolven creature with dripping jaws and now crouched low on the bloody floor. He sprang up and, in a single enormous bound, took the nearest two vampires down with a thud. Nat grabbed the moment and, feeling the Wolven strength coursing through his body, propelled himself forward. He rammed the stakes simultaneously into the surprised bloodsuckers' hearts, closing his eyes as their bodies exploded and he was covered in black gore from head to foot.

Spurred on by the boys' success, the others clambered down from the exposed roof. Led by Maccabee Hammer, his coat protecting him from the sunlight, they advanced toward the vampires in a battle line. The remaining vampires were retreating!

"Don't let 'em get away!" shrieked Fish. "We need to get all of them!"

Woody slipped around the back of the retreating horrors like a demented sheepdog.

He's rounding them up! thought Fish. The confused vampires surged forward, away from Woody's deadly teeth, straight into the line of slayers and their devastating stakes.

The vampire slayers finished the job. The hive was dead. In the windowless room, the last traces of the vampires hung in the dank air. All that could be seen of the slayers was the gleam in their eyes; they were covered from head to toe in the black blood of the undead.

"Oh man, oh *man*!!" yelled Fish. "We did it!"

Nat wiped the vampire gunk from his eyes. "I've just remembered something," he said tiredly.

"What's that?" asked Fish.

"It's Christmas Day," he said. "Merry Christmas, everyone."

CHAPTER 25
HUNTING WITH THE HOWLERS

Safely back at the camp, in the orange light of the fires, the Twilighters rejoiced. It was, after all, Christmas night, and thanks to the slayers, the hive was dead! From their cozy cardboard boxes by the biggest bonfire they had lit all winter, Woody and Fish told the story between them, the others chipping in with the bits they had forgotten. But for all the rejoicing, Nat was quiet. The hive might be dead, but there was still the unsolved problem of Lucas Scale. He still remembered the heart-sinking feeling of discovering the eye in the snow globe, and it made him feel sick and uneasy. He could think of nothing else.

He felt uncomfortable in Crescent's presence, too. There was something different about her—a different smell. And she looked different: sort of scruffy, like she hadn't taken a bath for a while. It seemed she had given up sulking, but she still hadn't offered Nat an apology or any explanation for her cowardly behavior during the vampire attack. And now she was rounding up the Howlers for a hunt.

"Come with us," she urged Woody. "We can help you look for your clan. That's what you came here for, wasn't it?"

Woody hesitated. He *had* felt frustrated not being able to search for them, but he could sense that there was something wrong with Nat. Instead of celebrating like everyone else, Nat seemed strangely quiet, *miserable*, even. Woody didn't want to find the clan with Crescent in tow, either.

"If you're coming, hurry up," whined Ramone. "I'm starving."

"You're such a greedy pig," sniffed Crescent, lifting her lip, showing less than clean teeth. She turned to the others. "Did you know he eats roadkill?"

Ramone flushed. Crescent had no business telling anyone his secrets. "Only if it's fresh," he muttered. "It's a waste otherwise."

"Come on, Woody," urged Otis. "It's about time you came on a run with us."

"Go on, it's fine," said Nat. "I don't mind, honest."

"Tell you what," said Crescent, turning to Nat. (*Even her eyes look odd*, thought Nat. *Sort of far away, as though she's not really here*.) "I'll bite you if you want. Can't be certain you'll live, but it's worth a try. At least you wouldn't be a mutt anymore!"

If Nat felt stung by Crescent's spiteful words, he hid it well.

"If I throw you a stick would you leave?" he said, enjoying the look of outrage on Crescent's face.

"Well, sorry, but it's true, isn't it?" Crescent smirked. "You're neither human nor Wolven."

Woody frowned, then his face lit up. "I know," he said to Nat, "you can run with me, then when you get tired, I'll come back with you. How does that sound?"

"Sounds like it's not going to work," snapped Nat, more sharply than he'd intended. "I've only got two legs, remember?"

Woody looked crestfallen.

"Oh, just *go*," said Nat, getting up from his box. "Crescent's right, I'm neither human nor Wolven. I'm a bloody *mongrel*."

• • •

The ancient ritual of dung adornment was a solemn and serious matter, not to be taken lightly, and Woody realized worriedly that Crescent intended him to be part of the hunt, too. This meant Woody had to be initiated into the werewolf pack in the traditional manner.

Salim had found a pile of steaming wild boar droppings, and Crescent, as the alpha wolf, was the first to roll on top of it, taking care to smear it commando-style on her furry face. Woody, as an honored guest of the pack, went second, his white fur streaked with the whiffy dung. Ramone and Salim rolled around in whatever was left, hoping to confuse their quarry with the smell of its own dung.

Woody's blood fizzed and crackled in his veins. His heart rate increased as he gulped in lungfuls of ice-cold air and sped after Crescent and the Howlers, the wild, dangerous smells of the forest flooding his senses as his paws flew across the snowy ground. The Howlers had picked up the ripe, musky smell of a large male boar, a tricky creature that carried with it the dark, damp smell of fungus and death. Woody had no doubt about what would happen to the boar when the Howlers tracked it down, but shocked himself by becoming so caught up in the thrill of the chase that he pushed it from his mind. Crescent streaked ahead, her russet coat easy to spot in the moonlight. The darker wolves followed and called to each other joyfully as they ran in pursuit of their prey. Woody brought up the rear, enjoying the freedom and excitement of the chase, savoring each moment to remember later.

"AAAAAOOOOOOOOOGhaaaaaaaaaarrr!" Crescent had spotted the boar at last. It was enormous, easily out-weighing the wolves. Ramone, Otis, and Salim had formed a close protective shield around her, flanking both sides while they calculated the size and weight of their prey. Woody hung back, still not sure what to do. The boar ran for its life, its body hunched into a bullet shape, trying to make itself appear smaller. Ramone and Salim raced ahead, closing in on the unfortunate boar as Crescent and Otis were now almost close enough to snap at its heels.

Woody willed himself to watch what happened next. The boar, knowing it was time to fight to the death, did a neat trick and stopped abruptly. It turned and faced the pack, its small red eyes glinting defiantly. The werewolves skidded into it, sending it sprawling. It quickly recovered and faced them, its razor-sharp tusks gleaming bone-white in the moonlight. The werewolves crept toward it, saliva dripping from their fangs, the hackles on their backs making them appear bigger and meaner.

But the boar wasn't fazed by the snarling werewolves at all. It prepared to fight. It charged and the Howlers broke formation, Salim now yelping in terror. Crescent rounded on the boar, her lethal teeth extended toward it like those of a great white shark. Woody howled a warning, but it was too late. The boar turned neatly, avoiding Crescent's teeth, and lacerated Salim's flank with his tusks, ripping it with the ease of a cutthroat razor.

There was no sound. The boar swung around again, sensing it had a chance for survival after all. Salim lay on his uninjured side, stunned and panting, bleeding heavily from the jagged wound. The shock had made him morph between wolf shape and human shape, the effort making the blood flow even faster. Otis and Ramone pawed at him in concern, but Woody noticed that Crescent seemed oddly unconcerned, even eager to leave Salim behind. *She doesn't smell right*, he thought to himself. *She smells bad, like some part of her has gone rancid.* And when he looked into her eyes, he thought he could detect a mean gleam in them.

With an enormous effort, Salim calmed himself by breathing deeply and allowing his body to deal with the pain.

Woody trotted over to Salim and sniffed. Satisfied it wasn't as deep as he first thought, Woody bent his head and licked the wound carefully, cleaning the blood away. Salim whimpered as he worked, and then relaxed as he felt the healing warmth begin to repair the flesh. Fifteen minutes later, he rose unsteadily to his feet. Woody drew away and turned back the way they had come, anxious to be on his way. He'd had enough. He wanted to go home to his little bunk in the *Silver Lady*, where Nat would already be asleep. But the others hung back, ears pressed to their heads, tails wagging slowly, hungry for blood. Woody stared at them. *Surely they weren't going after the boar again?* He tried to brain-jack Crescent for an answer. There was nothing there anymore. It was as though she had gone.

CHAPTER 2
WHITE WOLF FALLS

The Howlers were out of control. Woody ran a little way, then ran back toward them, doing it again so they'd get the picture and follow him. Crescent stared at him dully. Before he could react, she turned, vanishing back into the deep forest with the Howlers, who were following close behind, calling to each other in joyous yowls.

Woody shook himself. *No way*, he thought. He could still hear the Howlers hollering to each other as they crashed noisily through the undergrowth. He thought again of his cozy little bunk bed and trotted in the opposite direction. He felt cold and lonely and suddenly very miserable without Nat. *Why had he come? Of course Nat felt left out — with his two human legs instead of four, he would never have been able to keep up!* Woody felt guilty, too — he should have stuck up for Nat when Crescent had been so spiteful. Why was she being so mean? He decided that as soon as he got back to the *Silver Lady*, he would wake Nat up and they would have a midnight feast and Woody would apologize for deserting him, and everything would be all right again. Now that the hive was dead, they could hunt for his clan together as he had always imagined they would.

Encouraged by his plan, Woody gathered speed, becoming a white blur through the trees. As he sped along, he tried to think of what he would say to Nat and wondered if Crescent and the Howlers would catch the boar. He hoped the wily old boar had got a good start on them — it didn't deserve to be ripped apart by werewolves. Woody was so busy putting his world to rights, he didn't notice a shimmering pale shape shadowing him.

The mysterious shape mirrored Woody's actions with perfect harmony. If Woody swerved, the creature, who was lurking about ten feet deeper into the woods on Woody's left, swerved, too. If he jumped, the creature did, too. When Woody sensed he was being followed, he was more curious than scared. His first glimpse out of the corner of his eye showed him a large pale creature that ran on four legs, and it smelled . . . Oh, it smelled so *familiar*! He decided to draw the creature out from its cover. Woody ran in and out of the thick trees and, to his delight, the other did the same. Then he ran as fast as he could to see if the other creature could match him. It did so with ease, and Woody stopped to see if it would show itself. The snow, which until now had teased and dusted the forest paths with delicate, insubstantial flakes, decided to step up production. Woody's eyelashes were crusted with the stuff and it made his vision blurry. He peered through the clearing, but all he could see was a monochrome landscape of black trees, white snow, and black sky. *There! There it was—movement!* Woody held his breath. His Wolven senses, so fabulously enhanced to suss out any situation before any other cryptid creature he had ever met, had failed to identify the one thing he sought most.

An enormous white Wolven emerged from its cover of trees, its fur bright in the moonlight, its eyes glowing softly like topaz gems. Woody thought he must be dreaming—or hallucinating. He had waited for this moment since Iona de Gourney had revealed there might be survivors from his clan. But with all the bad vampire stuff kicking off, he had almost given up hope of finding them. And now he could scarcely believe his good fortune: A Wolven—maybe even a member of his clan—had found *him*! Woody hesitated, not sure how he should approach this white, shimmering creature. *Here goes nothing*, he thought. He took a deep breath and tried to stop himself rushing up and risk scaring it off. Cautiously, Woody trotted forward in polite friendly mode, his tail wagging slightly, ears erect, lips drawn slightly back in an openmouthed, friendly grin, and prepared himself for a little social sniffing. The other Wolven chuffed gently and danced before him encouragingly. Then it sped away, with Woody following closely, deeper and deeper into the forest. The pair of Wolven weaved in and out of the dense trees like white smoke. Woody lost all sense of time and direction as he concentrated on following the Wolven up ahead.

Nat had hung around waiting for Woody to come back from his run so that he could apologize about earlier. Worst of all, either the two-way thing wasn't working, or Woody was out of range.

Nat had left the Twilighters celebrating around the roaring fire, and he could still hear the music from Maccabee Hammer's fiddle, and hearty laughter drifting on the freezing night air. Nat didn't feel there was much to celebrate. The shrieks of the undead as they writhed on the floor of the factory still rang in his head, and there was the small matter of Lucas Scale, too. The cold fact that he was still alive was hard to bear, and without Woody to share his fears it felt worse. Nat felt himself tense and sniffed the cold air. Above the racket of celebrations, he could hear stealthy footsteps in the snow. *Fish.*

"What're you doing?" asked Fish in surprise. "It's *freezing* out here."

"Same as you, I expect," said Nat. "Thinking about what happened this afternoon."

"I wouldn't dwell on it for too long." Fish smiled wearily. "It'll give you bad dreams."

Nat gave her a ghost of a smile. "How's Del?"

Fish shrugged. "Same as he was before. Nat, I'm—"

"Scared," broke in Nat. "We didn't get the head vampire, did we?"

Fish shook her head miserably.

• • •

Back in the moonlit forest, Woody still chased the other Wolven. It was bigger and faster than he was, and there were times he thought he had lost it, but then he would spot it in the distance, waiting up ahead, tongue lolling, tail wagging. But when at last Woody felt he could run no more, the other Wolven disappeared from view. Woody looked around him, sniffing the freezing night air, but he could neither smell nor see it anymore. Anxiously, he paced the perimeter of a circular clearing in the trees.

Despite his disappointment at losing the Wolven, Woody felt he was in a special place. In the thaw it would be a perfect oasis with a pool of fresh water fed by a gushing waterfall. But with the current temperatures way below freezing, the waterfall hung in suspended animation, a thick curtain of enormous icicles and sheets of ice above the frozen pool. Woody ate some snow and let it melt in his mouth as he figured out what to do next.

Where'd it go? Woody chuffed and whined, hoping the other Wolven would hear him and come back and show itself. His keen vision could make out the scene as though it was daylight. The ice shone midnight blue in the light of the moon, and the waterfall glinted and sparkled like cold diamonds. Panting, he leaped easily onto the rocky ledge beneath the waterfall. Negotiating his way around the back of the frozen curtain of water was tricky, and his claws were barely able to stop him from sliding off the frozen rock, but when he edged his way farther in he realized he was in a cavernous chamber. *So this is where the other Wolven went!* Excited, he trotted to the back of the cave, where there was a small fissure in the rock. Woody could feel the difference in the air temperature. Warmer air filtered through the crack, which was just big enough for a large wolflike creature to squeeze through. Pressing his body low onto the rocky floor, Woody crawled forward on all fours, gripping the rough surface with his claws. Flattening himself as much as he could, he pulled himself through, scrambling down from the rocks on the other side into what seemed to be another chamber, a subterranean cavern below the cave.

Woody had been in the presence of magic before, and this place fairly thrummed with it. The chamber was as big as a medium-sized village church, and about the same shape. Up ahead, nestled in niches within the rocky ceiling were hundreds — *No, make that thousands*, thought Woody to himself — of tiny twinkling orbs of golden light, which gave off a warm glow, like a sunrise on a summer dawn. Toward the front of the chamber were placed a number of oblong objects in a large circle, each about the width and length of a man. Woody padded over to investigate.

He growled in surprise. The oblong objects (and Woody counted twelve) appeared to be stone tombs. Each tomb had the effigy of the occupant in delicately sculpted marble on the top, and he stared at these in morbid fascination. It looked to him as though the gentlemen whose remains lay at rest underneath were reclining in the armor of the Knights Templar, and he shivered up to his hackles at the expressions on their marble faces. Each grave face looked rather haughty for Woody's comfort, some appearing cross, as though they had been greatly inconvenienced at finding themselves dead. Each effigy was armed with a huge sword, and lying at each pair of marble feet was an enormous marble wolf creature — a *Wolven*!

What is this place? Woody asked himself. He was beginning to feel well and truly spooked by the whole thing, and wished again that Nat was there to share it with him. But on reflection, Woody doubted that a human could have squeezed through the gap in the cave unless there was another way in, and anyway, Nat was claustrophobic—he hated being underground. There was a sort of raised area behind the tombs, like an altar, and under the strange lighting shone a stronger light, like a great golden halo. Woody walked into the light, and if he had been in human shape he would have gasped.

Coffers of golden treasure shimmered and glimmered in front of him, winking under the sparkling lights. Treasure far beyond a king's ransom lit up Woody's fur with an eerie Midas glow as he tried to take it all in. He narrowed his eyes to blot out the light and mentally added another question to the list forming in his mind. *Was this the lost cargo of Templar treasure—treasure searched for across the globe for almost a thousand years?* Iona de Gourney had told both Woody and Nat about the legendary lost Templar gold, which had fueled the imagination of millions of people for centuries. Iona's ancient ancestor Sir William de Gourney had even speculated in his chronicles that the treasure included priceless holy relics such as the Grail or even the Ark of the Covenant! Woody panted with excitement and awe. *What if the two things that humans had searched for over hundreds of years were here in this underground church, guarded by the King's Wolven? What if—?*

Woody forgot about the gold abruptly. Sometime during his ponderings, the other Wolven had come back. To Woody's overwhelming joy, more followed, their eyes alight with the same wonder that Woody felt as he gazed upon his clan. Then they were upon him, squealing with delight, tails wagging ecstatically, all wanting to touch him.

"Dear one." The Wolven clan spoke as one. *He was home.*

Deep inside Crescent's soul lurked the mind of Lucas Scale, and it hurt her. The viselike grip was back. Crescent's will was no match for the evil Scale's; his manipulating presence inside her head was steering her away from reason and sanity. Even when the boar had gored Salim and Woody had licked his wounds clean, she had known she would betray them all.

Scale wanted her to spy on Woody, to follow him and find his clan. Only then would he let go of her mind.

Crescent had her chance. The old boar was brought down at last and Otis, Ramone, and Salim had been too busy ripping it to shreds to notice her skulk away. She tracked Woody swiftly and skillfully, staying far enough back for the freezing wind to hide her scent. She followed his trail, stopping at a deserted clearing in the forest. There were two sets of tracks in the snow! Putting her head down, she sniffed. One set was Woody's, but whose was the other? She stared at the sheet of frozen water sparkling like diamonds in the moonlight. Crescent loped toward it, her slim body squeezing through the narrow opening easily. She closed her eyes against the pain of her brain being gripped by another. When they opened again, they belonged to Lucas Scale.

CHAPTER 27

T.R.A.P.P.E.D.

Agent Alex Fish felt the stirrings of unease. Before she had left NightShift HQ, she had brushed up on all reported cases of vampirism archived in the creepy underground vaults in Middle Temple Lane, and re-examined the first and, up until this afternoon, the *only* vampire hive she had exterminated. In all the cases she had read about, any victims of vampire attacks recovered fully *so long as the head vampire was slain*. In the case of the Threadneedle Street Hive, this had been proven when some builders had been attacked. As soon as the hive was really and truly dead (not just undead), the victims made a swift and full recovery. NightShift agent Jack Tully had followed it up and reported the improvement was almost immediate.

But when Del Underhill failed to show up at the celebratory dinner to rejoice in Christmas and the extermination of the hive, the nagging doubt she had felt earlier turned into gut-wrenching feelings of dread. Fish had hoped to give Del the best Christmas present ever, by slaughtering the hive and giving him his life back.

She knocked gently on the door of the satyrs' trailer. When Paddy answered her knock, she knew by the expression on his face that things had not improved. Following him into the cozy depths, she had to wait for her eyes to adjust to the gloom.

"He can't stand the light," explained Paddy. "It hurts his eyes, so I keep it dark."

Fish went over to the bunk where Del lay. His white face shone unnaturally in the dim light, and his long, black lashes contrasted starkly with his pallid skin. Fish's heart sank, because if anything, the poor satyr looked as though he was getting worse. His skin was clammy and his breathing shallow and wheezy. Every now and then he would moan in his sleep: a lost, despairing sound. Careful not to awaken him, Fish gently examined the spiteful wound on his neck and was horrified to see it still looked as poisonous as it had at first bite. Then Paddy reported that his brother still couldn't eat because food made him sick, and he couldn't tolerate the tiniest chink of light peeping through the curtains. Alex Fish's fears were real.

Alex Fish knew that being a successful NightShift operative was all about having a backup plan. Looking back, she admitted it had all been too easy. Maybe there was another hive hiding somewhere else. She shuddered at the thought. *How many were there?* The head vampire wouldn't be as accessible as the rest of the hive; she should have known that. Closing her books thoughtfully, a brilliant but very risky plan formed in her mind.

When Nat found out that Fish's cunning plan involved communicating with the dead, he was slightly uncomfortable. But Fish was firm.

"So, like, how many people d'you need for a séance?" asked Nat as they went in search of likely candidates. Fish admitted she didn't actually know, but thought that four would be an even number. Natalie and Scarlet were her top choices to join them, as they were sensible enough not to mess about and give "negative energy" to the proceedings. It wasn't much use asking anyone else; the grown-ups would be horrified and the cryptids and shape-shifters would be too scared to take part, as they were frightened of spirits. Fish had the devil of a job persuading Scarlet and Natalie to leave the celebrations until she shared her fears with them. She had given Nat a list of stuff they needed for the séance and she had set up a table in the black circus tent, onto which she placed three candles, a pack of Lexicon cards with the alphabet, and an empty glass.

"Have you done this before?" asked Scarlet, watching Fish's face glare orange in the momentary light of the match as she lit the candles.

"Loads of times," said Fish airily. "It's better than the Internet."

"But *why* are we trying to contact the dead?" asked Nat. "How can they help us find the head vampire?"

"We're going to try to contact the *half* dead, the revenants," explained Fish patiently, "beings who were once human and who have served the vampire for one or more centuries. When they are too old to be of any use, they can't die. They remain in purgatory, neither dead nor alive. Only when the head vampire is killed once and for all can their souls be released."

"That's *awful*," cried Scarlet.

"Is . . . is it safe to contact the half dead?" asked Natalie, shivering slightly.

Fish polished her spectacles with the tiny piece of cloth that fastidious people keep in their spectacle cases specially for polishing.

"As long as we are respectful and don't mess about, it's safe," assured Fish, pushing her specs firmly into position. "All we're doing is connecting with half lives on another frequency, but just to be on the safe side, if anything unsettling happens, Natalie, you turn the lights on and I'll blow out the candles, signifying the end of the séance."

"*Whoa*, hang on," said Nat nervously, "what d'you mean by 'unsettling'?"

"You'll know if it happens," said Fish grimly.

As they sat down, Fish placed the Lexicon cards around the table and the glass tumbler in the center. Every letter of the alphabet was laid out in a circle with "Yes" and "No" at strategic points.

"Now, place the index finger of your right hand on the top of the glass," instructed Fish, "and good luck, everyone."

Nat pressed his lips together firmly. Although he was a bit scared, he still thought séances belonged in stupid old horror movies or to old ladies trying to find out which loose floorboard their dead husband's money was under. The thought of Fish chatting to dead people seemed more ridiculous than frightening.

Agent Fish closed her eyes and drew a deep breath.

"Dear revenants of the undead, we respectfully ask that you honor us with your presence this Christmas evening," she intoned, her eyes still closed. "We respectfully ask for your help with an urgent matter of life and death. *Is there anybody there?*"

Nat had been prepared to go along with it until that point. A loud snort of laughter shot out of his mouth and nose, followed by a fit of explosive giggles from Natalie and Scarlet. Fish snapped her eyes open and gave them her most withering of withering looks, but it was a good two minutes before she had their complete attention again.

"*What?*" She glowered at them. "What's so funny?"

Nat was wiping away the tears of hysteria. "Sorry, sorry," he mumbled, trying to smother another gale of laughter that threatened to bubble up. "It was just when you said the last bit, it . . . well . . . it was really funny."

Fish gave him another narrow-eyed look of disgust. "What was? The bit where I ask is there anybody there?"

Natalie and Scarlet covered their faces, their bodies trembling convulsively as they tried to stop laughing again.

"Oh, don't . . . don't say it again," cried Nat weakly. "It . . . it just sounds so . . . *corny!*"

He knew it wasn't professional or big or clever to laugh at such an important moment, but he just couldn't help it. It was like listening to a really duff line out of a rubbish movie.

"That's the recommended dialogue in a properly conducted séance," said Fish grumpily. "We'll have to start again now."

They placed their fingers on the glass again, and this time when Fish asked the question, no one laughed. Nat made himself concentrate and banished all other thoughts from his mind.

"Is there anyone there?" repeated Fish. Nothing, *rien*, nada, zilch. The glass tumbler stayed innocently in the center of the table.

They sat like that for some minutes. Nat wondered if Scarlet and Natalie felt as daft as he did. His head filled up with random thoughts as he tried to brain-jack Scarlet. Her aura was the deep purple color of concentration. *Good for her!* Then he tensed. He could hear other voices in his head, faint at first, then increasing in volume until the noise became massive, as if the voices were competing with each other, clamoring to be heard. A sickly taste came into his mouth: a familiar, sweet taste of roses.

Then, incredibly, the glass began to move. Trying to focus on it, Nat looked at the others. Fish had a feverish smile of triumph on her lips, while Scarlet and Natalie looked as though they were ready to get up and run away as fast as they could. The glass moved smoothly across the table toward Nat and came to a brief stop at the *T.* It journeyed back into the middle of the table and set off again toward Nat but dipped slightly to his right to stop at the *R.* It moved backward and forward, to and fro, five more times until it had spelled the word:

T. R. A. P. P. E. D.

A ringing sound like a glass makes when you rub a wet finger around the rim filled Nat's brain and *Ow, it hurt!* He was no longer aware of the other three sitting at the table. All he was aware of was the rich, cloying taste of roses, which was so overpowering it made him want to vomit. *Oh no! Not again*, thought Nat in panic, knowing what was coming next. The ringing sound had reached an almost unbearable pitch and, paired with the smell of roses, Nat felt as though he was going to pass out. And then there was nothing but freezing darkness and he felt a horrible twisting sensation in his stomach, as though he was being sucked out of the world by an industrial-strength vacuum cleaner.

When Nat opened his eyes, he knew immediately what had happened, but it didn't stop him from reeling in shock. He was no longer in the black tent; Fish, Scarlet, and Natalie had all disappeared. Above him, the darkening night sky sparkled with frosty vapors of cold air, framing the glittering moon and stars. In the near distance loomed the unwelcoming silhouette of the Black Chateau, where he and Woody had fled the giant mosquitoes.

He had gone over, gone backward in time! It had happened to him twice before. Once, when Iona de Gourney wanted to show him something important, and the other when Lucas Scale had almost killed him. Iona had told him that at times of great stress, worlds sometimes collide and get mixed up. *Well yeah*, Nat thought to himself, *you could call this a stressful moment. I've gone from the vampire-infested South of France back in time to who knows when? Without a coat. In the dead of winter. I'm freakin' freezing!*

The Black Chateau looked dead. There were no lights shining in the windows, or any other sign of life. Nat hugged himself for warmth, his teeth chattering, trying to make sense of this latest unwelcome adventure. Iona de Gourney had warned him the potion could repeat itself, and Fish's séance must have been the trigger. And the fact that he had been catapulted into the Salinas plains near to the Black Chateau could only mean he was about to be shown something interesting. Or *terrifying*.

Darkness came and a young moon looked down on him, huge in the clear black sky. Nat saw in horror that the dark and light areas on the surface of the moon seemed to shimmer for a moment, rearranging themselves to form the shape of a skull.

I'm not seeing that, Nat told himself firmly. *That didn't happen.*

He tried Woody again on the two-way thing; if ever he needed a friend, it was now. Then he was struck by an awful thought. *If he'd gone back in time, even a little bit, he wouldn't be able to contact Woody by the two-way thing. It would be impossible.* This was *bad*. He decided that, whatever happened, he couldn't stay out on the plain—he would freeze. He set out for the chateau, thinking perhaps he could find an outhouse or somewhere to spend the night. At least it had stopped snowing for now.

Suddenly, a movement caught his keen Wolven eyes. Someone was running down the rock-strewn path leading from the front of the chateau, the same one that he and Woody had fled down, escaping from the swarm of bloodsucking skeeters! Instinctively, Nat glanced around for somewhere to hide himself. From the safety of a tiny copse of trees he watched as a slim girl—he was certain it was a girl—ran down the path. Nat could feel her panic as she ran, her fair hair shining in the light of the young moon. She ran as if the very devil was after her! He searched for her mind in the darkness, and felt she was running for her life. *Whatever she ran from would soon be awake.* Nat half ran, half fell down into the incline to meet her, but he promptly lost sight of her. He tried to ignore the voices that had returned inside his head, the same voices he had heard when Fish had conducted the séance. He continued running toward the path, hoping he would see her again before it was too late. The voices were calling the same word over and over again. It sounded as though they were calling to someone named "Saffi." *The missing girl!* thought Nat excitedly. *She must have been here the whole time.*

Then Nat spotted her again. At the bottom of the incline surrounding the chateau was a lake, frozen for the winter, and Nat could see the girl was trying to cross it, her face a mask of fear. She could hear the voices, too; Nat could feel her thoughts as she tried to hurry across the lake. Quickly he estimated how far away she was from him and the cover of the forest. Roughly one hundred feet. His heart almost stopped as dark shapes moving under the ice came into focus. They must be the revenants Fish had told them about, the half lives in purgatory, trapped in this world until the head vampire was slain! The girl, Saffi, was getting nearer, and Nat could see the panic in her eyes and the look of sheer exhaustion as she picked her way across the frozen water.

As Saffi lifted her right foot to take her final step off the ice toward Nat, she stumbled, falling with her frozen cheek pressed to the hard surface.

"Saffi! Come *on*, get *up*!" shouted Nat.

With fresh hope in her eyes, Saffi reached for Nat's outstretched hand. She scrabbled to her feet, her hand not quite reaching across. A strange keening sound echoed around the ice from the revenants below.

They're warning her about something, realized Nat as he tried to grab her hand again.

Way above the ice came a blackness so dark that the light from the moon was blotted. Nat was still yelling her name, but Saffi turned around slowly, as though resigned to her fate. Then Nat heard the dreaded sound of leathery wings, *THWACK THWACK,* and understood. He caught a glimpse of a triumphant red smile and matching eyes as the vampire swooped from the sky to snatch its prize. Nat saw Saffi's stricken face in high-definition close-up, her lips moving silently as the dark vampire enveloped her in its wings and the revenants under the ice made their wild keening noises, which echoed around the deserted plain. It happened so quickly that by the time the moon shone again, Saffi Besson had vanished. It was as though she had never been there at all.

Nat's trip back in time had shown him Saffi's fate. He howled in despair and once more his ears were filled with the ringing sound, like a wet finger on the rim of a wine glass. Then it was dark again.

CHAPTER 28
NAT AND FISH

When he found himself lying flat on his back on the floor of the circus tent, Nat was dimly aware of three astonished faces looking down on him.

"*Ooof*" was all he managed to say. He tried to sit up, but his world was whirling like a dervish. He could still taste roses.

"Better give him some air," instructed Fish hastily. "He looks like he's going to throw up."

"*Eurgh*, thanks," Nat groaned, and smiled weakly. "I just need to sit quietly for a while."

But although Fish tried very hard for a nanosecond to be patient, she fired questions at Nat like a machine gun.

"What *happened*? *Where'd* you go? *How* did it happen? What *did* you—"

"I went back in time. It's complicated," said Nat, struggling to his feet. "But I know where the head vampire is."

• • •

Boxing Day at dawn, and Nat Carver had spent a miserable night trying to get to sleep. The morning brought new and worrying developments and a snowstorm of such violence it was difficult to stand up outside. The Howlers had arrived back at camp disheveled and exhausted shortly after midnight. There was no sign of Crescent or Woody, and the Howlers were no help in shedding any light on their whereabouts.

"Woody's *got* to come back," Fish told Nat later. "Do that two-way thing. Tell him we need him."

But Nat had already tried the two-way thing a dozen times that evening, twice after he found himself transported back to the Black Chateau. Something had happened, something important, Nat was sure. He felt sick again, but this time with worry. *Where were they? Were they together?*

It was still dark when Fish had knocked softly on the window of the *Silver Lady*. It had been a huge blow to find there was still no sign of Woody or Crescent. She was shocked at Nat's appearance; he looked tired and pale, and Fish wondered if he was going to be strong enough to carry out the next stage of her plan. They crept toward the stables, where Nat could see the outline of two horses and two humans, their warm breath joining with the early-morning mist, giving them an unreal, ghostly appearance. Scarlet and Natalie handed the reins over anxiously, worried for their friends and the task that awaited them. Fish felt heartened as Nat vaulted easily onto Rudi, while she struggled a bit with Nikita, Scarlet's own Russian Don horse, a breed famous for once leading the Russian Cossacks into battle, which in the circumstances, thought Fish wryly, was quite appropriate.

"Don't tell JC we've gone until it's too late for them to follow," said Fish. "With any luck, we can do this thing before nightfall."

Scarlet and Natalie watched in silence as the two black horses and their riders were swallowed up by the dense fog and the swirling, deadly snow.

By the time Nat and Fish reached the plain, the sky had lightened, but because of the fog, visibility hadn't improved at all. It crawled over them like a freezing, damp cloak, thick enough to absorb any noise from the hooves of the horses and the creak of their leather saddles. Nat felt his internal GPS take over and help him guide Rudi back to the Black Chateau once again. It was he who had persuaded Fish not to share her plan with the adults until they had gone; his mum would have tried to stop him or, worse still, want to come with them, and frankly he had a hard job imagining his mum as a vampire slayer. *If only they had been able to investigate the Black Chateau sooner.* Saffi Besson had been alive when the vampire had swooped out of the sky and snatched her away from Nat, but he couldn't be sure how far he had gone back into the past. He had to admit to himself that it might be too late to save her from her fate. For all he knew, she could be a vampire by now.

The closer they got to the Black Chateau, the more uncomfortable they felt, their unease transferring to the horses as both Rudi and Nikita spooked and shied away from the slightest snowdrift. Fish gamely urged Nikita into a gallop when the snow thinned slightly, but promptly fell off. As for Nat, it was difficult to enjoy the ride when there was the head vampire waiting to be slain at the other end, and just when things seemed to be as glum and as gloomy as they could possibly get, the weather worsened again. The fog was joined by a fierce blizzard and the whiteout made visibility almost nil, but Nat sensed something moving up ahead in the swirling snow and fog. Then he saw something. *Something big and black.*

"*Now* what?" he muttered, more to himself than to Fish. He motioned to her to stop.

There appeared to be a number of black shapes moving ahead, just visible in the whiteout. Fish couldn't see a thing; she peered into the whiteness, but couldn't see as keenly as Nat, her human eyes being too weak.

"What is it?" she asked nervously. "What do you see?"

"I'm not sure," said Nat, his face a mask. "There's something coming toward us."

Fish's heart was in her mouth. *Vampires!*

On the open plain, there was nowhere to hide. Fish slithered onto the ground, pulling the lethal wooden stakes from her saddle bag. She was just about to pass them to Nat when she saw his expression change to one of relief. Then he smiled at her.

"It's OK," he said. "I can see their hearts. Whatever they are, they're alive."

The black shapes came steadily nearer, and Fish could see plumes of condensed air. She exclaimed in delight as out of the snow emerged a small family of the most beautiful animals she had ever seen. Time stood still for a few seconds as the exquisite black palominos filed past Nat and Fish, seemingly unbothered as they tossed their blueywhite manes and disappeared back into the fog. The sight of the wild horses cheered them like a good omen, making them feel how good it was to be alive.

Roughly half an hour later, as the outline of the Black Chateau rose out of the fog like a brooding monster, their spirits sank again. But this time the fog proved to be their friend, as they found a shelter to hide their horses from prying eyes while they carried out the next part of the plan on foot. Drawing closer to the chateau, Nat made his mind empty of everything except the memory of what he thought he had seen when he and Woody had been in the horrible garden with the creepy statues and farty smells. He found the archway again, and under the cover of the fog they slipped into the gardens, Fish exclaiming every now and then under her breath every time she was taken unawares by one of the ugly statues.

"I just want to check something out," whispered Nat, and Fish followed him through the archway. Someone, Saffi—Nat was sure it had been Saffi, or someone else unfortunate enough to be kept locked in the tower—had thrown something from the window. It seemed a good place to start. Judging the distance from the tower to where the thing would have fallen, Nat and Fish dug in the deep snow in search of it. It was Fish who found it. With a muffled cry of triumph, Nat watched as she held up something that glowed unnaturally bright in the miserable fog. Nat grinned. It was a delicate gold crucifix.

"Is she still there?" whispered Fish. "Is she still in the tower?"

"SAFFI! ARE YOU THERE?" yelled Nat. "IF YOU CAN HEAR ME, SHOUT!"

Fish almost jumped out of her designer ski suit. *"Shut up, you idiot,"* she hissed. "What on earth are you trying to do?"

Nat looked hurt. "I was seeing if she was still there like you asked," he said.

"I *know*," said Fish, "but I didn't expect you to shout like a foghorn! I thought you could sense these things."

"Sorry," said Nat. "Sometimes it's quicker to just do stuff normally."

But Fish was annoyed. "If anyone heard that, we've had it."

"But it's daylight now," protested Nat. "The vampires'll be asleep."

Fish shook her head in exasperation. "Yes, but if the rest of the hive *is* here, they've been well hidden. Remember, Teebo Bon searched here when the people started to disappear. It's possible the vampires have had some help from their familiars: servant drones who can walk in the daylight."

Nat closed his eyes and tried to see Saffi in his mind. He could see her face as he had seen it when he had flipped, but he couldn't see her in the tower. But she was still alive, of that he was certain. They had come to a formal walkway, each side lined by skeletal black trees. At the top of the walkway loomed a high bridge, made of what appeared to be black marble. The bridge led over the vast expanse of frozen water to a tiny island on which was another, much smaller building, also in black marble. It had probably been beautiful once upon a time, but now it just looked desolate and creepy.

"Do you see what I see?" asked Alex Fish, her eyes shining in the gloom.

"That's where they put the dead people, right?" asked Nat with a shudder.

"Yep," said Fish, "it's not so fashionable nowadays, but in the olden times they used to put the whole family in one of these, obviously when they were dead. The posher the building the better."

Nat winced. Personally he thought it was a horrible idea, but followed Fish reluctantly as she sprinted across the dangerous-looking bridge to check out the weird building.

Above the entrance, etched into the black marble, were the words *Vitam Eternam*.

"Wonder what that means," whispered Nat.

"It's Latin," whispered back Fish grimly. "I've seen it before."

"Where?"

"On a vampire's coffin at NightShift HQ," Fish answered. "It means *immortal*."

Nat didn't trust himself to say anything. It was real, then; it was here.

"You sure you're up for this?" asked Fish, concerned. Nat looked scared to death.

No, I'm not up for this, he thought to himself. *I'm not up for it at all. I want Woody to be here; I only feel safe when I'm with him.* He took a deep breath. "Seems like as good a place to start as any," he said, trying to sound nonchalant.

Fish gave him a knowing look, then busily emptied her rucksack, passing some stakes to Nat. She pushed the rest back so that they stuck out of her pack like arrows.

There was a chunky padlock, which looked brand-new, hanging by a chain on the sturdy door. It didn't put Fish off for a second. Reaching inside one of her many pockets, she produced a tiny leather pouch and retrieved a small, decorative silver key.

Nat watched with interest as she pushed the key into the padlock and turned it. The padlock sprang open and dropped onto the snow.

"Cool," whistled Nat, impressed.

"It's Egyptian," whispered Fish. "It's thousands of years old. The story goes it can open any door in any time or place."

"How come you have it?" asked Nat.

"It's part of a collection of Egyptian artifacts that used to belong to Cleopatra," said Fish.

"'Course it is," said Nat, bemused. "I should have known."

Fish grinned. "If you come back to NightShift HQ after all this is over, I'll gladly show you around the vaults. Man oh man, you wouldn't believe what's down there."

"What time you got?" asked Nat, glancing down at his wristwatch.

"I have 0900 hours," said Fish smartly. "We've got *bags* of time until sunset."

Nat hesitated as Fish disappeared inside the yawning mouth of the mausoleum, gingerly checking it out with her flashlight. It was crowded with coffins. Some were stacked on top of each other, and Nat groaned inwardly. This was going to take longer than he thought. He tripped over the nearest coffin and banged his knee.

"Careful," warned Fish. "Don't forget, all these dead dudes could be innocent — free of vampirism. We have to treat each one with respect."

"Or they all might be undead," said Nat, rubbing his knee. "It's going to take ages—there's got to be at least thirty coffins in here."

"Then let's get on with it," said Fish primly.

At the first coffin they paused to read the name from the plaque on the top.

LE COMTE LOUIS DE MORDAUNT
1808–1881

"Le Comte!" gasped Nat. "That's like royalty, isn't it? Or nobility? I think it means *count*."

Fish nodded. "Better go careful, in case we get sued or something by the blue bloods."

Great. More blood, Nat thought. He swallowed and lifted the lid while Alex Fish stood poised with a stake. Nat had offered her Saffi's cross, but she had grinned and lifted her own humungous one out of the top of her ski jacket. It was the flashiest piece of bling Nat had ever seen, and at least five times the size of the real gold cross he had found.

"Only ten quid at the flea market," said Fish with a grin.

With the coffin open, Fish shone her light inside. Nat had been holding his breath in case it smelled of rotting flesh like it does on the TV, but actually it smelled kind of musty—at best like old library books, at worst like old people's hallways when they keep cats. Despite the obvious fact that it was quite unusual to be peering into strangers' coffins armed with stakes, it really wasn't bad at all. The sight of the long-dead aristocrat was sad rather than horrible, his once-fine clothes stained and rotten, his bones long dead and forgotten.

"I think we can rule out ol' Louis as the head vampire," said Fish, relaxing slightly. "That's one down, another twenty-nine to go."

They repeated the process another nine times before they found what they were looking for.

The coffin stood slightly alone from the others on a plinth under a tiny window, which was more like a slit in the marble than a proper window. Fish dusted the plaque off with her sleeve and read:

COMTESSE SEVERINE DE MORDAUNT
1815–1840

"She was young," remarked Fish. "Only about twenty-five when she died. How sad."

But Nat was concentrating on opening the coffin lid. It was stuck. He bent down to get a better purchase on the lid and it flew open suddenly, as though on a spring, making them both jump. They both peered inside, Fish flashing her torch, expecting to see the now familiar sight of old rags and bones. The coffin was shocking in its emptiness.

"Jackpot," said Fish softly.

"The queen of the hive," agreed Nat, "but where on earth is she?"

Even as he spoke, Nat sensed movement behind him. He spun around just in time to see the door of the crypt slam shut. They were trapped!

CHAPTER 29
NAT MEETS THE QUEEN

"That *so* wasn't supposed to happen," said Fish, sounding on the verge of tears. Nat couldn't blame her. He knew how she felt. From the sliver of light shining dully through the tiny slit of the window, Nat could see Alex Fish's stricken face. As soon as the door had slammed shut, sealing them inside the mausoleum, Nat had run to it and pushed against it, hoping his Wolven strength would have budged it. But it was useless. Whoever had seen them enter the crypt had only been biding their time before locking them in. They heard the chunky padlock being snapped firmly into place again on the other side of the door, and Nat's awful claustrophobia was back with him, made worse by the fact that they were sharing the small space with a bunch of skeletons.

"D'you reckon it was her?" asked Nat. "The comtesse?"

Fish shook her head miserably. "It's still light; she'll

be sleeping. Like I said, she'll have others to do her dirty work."

Nat thought on this for a while. "Her familiars?"

"Imagine a hive of bees," replied Fish. "Every queen needs helpers. It's no different with a vampire hive — some are workers, some are drones, and they're beholden to the queen for their entire lives, or until she dies."

"They'll come for us, then," said Nat, his eyes burning, "when the sun goes down."

"Or not," said Fish moodily. "Maybe they'll just leave us to suffocate in here with the dead."

"There you go again," said Nat, trying to cheer her up, "always looking on the bright side."

But there appeared to be no way to escape their marble prison. Fish scrabbled around on the dusty floor trying to find a trapdoor while Nat systematically checked the roof and the walls. The crypt was apparently seamless; nothing could get in or out.

"We're toast," said Fish. "I think you're right — when it's dark, she'll come for us."

"Yeah," said Nat thoughtfully, "and we'll be waiting."

• • •

In the dark mausoleum, time passed slowly among the dead. Nat paced up and down, trying to forget about his claustrophobia, refusing to accept they were locked in and there was nothing they could do. As hour after hour crept by, he could only hope that his dad and JC were on their way and would make it in time to rescue them before the vampire, wherever *she* was, awoke, but he only said that to give Alex Fish hope. He knew that the blizzard would have seriously stymied any rescue attempt by the Twilighters. It would have been madness for anyone to try to find the Black Chateau without the benefit of a map or Wolven GPS. He felt hot and strange and angry. Dozens of emotions sped through his brain as the reality of their deadly situation sunk in. Fish was angry, too, blaming herself and wondering how NightShift's best agent could have left the padlock in the door.

"Try the two-way thing again," she said for the umpteenth time. "Try Woody."

Nat knew that if Woody could pick up on the two-way, or sense they were in trouble, he would be there in no time. To Nat, Woody's failure to come back after his run with the Howlers was more worrying than the predicament in which he currently found himself. He refused to believe that Woody was choosing not to respond to the two-way thing. He needed to find out what had happened, but first there was the small matter of getting out of the crypt and hunting down the vampire queen. *No pressure.*

1700 hours. The sliver of light from the tiny window had almost disappeared. Somewhere behind the blizzard the elusive sun was setting. Nat's keen ears caught a tiny sound from outside.

"Something's coming," he whispered to Fish. "Get ready."

Alex Fish stood in position while Nat waited, heart pumping inhumanly fast, blood rushing noisily in his ears. They had nothing but the two crucifixes, a batch of stakes, and their faith in each other to fight whatever was on the other side of the crypt door. Alexandra Fish was a NightShift agent who believed in herself, despite the blip with the padlock, and Nat Carver was a mongrel by his own admission—neither boy nor Wolven. He decided to go Wolven.

Crouched in front of the door, he thought he could feel his body changing. The hairs rose on the back of his neck like hackles, and his muscles felt pumped and tingly, as though just by tensing them he could make them twice their size. Although Fish was hindered by her human eyesight and couldn't see Nat properly, she could see his eyes flashing again with a fevered topaz light, and suddenly he wasn't Nat anymore. Oh, he still *looked* like Nat Carver; he hadn't morphed into a wolf or anything. Except that he sort of wasn't—he was bigger, somehow, and his face was set in a hard, un-Nat-like expression, *brutal*, almost. Fish shivered all the way to her toes.

When the old door groaned open, Nat felt himself leap upward as if he had no control over his own body. The small vestibule of the crypt was filled with the most bloody of bloodcurdling growls, which chilled Nat to the marrow of his bones. Then, shockingly, he realized that the growling and snarling was coming from *him*— bloodcurdling noises came again from way down deep inside his chest—*he was growling and snarling like a wolf.* He used the open door as a board from which to spring out, and prepared to fight whoever was waiting for them.

There was nothing there.

Nat gulped in great lungfuls of snowy air as he looked

around him. Fish followed him, glad to be out of the crypt and breathing fresh air again, even if it was freezing. She stared at Nat. His eyes still blazed, but he looked as though he was regaining some control.

"What's happening?" she shouted against the roar of the wind. "Why have they let us go?"

"Don't know," yelled back Nat. Through the swirling snow, he scanned the bridge and then the gardens, satisfied there was no one there.

"What now?" he asked Fish.

"We split up," said the agent firmly. "Don't tell me you're scared—I've just seen you wolf out. You scared *me*, and I don't scare easily."

Nat grinned. "You know this is bad, don't you? Whoever let us out is playing with us."

Fish shrugged. "You want the chateau or the grounds?"

"I can run faster than you," said Nat. "I'll take the gardens and you find the best way inside the chateau. I'll find *you*, OK? Promise you won't go inside alone?"

Fish nodded. "Good luck," she said.

Nat wasted no time and was away on his toes. Across the precarious bridge and down into the horrid, dead gardens again. He got his breath back, grateful for the cover of the trees and statues, even if it did stink of sulfur—or *fartz*, as Woody had described it the first time they were there. Nat smiled slightly at the memory and closed his eyes, wishing that Woody would materialize and tell him what to do now. It was all right for Alex Fish to insist they split up. (What *was* her fixation about splitting up, anyway?) He was fed up with people like Fish and werewolves like Crescent bossing him about all the time.

While he searched, Nat tried to zone in on Saffi by holding her crucifix tightly in his hand. If she was still here, and he was sure she was, maybe somewhere inside the Black Chateau, they would find her. He tried concentrating on the crucifix, but he couldn't get anything from it. Satisfied there was nothing worth investigating in the immediate grounds, he ran stealthily into the courtyard. His Wolven eyes searched the darkness for Alex Fish. *Where was she?* Then he had a thought. *The key! I bet she's used the Egyptian key, and gone in on her own!* To make sure, he loped around the other side of the chateau, keeping close to the building, using the shadows to hide himself. *Nope—no sign.* He tried the nearest door to him.

Locked! No surprise there. Scanning the walls, he noticed a narrow glass door leading to a type of glass structure that he thought was called an orangery, or a conservatory, and ran swiftly toward it. As he approached, the door banged open as though the wind had caught it. Forgetting his advice to Fish, he held his breath and stepped across the threshold, allowing his eyes to adjust to the candlelight inside. There was something here, something monstrous, waiting in the shadowy darkness.

Welcome, it said.

Nat felt the voice rather than heard it; it crept into his head like a spider, its eight legs scrabbling through his brain, delving and rummaging, as if choosing what to take first.

He didn't know what he had expected when he came face-to-face with evil, but the scene in front of him definitely wasn't it. For a start, there was a lovely smell in the room, like Christmas, all cinnamon and mulberries and hot apple cider. His Wolven senses were screaming *VAMPIRE* at him, so there was no doubt what now confronted him — but this vampire looked nothing like he had imagined. She — *it* — was sitting on a squashy, comfy chair dressed in quite ordinary clothes. OK, so Nat didn't know much about fashion, but the black pantsuit she wore wasn't his idea of vampire clothing at all. At her throat was an enormous orb of light, which Nat assumed was a ginormous diamond. The candlelight bounced off the diamond, sending rays of light around the room, illuminating the bare windows with a magical golden glow. Nat thought that, despite being a vampire, the woman — *Stop thinking it's a woman*, Nat told himself — smiling at him beguilingly, was probably the most beautiful creature he had ever seen in his life.

He swallowed and waited for her to say something else. He had expected to feel different . . . expected to feel revulsion and fear. *But how could such beauty be so evil?*

The vampire queen was sewing, her long fingers swiftly passing her needle in and out of the complicated tapestry on her lap.

Nat coughed. If she was going to fly at him, he wished she would hurry up. As if she could read his thoughts, she put her needle down with a little sigh and smiled. She held out her hand regally and, although she was a fair distance away from Nat, her hand seemed disembodied somehow, moving toward him like a snake. He tried to pull away but she was strong, her grip like a vice. She drew him closer and guided him to a chair.

"Master Carver, I presume?" she asked him, her voice smooth and low, and slightly mocking.

Nat opened his mouth to speak but nothing came out.

She smiled warmly. "If you'll allow me a little joke," she purred, "I have been undying to meet you."

Nat didn't think it at all funny. He still couldn't speak.

"You and your friend have caused me a great deal of trouble," she said, still smiling, "and a great deal of amusement."

"Why did you lock us in?" asked Nat, finally finding his tongue.

The vampire laughed. Her laugh was pretty; it sounded like tinkling little bells.

"I wanted to meet you on my terms," she replied, "after dark and alone."

"Who let us out?" asked Nat. "Why didn't you just finish us off?"

"Finish you *off*?" The vampire looked shocked at the

idea. "I don't want to finish you off—you're no good to me dead . . . not yet. Your spiky-haired friend, on the other hand . . ."

She laughed again when she saw Nat's expression.

"Letting you out was part of the game," she said. "You humans are funny little persons. So *tenacious*! Making your futile plans to escape. Tragic, really."

"You were saying about Fish," said Nat.

"Fish. *Poisson*. Curious name." The vampire smiled. "I'm afraid the little fishy is superfluous to my needs. But . . . she will be useful in other ways."

"Like Saffi Besson?" asked Nat, forgetting to be scared.

"So many questions." She smiled again. "The little *mademoiselle*, Saffi, is still alive . . . if a little drained."

"Is she . . . is she still human?" asked Nat. "And what about the others?"

"All in good time," soothed the vampire. "We have all night, after all."

"But what about Saffi?" insisted Nat.

A momentary flash of irritation crossed the vampire's lovely face. "I was warned you are still human enough to worry too much about others."

"*Who* warned you?" demanded Nat. "What do you know about me?"

The vampire comtesse smiled again and picked up her needle and thread. "Everything," she said. "I was supposed to destroy you and your little band of gifted friends."

Nat paled.

"I cannot call him a friend," said the vampire, concentrating on her needlework, "more of an associate, with whom I share a mutual loathing of the human race."

"*Scale,*" whispered Nat. "So why didn't you? Kill me, I mean?"

"*I* want you," said the vampire, still sewing. "I'm not prepared to hand you over to him. You are mine now, Nat Carver. All you have to do is to become my apprentice. In return, everything you ever desired will be yours."

"Er . . . ," mumbled Nat, "thanks, but no thanks. I'd rather not, if it's all the same to you. I like being human."

The vampire raised her eyebrows. "*Human?*" she said softly. "You are no more human than I am! You have the wolf in you, Master Carver, and the wolf is stronger than the boy."

Nat was silent. He watched her hands as she sewed.

There was dirt in her fingernails, as though she'd been doing some heavy-duty gardening, or perhaps *digging herself out of a grave*. He shuddered. The empty coffin in the mausoleum had been unsafe for her, too obvious if someone came looking. He had an image of her digging her way out of the frozen earth, and it sickened him.

"Let . . . let me see Saffi and the other children you took," he said at last. "If . . . they're still alive, then we can talk."

"Ah, Saffi," said the vampire, regret in her voice. "She is with the others now."

"You . . . you haven't . . . ?" stammered Nat.

The vampire licked her lips, her tongue flicking in and out of her red mouth like a snake. "Of course they are alive—the Besson girl, too. They have restored my youth. Without them I would not be beautiful."

Fair enough, thought Nat dreamily. For she *was* beautiful, even more beautiful than Angelina Jolie. She wasn't like the other vampires, all scaly and leathery, with their red eyes and skeletal faces. Her quick hands still sewed, the needle moving in and out of the tapestry, in and out, in and out . . . He found himself wondering what it would be like to be her apprentice. *Would he really live forever?* That actually sounded quite cool.

Nat felt his eyes grow heavy as he watched the vampire sew, forgetting about the reason he had come here, forgetting about Fish, Woody . . .

A tiny familiar sound drew him out of his stupor. It was like a faraway dentist's drill. The vampire stopped sewing and looked at the source of the noise in annoyance. Nat turned his head toward the sound. A mosquito, just like the ones he and Woody had fled from, was buzzing around the vampire queen's head. There was a flash of steel as the vampire, faster than light, snipped the mosquito in two with her scissors. The two halves dropped abruptly onto the floor, spilling dark blood. For the briefest of moments the vampire and Nat stared at it as it oozed across the floor. Then she grinned like a velociraptor and the spell was broken.

"You've been trying to brainwash me!" yelled Nat.

She was close, *too* close; he could smell her breath. It smelled as meaty and rank as a fly-blown carcass. He recoiled as her face seemed to ripple like she was under water, and Nat realized he was seeing what was behind her facade of humanity. Beneath the mask she shifted into a raddled old crone, her body twisted and ancient, her vampire teeth yellow and protruding over her chin, and her hair little more than a covering of coarse scrub; and then to something far worse. Nat glimpsed a monster: a great black spider with four pairs of eyes and a squat, bloated body.

"I will trade the children for you," said the vampire, regaining its human shape. "You will stay with me and I will show you everything. In return, you will bestow me with your Wolven gifts."

"Like I said," said Nat, coldly brave, "show me the children and maybe we can do a deal."

The candles started to flicker as though a sudden wind threatened to extinguish them. The room grew dark and the vampire queen laughed: a horrible, cracked cackle.

"I deal in illusion just like your grandfather," it said, as all humanity left it and it stood in front of Nat a blackened, leathery horror. The glass conservatory shuddered and shook. To his horror, it started to crack, splinters of glass falling from the ceiling. He felt in his pocket to where Saffi's cross glowed warmly, but it was too late. The vampire enveloped him in darkness, and Nat was lost.

CHAPTER 30
COCOON

Where is he? thought Alex Fish. It had been ages. Nat had told her not to go inside the chateau on her own, but he was nowhere to be seen. Surely he must have finished searching the gardens? Fish had waited by the chateau and when he hadn't turned up she had gone to find him. *They must have passed each other. Tarnation!*

Just about everything had gone wrong that could go wrong. They'd been cooped up in that horrible mausoleum all through the daylight hours, and now it was the vampires' time. It was a whole lot easier staking them in their coffins than chasing them around. Fish waited at least ten more minutes, then, almost frozen solid and fed up with being battered by the wind, she made a decision. The moon had disappeared behind the raging blizzard, and without the benefit of supernatural eyesight she had trouble picking her way back to the courtyard. She considered using her flashlight, but was worried the beam would be seen by someone. Fish felt vulnerable and alone, although tons better now that she was on the move again, and she could feel the comforting shape of the little Egyptian key nestling in the pocket of her ski jacket.

Where would the vampire queen be? Fish asked herself as she moved in the shadows around the back of the vast building. There was a door by a small plot of land, which Fish thought could be a kitchen garden. She rummaged in her pocket and pulled out the little silver key, hearing the satisfying click as the lock yielded. Opening the door slowly, she found herself in a narrow hallway lit by a single ugly lightbulb: nothing like you would expect in a medieval chateau, thought Fish, disappointed. She had two stakes in each hand and backup stakes sticking out of the top of her boots; she looked like a walking cactus. There were two choices. One steep set of stone steps led upward, one equally steep set led down, a black hole yawning at the bottom. Fish grimaced. Neither set of steps looked very inviting. She drew a coin out of her pocket and flipped. Heads up, tails down. *Tails!*

• • •

Nat's world had turned upside down again. The glass room had shattered along with the rest of the vampire queen's clever illusion, and someone had trussed him up like a Christmas turkey.

He had no idea where he was. He had no idea how long he had been unconscious—or if he had been unconscious at all. All he knew was that it was freezing cold and still dark. He sensed he had been moved to another part of the chateau. He was alone, tied up, and his chances of surviving the night—unless he agreed to the vampire's demands— were approximately nil. He tried looking for Fish with his mind, but he couldn't feel her anywhere close. Nat tried to look at his watch, but the rope had been tied so tightly he couldn't free his arm. He forced himself to breathe deeply and consider his options. He thought about his Wolven gifts first. *Strength.* He flexed his muscles and tried to break the rope by bursting out of it. He had to give up when his eyeballs threatened to burst out of his head with the effort. *OK, so that didn't work*, Nat told himself calmly, when his heart rate had slowed down. His new senses were no help in this. Dismally, he looked down at the thick rope wrapped around his chest. *Bite it.* Nat rested his head on his chest and gripped the thick rope in his teeth. *Eurgh!* It made him want to gag. He bit down hard, his jaws aching with the effort. At this rate he'd be free just before next Christmas! *I can't stay here*, he thought to himself. *I can't just sit here and wait for that . . . that thing to come near me again.* He closed his eyes and thought of Woody. Then with all his remaining strength he let rip a desperate mindhowl and sent it out to find Woody. . . . *AAAAAAaaaroooooooghhhhh!WOODYCOMEQUICK OHWOODYNEEDYOUPLEEEEEEAASE Aooooooooowwwwwwww!*

For centuries, French nobles had come to Salinas from as far as Versailles to sample the fine wines stored deep in the bowels of the Black Chateau.

But something else was stored there now. The doorway to the cellars was barred by a gross curtain of thick spiderwebs, thickened with the bodies of small unfortunate insects, rodents, and filthy dust. The stone walls were strewn with the same thick webby shroud. On first inspection the cellar appeared empty, but if you were to look closely, you would see something you hoped you would never see again. But then if you had got this far, it was unlikely you would make it out alive to see anything again anyway.

Suspended within the walls were a dozen or more cigar-shaped cocoons. Each cocoon contained the body of a child, their noses and eyes just visible. The younger children had been stricken dumb, almost catatonic with blood loss and shock, for this was Madame Vampire's larder.

In her own uncomfortable cocoon, Saffi Besson still lived. While her own blood still flowed through her veins, while her heart kept beating, Saffi still hoped the boy she had seen at the lake would come back. Although her voice was fading, she sang the songs her mother had sung to her when she was little, hoping her muffled, off-key voice would give some comfort to the others.

Drifting in and out of consciousness, Saffi had no idea if it was day or night. The only way to tell was if the vampire came to feed. She closed her eyes again, hoping to fall asleep and dream of home.

An almost imperceptible sound made her eyes snap open and her frail body stiffen within its cocoon. *Something was coming!* The sound she had heard was the heavy door opening in the kitchens above. Saffi knew the layout of the lower floors from her brief moment of freedom. The door creaked and moonlight bathed the cellar floor as it opened.

She held her breath as the outline of a girlish figure stepped lightly into the room. Whoever it was had a flashlight in their mouth and spiky hair. Sharp sticks stuck out of their pockets and boots, and in each hand they carried two more. Saffi realized with mounting joy that the sharp sticks were stakes! *Stakes to kill vampires!* She couldn't see the person's face clearly because of the flashlight, but armed with the stakes, the mystery slayer looked like a cross between Van Helsing and a large hedgehog. Saffi opened her mouth and screamed. All that came out was a tiny rush of stale air. The spiky-haired person didn't hear, too busy pointing the flashlight into all the corners of the cellar. Saffi was terrified the person would leave. She struggled inside her cocoon, trying to break out, but she was too tightly wrapped in the disgusting web. She thrashed inside her tight bonds. *Please, God,* she prayed. *If you can hear me, please help me!*

Saffi Besson was so dehydrated she couldn't even cry. What came out was a desperate, dry sob. But perhaps God had heard her at last, for it was enough to make the spiky-haired person stop and shine their precious light up toward Saffi's cocoon.

"Aide-moi. Help me." Saffi managed one last cry for help. It was all she had. Blinded by the powerful beam of the flashlight, Saffi could hear the person exclaim in horror.

"Hello?" It *was* a girl's voice. She was shining her flashlight, searching around the cellar, suddenly seeing for the first time the extent of the vampire's greed and cruelty. Saffi watched as the girl put out her hand to steady herself and swallowed hard as though to stop herself from vomiting. Then she reached up and gently pulled away the threads covering Saffi's mouth.

"Merci," whispered Saffi through swollen, parched lips.

"Saffi? Saffi Besson?" asked her rescuer.

Saffi managed to nod her head slightly.

"My name is Fish. Alex Fish," said the girl with spiky

hair and a sharp little face. "Saffi, you must listen very carefully, I hope you can understand me." She held Saffi by her shoulders and spoke very slowly to make sure the girl understood. "I'm going to get you all out of here, I promise."

CHAPTER 31
MINDHOWL

AAAAAAaaarooooooghhhhh!WOODYCOMEQUICK
OHWOODYNEEDYOUPLEEEEEEEEEAASE
Aoooooooooowwwwwwww!

The desperate mindhowl for help smashed through
Woody's brain. He had been thinking about Nat, feeling
guilty he had left without a word. He felt split between
Nat and his clan—the two worlds they inhabited were
so different that Woody didn't know where his true path
led. Until he had met Nat, he would have said his place
in the world was with his clan. Now he wasn't so sure. He
had been running with them, getting used to being one
of them, when Nat's mindhowl had blasted him, catching
him right between the eyes at about ninety miles an hour
and knocking him clean off his feet. He hit the snow tail-
first and rolled backward, over and over, until he looked

like an enormous ball of snow with four legs and a head. Woody shook the snow from his fur and led his clan back to the frozen waterfall. Something huge had happened. *Nat needed him!*

Scale was still hiding in Crescent's body. He too had heard Nat Carver's mindhowl for help, and was glad. He was operating the she-wolf like a puppet, guiding her body and seeing through her eyes. He had made Crescent hide in the caves behind the curtain of ice, spying and listening to the Wolven's plans. This was better than perfect. The Wolven were going to fight and lead him straight to Nat Carver! He would see to it that they would die trying. He could read the vampire queen's mind like a well-thumbed book — he knew she had double-crossed him. No matter. He would see to it that she would pay the ultimate price. And so would Nat Carver.

While Scale was making his sick plans, the vampire queen scanned the snowy horizon from the top of the north tower. Her red eyes sought her hive in the darkness. *Two hours until dawn!* Her search scouts had reported that the small band of Wolven were on the move at last. The Carver boy was safely out of action for now, and when the Wolven clan came to his rescue they would be wiped out by the hive. *All except the young one—the one they called Woody.* The vampire was grateful to the demon wolf creature, Scale, for awakening her from her long sleep after her own *husband* had put the stake through her heart all those years ago. But not so grateful that she had any qualms about double-crossing him. Let Scale think she had destroyed the boy and his pet Wolven; she had uses for them herself! She had enjoyed showing the boy how powerful she was just by the simple illusion, and his face had shown her better than any mirror could how her appearance was improving all the time thanks to her moonlit blood baths. And the future? She would bewitch humanity! She would create legions of vampires and be more powerful than any vampire in Europe. Then she would spread her wings farther across the world. She smiled to herself. *Things were working out beautifully.* She leaned over the top of the tower and called for her last remaining hive, listening keenly for the *THWACK THWACK* of their beautiful strong wings.

• • •

Somewhere deep inside the Black Chateau, Nat was dozing uneasily until a small, freezing cold hand was shoved roughly over his mouth.

"This is no time for a nap," whispered Fish. "Let's get you out of here."

Nat thought he was dreaming until the pain from the tight ropes sharpened his senses.

"Easy does it," said Fish as she cut through the thick rope with her penknife, helping him to massage his limbs to get the blood flowing again.

"What's going on?" whispered Nat. "Wha—?"

"Tell you later," said Fish. "You need to know two things for now: The good news is that Saffi Besson and the other missing kids are still alive. They're safe for now. The bad news is that the chateau is heaving with vampires."

Nat stared at her in awe. "Crone was right about you," he muttered, "you really *are* superhuman."

Fish smiled modestly, although inside she agreed with every word. She pulled him to his feet and together they left the hateful room behind them, stepping out into the long passage.

"C'mon," said Nat, feeling his strength return. "Something's about to happen. I can feel it." It was true; familiar feelings were stirring in his body. His hairs — *hackles* — rose and stuck up like quills at the back of his neck, his eyes felt like they were bugging out, and his breath was coming in quick short pants, like a wolf. And then it came. Loud and clear. No mistake:

NATHOLDONAMCOMINGWILLHELP SOOOOOOOOOOONNN!!!!

It was Woody.

Woody led the King's Wolven out from behind the ice curtain and onto the frozen plain. He had locked onto the echoes of Nat's scream for help and it still played like a movie in his brain. Pinpointing Nat's whereabouts had been easy, and the vision of the Black Chateau helped guide both his clan and his Wolven GPS. Woody ran tirelessly, his thoughts jumbled with the visions he had picked up from his friend. *VAMPIRES!*

The clan was willing to die in the fight for Woody's friend, and this made the choice Woody would have to make all the harder to deal with. *If I'm still alive,* he thought grimly.

As the Black Chateau came into sight for the first time, Woody skidded to a halt and turned to face his clan. Then, placing their power, their loyalty, and their trust in him, the twelve Wolven — together for the first time in the new millennium — prepared to fight.

CHAPTER 3

BLACK SNOW

The twelve Wolven came, manes flowing, eyes glowing.

From the north tower of the Black Chateau, the vampire queen saw them arrive through the blizzard, her bloodred eyes narrowed against the sting of snow. For the first time she felt unease. The Wolven's white shimmering coats blended perfectly with the deep snow, and it was almost impossible for her to track them. She couldn't help feeling a grudging admiration at her first sight of them and the speed with which they traveled. Not even the frozen wasteland of the lake could slow them, their lithe bodies moving like soft white smoke. *Then, suddenly and impossibly, they had vanished!*

The vampire hovered a little above the parapet of the tower, a small cry of dismay escaping from her strange mouth. *They had disappeared!* She tried to calm herself. She could see her hive clearly, like big ugly ants as they waited to attack, some in the trees, some on the ground at the bottom of her tower. She drew comfort from the fact that her army could attack from the air. The Wolven had no choice but to stay grounded. Her job was to see it all when it happened, to command the battle like a general, guiding and directing, but never endanger her own life. *But how could she do it if she couldn't see the enemy?*

Woody had led his Wolven clan across the ice. He remembered the layout of the Black Chateau and could feel that Nat was somewhere close. Burrowing under the deep snow, he tunneled out of sight, the others following eagerly. Their movements were so smooth that there was no evidence on the surface of anything traveling quickly beneath. Then Woody's nostrils were filled with the familiar stink of the vampires. *They were close now.*

The vampires at the bottom of the tower were ready to fight and were picking up on the queen's ugly mood. They were unsure from which side the Wolven enemy would approach. The vampire lieutenant had warned them that the Wolven had temporarily disappeared from sight, and this made them very nervous. The survivors of the onion soup attacks had seen what a werewolf could do, let alone a Wolven. Wolven were rock hard, the stuff of legend and—

"*AAAAAAAAAAAAAAAAAAAAAAAAA OOOOOOOOOOOOOOOOOOOOOOOO WWWWWRRRRRRRRRRRRRRRRRRRRRR!!*"

The nearest vampires were hit by a snow tsunami as the Wolven sprang out like demented jack-in-the-boxes. The noise of their howls was immense, so loud that some of the vampires tried to run away, their hands clamped awkwardly over their pointed ears. The vampire queen watched in horrified dismay as the Wolven paired off and repeatedly and tirelessly attacked the vampire hive, ripping and tearing at the blackened shapes. They bit easily through the vampires' scrawny necks, disconnecting their loathsome heads from their bodies, although some still ran around like headless chickens. The snow had turned black with their foul blood.

The queen looked feverishly toward the eastern sky, searching for signs of dawn. The Wolven had dispatched the vampires on the ground in minutes. Shrieking like a banshee, she called again and the sky became black with dark angel wings as the rest of the hive flew down from the trees. With a last glance at the battle below, the queen crawled down the side of the tower like a monstrous spider.

"They're here," said Nat.

Fish looked at him, thrilled. Nat's eyes were glowing a warm orange in the darkness.

"You mean, *he's* here," said Fish, a little shiver running down her back.

Nat shook his head. "No, it . . . it's not just Woody. There's more. *I can sense more—more Wolven!*"

"Noooo!" said Fish, her excitement reaching fever pitch. "Are you sure?"

Nat was just about to reply when unearthly shrieks interrupted him.

"Something's happening," said Fish. "Quick."

They ran to the bridge and peered over the parapet.

"No way!" said Nat. "*Oh*, look at them!"

Nat knew they were witnessing something incredible. *The King's Wolven, just as his friend Iona had described them. Woody had found his clan! That was why he had disappeared.*

Fish strained her eyes. Hampered as she was by human eyesight, all she could see was the black sky and white snow. But then she caught a glimpse of an enormous white wolf, and then another and another. They glowed bluey-white in the darkness, their eyes shining with topaz colors. They were leaping up into the air, bringing down writhing black shapes, then shaking them like a dog shakes a rag. The Wolven were fighting the vampires!

Nat counted five . . . *no* . . . *eight* . . . *ten* Wolven, but there were too many vampires to count; they seemed hopelessly outnumbered. But the Wolven were equipped with teeth, claws, and incredible strength. The vampires were strong, but the white wolf creatures had an advantage over them: The bloodsuckers had to get up close and really personal to use their teeth.

"We need to get the kids and leave," said Fish, interrupting his thoughts, "and we can't stay up here. We're too exposed."

Nat agreed reluctantly. He thought about blasting Woody again, but he worried he might knock him off his guard. He hadn't seen his friend in the midst of the fighting, but just the knowledge he was nearby was comfort enough. He glanced at the sky in hope. *How long before dawn?*

The Carver boy was gone!

The vampire queen surveyed the room. It was empty except for the rope she herself had bound him with. For the first time since the rats had reanimated her with their blood, she was frightened. Her fears were confirmed when she reached the cellars. The cocoons lay in tatters — *the children had gone, too.*

She stared at the empty cocoons. If the hive lost the battle, the Wolven would come for her. She needed to find Nat Carver quickly. The others could rot in hell, but Carver was her insurance. *He could not leave the chateau!*

"You put them *where?*" asked Nat incredulously.

"In the mausoleum," said Fish. "I used the Egyptian key to lock 'em in."

"If they didn't need therapy before, they will now," said Nat, shaking his head.

"It's safer than anywhere else," said Fish defensively. "The comtesse sleeps in the chateau, and the other coffins were full."

"We'd better—" Nat stopped abruptly. "Can you hear that?"

Fish could hear nothing apart from the howling wind, and shook her head.

Nat concentrated. The voice in his head was familiar, but very faint. And it kept phasing out like a bad radio signal. . . . Then . . .

Cominwhereareyaaaaaaa????

It was Woody!

Meetyaattheblackbridgecominnow!!!! Nat blasted back, and hoped he had done it hard enough. His head aching with the effort, he grabbed Fish's hand and ran.

"C'mon," he shouted. "We'll meet him at the black bridge."

Their relief at hearing from Woody was cut short by another noise.

THWACK THWACK THWACK. Nat's reaction was instant. Pulling Fish with him, he shot under the cover of the archway between the chateau and the lower gardens.

Flattening themselves to the wall, they prayed they hadn't been seen by the circling vampires.

"The vampire queen must know I've escaped," panted Nat. "She wouldn't spare any of them from the fighting unless she'd found out."

Counting the seconds, Nat risked sliding out from under the thin arch. "They've gone," he said, his face white in the darkness. "C'mon!"

Still dragging Fish by the hand, he belted across the black bridge, trying not to look at the drop on either side. As they ran they instinctively ducked their heads, keeping themselves as low and small as possible. Reaching the enormous door of the mausoleum, Fish fumbled in her pocket for the Egyptian key. There was a truly horrible moment when her frozen fingers dropped it in the snow. Falling to her knees, she scrabbled about for it while Nat scanned the black sky, expecting to see red eyes and black wings and hear the *THWACK THWACK* of wings.

"Got it!" shouted Fish triumphantly, holding the key out to Nat.

But Nat wasn't listening. He was just standing there, grinning like an idiot. For galloping over the black bridge, tongue lolling, eyes glowing like headlights, came a large, white wolf creature. It was Woody.

Saffi Besson had been busy. She had surprised herself over the last dreadful weeks in the company of the vampire, and knew that whatever happened—whether they managed to get out of here alive or not—it wasn't because she hadn't tried to save herself. Now she was in charge of these shocked and freezing kids. Her mum always said that God helps those who help themselves. Well, she didn't know about that, but she—or God—had found some paraffin lamps and matches and, with the help of a couple of the bigger kids, she had smashed up a couple of coffin lids to get a fire going. And when she heard the key turn in the lock, she was ready. Brandishing a flaming piece of wood, she waited, wild-eyed and grim.

The heavy door crashed open, the kids by the fire cowering in fright, covering their eyes. Saffi, her breath held, her feet planted firmly so she could get a good swing at whoever it was, almost fainted in relief. *It was the girl, Alex Fish!*

But there was someone with her—a boy—a boy whom

Saffi had no difficulty in recognizing. *It was the boy from the lake!* The boy she had prayed would get help. *He was smiling at her.* But . . . this had to be a dream, for behind him there was — and Saffi took a few steps back — *behind him there was a great big white wolf!*

"It's OK," said Fish hastily as she saw Saffi raise the piece of burning wood. "He's harmless."

Then the boy with the dark blue eyes smiled. "Ready to get out of here?"

Saffi nodded, her eyes filling with grateful tears.

Gathering up the children, Nat opened the door of the mausoleum for the last time. The moon had come out from the snow-laden sky, showing the black bridge and the white ice in perfect monochrome. *And there were vampires roosted silently on the parapets.*

The vampire queen grinned obscenely as she stood in front of them.

"Caught like rats in a trap," she cackled. "And now I have a pet Wolven, too. How convenient."

CHAPTER 33
DEATH BY WOLVEN

It didn't take Nat and Fish long to realize they were out-numbered. Woody's lip was drawn into a deadly snarl that showed all his teeth. He looked terrifying.

"Down, boy." The vampire queen smirked, flanked by her deadly assistants, their red eyes glowing malevolently with thirst. "Master Carver, you'll have to control your beast; he's frightening the children!"

But Woody knew something else, and he hoped Nat was sharing his thoughts. *The clan had been victorious. They had all but demolished the hive and they were coming. Coming for the last of the hive and their evil queen.*

"A A A A A A A A A H W O O O O O O O O O O O RAAAAAAAAAAAAAAAGHHHHHHHHHHHHHHHH!"

The howling cut through the tension like a knife. Fish noticed the expression on the face of the vampire queen with satisfaction. She looked petrified. *Well, it serves her right*, thought Fish. *A good general never leaves the battle without making sure they're winning.*

In the moonlight came Woody's clan, so glaringly white it almost hurt Fish's eyes to look at them. In one minute flat, the queen had gone from triumph to dismay. Fish watched as the last of the vampire hive swooped to meet the approaching Wolven.

Woody galloped toward them, snarling and growling. Nat watched in horror as a red-eyed bloodsucker landed on Woody's back. In a trice, Woody had rolled over and grabbed the surprised vamp by the throat. Black blood splattered Woody and onto the ice. The Wolven were tireless. As the remaining vampires tried to flee, the clan leaped high into the air, bringing them down effortlessly and finishing them off, the snow melting with their stinking gore.

The queen stood alone. Smiling at them, she backed away, her wings quivering as she tried to unfold them.

"Get her!" screamed Fish. "She's trying to morph!"

The queen laughed, a harsh, grating sound, and leaped up onto the top of the bridge, preparing to morph into her wings. Just as her feet left the ground, a white blur shot past Nat and Fish and rocketed high into the air, just managing to lock onto her horrid long toes with its teeth.

"AAAAAIIIEEEEEEEEEEEEEEEEEEEE!!" A ghastly shriek came from the maw of the vampire's mouth as both vampire and Woody plummeted from the top of the parapet down onto the ice-covered lake.

"Get the children inside!" yelled Nat to Fish. "They're going to freeze out here!"

Fish hesitated; she wanted to follow the Wolven, not babysit. But common sense told her she had no choice. Reluctantly she agreed, and she and Saffi took the children back inside the mausoleum, out of the freezing wind.

Nat raced over to the edge of the bridge and looked down. All he could see was a black hole in the ice where Woody had taken down the vampire queen and crashed through. There was no sign of either.

He watched, his heart in his mouth, as the remaining eleven Wolven raced down the rocky path to the lake below. Remembering Mac's words, he hoped they were true: *I can even drown.* If Woody had survived the fall and was strong enough to keep the vampire under the water long enough to drown her, the reign of terror would be finished — at least for now.

As dawn came, there was no word from the lake. Nat slumped as his energy left him. The kids were safe at least; if only Woody . . .

He felt a movement behind him and turned around. A large, russet-colored wolf stood in the first light of the sun as it rose in the misty east.

Crescent! Did that mean the Howlers had tracked them? *But there was something wrong with her,* thought Nat uneasily. *Something wrong with the way she moved.* She looked awkward, almost cringing away before being propelled toward him, her ears tightly pressed to her skull as though she was moving against her will. And there was something else — *her eyes weren't her own!* Crescent's eyes were usually a vivid, orange color, filled with haughty excitement, full of life. The eyes that were narrowed and stared at Nat were a dull, malevolent orange; they were the eyes of a dead creature with no soul. *The eyes of Lucas Scale!*

Crescent's body launched itself clumsily at Nat. Finding himself on the ground, Nat scrabbled away from the werewolf, desperate to summon up some Wolven strength. He could feel his muscles stretching and pulling under his skin, could feel his strength increasing as the adrenaline made him wolf out like he had in the crypt, hours before.

But hold on—what else was happening? *It wasn't stopping!* Then Nat was aware of falling, his body lengthening out on the cold, cold ground. Something insane was happening. *My hands are changing!* Terrified, Nat saw his hands spread out in front of him. They were morphing into paws, great claws emerging from what were once his ordinary, human hands. *Oh God, what's my mum going to say?* thought Nat irrationally. And then his wolf side took over.

Inside Crescent's body, Scale felt the first frisson of fear. *This was unexpected, to say the least!* He stared at the silver-gray wolf who had until seconds ago been a teenage boy. The wolf who stared back at him, sizing him up, creeping toward him with dripping jaws, much bigger than the she-wolf that Scale now inhabited.

The two locked together in a deadly embrace, neither moving as they both clung on to each other with their claws, each trying to find purchase with their teeth.

Alex Fish and Saffi Besson stared at each other in dismay. What was going on? Fish had thought the noises were thunder at first, low rumbling sounds that shook the ground. But then, there was no mistaking it. *Growling.* The noise was somehow the worst sound Fish had ever heard. Leaving Saffi with the increasingly confused children, Fish sped back to the bridge to see a large silvery gray wolf grappling with a familiar russet she-wolf. *Crescent! But who was the other one? And what was going on?* thought Fish, confused. Then she saw Nat's ragged clothes in a heap. Her eyes widened in shock. *The beautiful silver-gray animal was Nat!*

As Nat pinned down his enemy and bared his teeth for the final time, Fish ran out from the shadows, yelling his name.

"Nat! *Noooo!* It's *Crescent!*"

Nat came to his senses and stopped. *If he killed this body, he wasn't killing Scale, but Crescent!* Then another thought popped into his head, sent there by Lucas Scale.

Yes, but isn't she your enemy? Isn't she always trying to break your friendship with Woody? Kill her!

Lucas Scale had lost this battle for now, he knew that. But if he could make the Carver brat finish off the she-wolf, well, that would almost make up for it! He would be an outcast!

Nat hesitated again, thinking about plunging his teeth into Crescent's soft furry neck. It was all Fish needed. She knew that to part two fighting werewolves was madness — she could end up dead herself. But she felt herself grabbing Nat by the scruff of thick fur on his neck, and *puuuuulling.*

Nat fell on top of Fish, almost squishing her. When he had scrambled to his feet, he saw the truth. It was just Crescent, lying in an untidy heap on the ground staring up at him, her eyes filled with molten tears. Of Scale, there was no sign. He had left Crescent's body and disappeared.

Alex Fish watched wide-eyed as the russet wolf shook herself and flexed her lithe body in the snow beneath her. She stared in fascination as Crescent's face and body started to change. Her snout flattened out, her ears shrank, and her body shortened into a human shape again. In seconds the russet wolf had gone, replaced by a naked girl, her body bruised from her fight with the silver-gray wolf.

The wolf who had once been Nat Carver watched as Fish pulled off her top layer of clothes and offered them to the exhausted girl. Crescent flashed her a grateful smile.

"Thanks," she said simply. Then Crescent turned to the gray wolf and smiled.

"Guess I didn't have to bite you after all," she said. "You could do it all along."

"D'you think he can turn back again?" asked Fish worriedly. "What am I going to tell his mum and dad?"

"Never mind that," said Crescent urgently. *"Look!"*

The first rays of the sun burned triumphantly through the mist, turning the sky and the snow radiant shades of orange. It lit up the lake as though it was turning the ice to fire. The gray wolf howled joyfully as he saw Woody among the victorious Wolven, soaking wet but in one piece, his clansmen nuzzling and dancing around him triumphantly.

And something incredible was happening! A rainbow of lights shone above the melting ice as the revenants were set free from their purgatory beneath. Which could only mean one thing. *They were free from the curse of the vampire!* The Wolven could feel the rush of warmth as the revenants' souls prepared to ascend high up into the heavens. They watched as the freed souls suddenly gathered force and sped upward like a million fairy lights, up, up, until the only light in the sky was from the sun.

CHAPTER 34
AMNESTY

With all British airports snowbound, fogbound, and generally at a complete standstill as they had been for weeks, a chartered Sikorsky helicopter containing Quentin Crone, head of NightShift, arrived in Marais just in time for lunch.

Agent Alexandra Fish had been up until the early hours writing up her report on the *Black Widow Vampire*, as she had proudly and inventively named the file. She couldn't wait to see the boss's face when he read it. Crone was met at the helicopter by John Carver and Teebo Bon (who had returned to normal and was now back with his wife, although he wasn't sure which was worse—the bloodsucking vampire or his wife) and it all became rather grown-up and official. A debriefing meeting was held in John Carver's cabin.

"I got here as soon as I could," said Crone, shaking

each person firmly by the hand. "JC has told me what a remarkable job you have done. Congratulations."

"Wasn't just us, boss," said Fish. "Woody's clan turned up just as everything was really kicking off. They were phenomenal!"

It had, thought Fish, *turned out nicely*. The revenants under the ice had their revenge at last; the evil comtesse had been dragged to the bottom of the lake and drowned. Her remains were burned by Teebo's men, and the ashes walled up inside the mausoleum for eternity. Nat Carver had eventually changed back into human form, but it had been hard for Jude to cope with. And Woody was missing again.

"What about Woody?" asked Crone, as if he had read her thoughts.

"He's gone," said Nat quietly. "Went with the clan."

"One minute they were there, watching the revenants, then they just vanished," said Fish, "like smoke."

"Any news of his whereabouts?" asked Crone.

Nat shook his head glumly.

"He'll be back," said Jude. "You'll see."

"It's *OK*, Mum," said Nat gruffly, frankly wishing that

his mum would shut up. He knew she was almost as upset as he was about Woody, but he felt like he might cry, and if he boohooed in front of Fish and Crescent he would feel like a major dork.

"Woody always wanted to find his clan," he said, "and I . . . well, I guess I understand how he felt. I just wish that the last time I spoke to him, I hadn't behaved like an idiot."

"Ah, your man Woody never struck me as being one who'd let a small thing like that bug him," said Del, who had fully recovered from his vampire bite and was making the hot chocolate and hunting for the last packet of oat cakes.

"How're things in London?" asked Fish, changing the subject.

"Slightly hectic," replied Crone, "and missing your expertise. Now that you've got the hang of this vampire lark, there's a few more waiting for you to extinguish."

"Bring it on!" said Fish, rubbing her hands together in glee. "Can't wait!"

"That's the spirit," said Crone crisply. "You're going to need plenty of that when you get back."

But Nat felt truly down in the dumps. He hated good-byes. Even Fish would be going back to England, and it would be hard having no one to share the experiences of the last weeks, especially the new development, which hadn't really sunk in yet. *He could shift!* Did that mean he wasn't a mongrel anymore? With no Woody to talk all this over with, he felt lost.

"What about you, Nat?" Crone asked Nat softly. "I've kept my promise, although I asked for nothing in return. You and Woody are no longer the World's Most Wanted. But NightShift and your country would still benefit from your gifts, not to mention your vampire-slaying skills."

Alex Fish was getting fidgety. With all this soppy sentimental chat going on, no one had asked the BIG QUESTION. Like, what was the lowdown on Lucas Scale now that he had failed to finish off Nat and Woody again?

It was as if the boss had read her mind. "MI5 have supplied me with valuable information about a werewolf they have in custody," he said. "He's known to us at NightShift, and to *you*, Nat."

Nat felt his blood turn to ice water. "N . . . N . . . not . . . *Lucas Scale*?" The name fell from his lips and seemed to hang in the air for about a thousand years before Crone answered him.

"I wish," he said grimly. "I'm referring to someone far less toxic, I'm afraid. Teddy Davis."

For all his Wolven gifts, Nat had to admit he didn't see *that* coming. "Oh" was all he could manage, his eyes wide with surprise.

"Teddy Davis was found naked and crying outside a wolf sanctuary at Cricket St. Thomas," said Crone. "He had a very worrying tale to tell."

"He's seen *Him*," said Nat, not able to speak the name again.

Crone nodded. "His ability to take possession of Crescent confirmed that his powers are increasing, even though he failed once again to get rid of you and Woody. He's back in his body in England and recruiting again."

Since Nat and Alex Fish had come back from the Black Chateau, there had been a carnival atmosphere at the Twilighters' camp. Teebo Bon had organized a massive celebration with Nat and Fish as the star guests. Nat was touched and grateful for all the fuss, but wished Woody could be there to share it. No matter how hard he tried to get through to Woody, it wasn't working. He couldn't believe that after all they had shared Woody had decided to cut all ties with Nat and his family, but the longer it went on, Nat had to admit to himself that it was over. Woody had gone back to his clan.

Later that night there was feasting and fire walking, with music from Crescent and the Howlers, who were all on their very best behavior. At last the Christmas presents could be given out, very belatedly, and Nat had a pair of socks and a big red sweater with a reindeer on the front from Apple and Mick, some books from his parents, and, best of all, a custom-made guitar from Crescent.

"But, this is yours!" protested Nat. "It's too much; I can't take it!"

"I know you've always liked it," said Crescent, in her new humble voice. "I'd love for you to have it. And sorry for behaving like a brat."

Nat was speechless. He'd never heard a werewolf say sorry. It wasn't usually in their vocabulary.

"I was jealous," explained Crescent awkwardly. "Jealous of you and Woody, I suppose, you being such best friends and everything. I guess the way I felt gave Scale the necessary power to take me over so completely."

Blimey, thought Nat. *This is surreal. Crescent never apologizes. Never.*

Then Teebo Bon made a speech thanking everyone who was involved in the cleansing of the hive, after which, to Nat's surprise, Crescent and the Howlers slipped away.

"We have a very special Christmas present for you, Nat," said Teebo. "Saffi, will you bring him in, please."

Then Nat realized why the werewolves had left. Saffi Besson rode into the entrance of the Twilighters' camp riding a shiny, jet-black horse with a long, blindingly white mane and tail.

"A black palomino!" he breathed.

"*Your* black palomino," said Saffi, dismounting and handing Nat the reins. "He comes with a big thank-you from the people of Marais."

"What are you going to call him?" asked Scarlet curiously.

Nat paused for a moment. "Arcadia"—he smiled—"after a very brave horse I rode a long time ago. When

I rode alongside Richard the Lionheart. But that's another story."

Quentin Crone and Alex Fish visited Nat and his mum and dad before they flew back to England the next morning.

"I was sure Woody would be back," admitted Crone, "but maybe it's better this way. If Scale is still out for revenge, Woody is safer here with the English Channel between them."

"But what about Nat?" asked Jude nervously. "Is *he* safe from Scale?"

"*No one* is safe from him," said Crone. "The more we can find out about him, though, and what his plan is, the better it will be for all of us."

"Is your offer still open?" asked Nat suddenly.

"Nat—" began Jude.

"No, Mum," said Nat firmly. "We've all seen things over the last few months that we never thought we would. I helped do something that would have turned out much worse if I hadn't been able to fight back. If my Wolven stuff can help find beings like Scale and make a difference, then I'm going to help NightShift."

"You're *thirteen*," said Jude desperately, "you can't save the world."

"Not on my own," admitted Nat, "but things are going to get worse. Mr. Crone is right."

"He won't be in the front line," said Crone softly. "He'll be guiding us, telling us where to look."

"You make it sound as though we have no choice but to let him go," said Jude bitterly. "I wish I'd never heard of any of you."

"Mum," said Nat, kneeling down by Jude's side. "You're right. We don't have a choice."

Forty-eight hours later, the snow on the plains glistened blue as it reflected the cloudless sky. Nat Carver rode out of camp alone, enjoying the crisp, bright morning and the comforting noise of Arcadia's hooves drumming on the compacted snow. He hadn't told anyone where he was going, but the night before he had had the most amazing dream. He guided Arcadia with his knees, never needing to touch his flanks with his heels, so in tune was he with the palomino; he still couldn't quite believe that the blue-eyed horse was his. He rode on until his belly started to rumble and stopped for a while, letting Arcadia drink from a shallow lagoon. He pulled out some bread, cheese, and sausage and sat on a log enjoying the fresh food. There was nothing like eating out of doors.

His ears pricked up at the sound of something moving cautiously to his left, something coming out of the forest. Nat stood up.

"I've saved you some," he called.

"Awe-*oooo*-some!" came a familiar voice. "I'm starving!"

The owner of the voice came into view out of the thick birch trees.

"You knew I was coming, then?" asked Woody, his breath pluming out into the cold morning air. "I wondered!"

"Got your message," said Nat, his mouth still full of sausage and bread. "It was in a dream."

Woody took the piece of bread and cheese and shoved it in his mouth. "It was the only way to tell you what was happening," he said between munches. "I thought you'd stopped talking to me until you howled—that was *loud*."

Nat nodded, bemused. "Same here, I thought you'd stopped talking to *me* . . . you know, after I had that hissy fit with Crescent."

"As if." Woody grinned. "I was in a cave network; two-way doesn't seem to work too well under rock. What's been happenin', then?"

"Nothing much," replied Nat, "not now that all the vampires are dead. Kind of boring, really. Oh yeah . . . I forgot. I . . . uh . . . I *did* it."

"Did what?" asked Woody curiously.

"I shifted." Nat grinned. "I turned into a wolf."

Woody looked stunned. "You're joking me, right?" But he could see that Nat was deadly serious. "But what hap—?"

"I'll tell you all about it when we get back to the *Silver Lady*." Nat smiled. "You *are* coming back, I take it?"

"I guess," said Woody. "They . . . the clan . . . they wanted me to stay—that's why I went back with them after the vampire thing, and there were brothers with injuries. I wanted to make sure they were OK."

Nat nodded. "It must have been really hard."

"I learned loads of stuff, though," said Woody, cheering up a bit, "and you know . . . I'm gonna keep in touch with them all."

"But you don't want to live with them?" asked Nat curiously.

Woody thought for a moment, then shook his head. "I love them . . . being with them. But it was different, you know? I think I've been away too long."

"Is it because they don't have a TV?" asked Nat.

"'Course not," said Woody, his eyes shining. "It's . . . I guess I want the best of both worlds . . . see them, but stay in the real world."

"I was hoping I'd get the chance to say I was sorry about everything," said Nat uncomfortably. "You know, with Crescent and that."

"Shake," said Woody, his mouthful of sausage.

"Shake." Nat grinned.

"We're two of a kind, we are," said Woody, still munching, "like Batman and Robin."

"Yeah," Nat agreed, "if they were covered in fur!" Then he looked at his friend in amusement. "What on earth are you wearing?"

"Oh, these," said Woody. "My clan don't wear real clothes. Only . . . ah . . . these pajamas."

"Right," said Nat. "They look a bit . . . . uh . . . *girly.*"

Woody looked down. "Oops. I must have put on Cassiopeia's by mistake."

"Who's she?" asked Nat.

"My litter sister," said Woody proudly. "We Wolven take our names from the constipations—you know, stars an' that. My litter brother is called Lupus."

"I think you mean *constellations,*" said Nat. "What's yours?"

"Erm . . . can't remember." Woody grinned weakly.

"Come on," said Nat, "what is it?"

"Uh . . . Crux," said Woody.

"*Crux?* That's a terrible name!" Nat winced. "I think I'd stick with Woody if I were you."

"Come on," said Woody, his mouth bulging with the last of the bread, "I'm gettin' cold. Wanna race back to the *Silver Lady?*"

"Last one back smells like moldy cheese," said Nat, vaulting expertly onto Arcadia's back as though he'd ridden all his life.

"AAAAAAaaargoooohhhh!" howled Woody, already half out of his girly pajamas.

As Nat watched, Woody's body shortened in a rush of silvery air and spread out onto four legs. His head shifted into that of an enormous Wolven covered in long handsome fur that shone like quicksilver in the noonday sun. The Wolven and the black palomino sped away neck and neck, the white Wolven almost invisible against the blinding white of the snow, until they had both disappeared in the distance.